The Vacation

A Jerry Wiley Novel

Jack Darnell

Author of Mary Ann and Finally Love

Printed in the USA

J & S Publishers

ISBN

978-0-9819507-8-5

Acknowledgements

Robert 'Sunny' Spencer was a senior member of the singing group, *The Sons of the Pioneers*. He was the master of twenty-two instruments. He passed away in 2005.

The Poems, **'Wanna Be Cowgirl'** and **'Here Lies a Cowboy'** were written by the Texas Cowgirl, **Pauline Lieck,** and used by permission.

The Greek Island of Corfu does exist. It is a beautiful Island that is host to the smaller ships of the USN's 6th Fleet and cruise ships. I first set foot there many years ago. I cannot remember ever being impressed more by another port or island. Corfu is a unique mixture of past and present, with a love of the past that is apparent.

There was a **Jerry Wiley**, a wonderful man, a minister who lived in Georgia. From what I have learned of the man it seems he and my Jerry Wiley shared many of the same traits.

Jeri Lyn's **Consignment Boutique** and **Creative Travel** are businesses in Belmont, aka Mount Bell.

Special thanks for editing and research to:

Stephen Darnell, JoAnn Trull, Evelyn Funderburk

Sherry Darnell

****

Praise for 'The Vacation'

As I read The Vacation, I appreciate more the love I have for my wife and how much I am enjoying growing older with her. This book is not only enjoyable but a blessing ....

Larry Wiley

****

Dedication

To my Sister **Shirl Darnell Wrap** who has always been supportive. She was the first to purchase my books.

I love you Shirl.

A Prologue

This is a stand-alone novel, but the characters have been together in several previous novels. The central figures here are Sherry and Jerry Wiley, seniors who married late in life. This is the first marriage for the colorful character Jerry. He is presently a very wealthy man. His money is old and new, but he has been his own man. Other characters you may remember include a doctor who became head of Duke Medical, a CIA operative known as Doc, a street person known as Rags, and the head of the MVA (Modern Vigilante Association) known as S'Gar.

It is the second marriage for Sherry, who is also a graduate of Duke with honors. She married another class mate, Brady Oxnard. Soon after graduation they operated a successful practice in Huntersville, North Carolina. Her husband, Brady, became involved in the drug trade and after a couple of legal attempts failed to shut him down, Jerry's MVA was unofficially invited in to short circuit the situation, and that they did. Their operation closed Brady down. Unfortunately for Brady it was permanent; he lost his life as a result of the MVA's attention. Sherry had been completely innocent of any wrong doing and was never charged with a crime.

Sherry, now a widow, and Jerry the bachelor, become close. They fell deeply in love and were married in an amazingly bizarre marriage ceremony that could have only been instigated by Jerry's own MVA crew.

Jerry and Sherry are two seniors in their 70's who live life to its fullest. They maintain two residences: one in Pittsburgh, an old home with staff on board and Jerry's home since childhood; the other one is in the development of Hawthorne in Mount Bell.

Mount Bell was a textile town for many years. The Imperial Mill provided homes for some of the employees. One of the streets was Hawthorne Street. When the jobs left, the Mill Village was razed and the upscale development of Hawthorne came into existence. Sherry had bought a home close to where her childhood home had been. Most folk in Hawthorne did not know that one of their neighbors was the former CEO of Wiley Industries. They could not know that he was also the head of the MVA (Modern Vigilante Association). Neither could they know that their nice neighbor was a certified billionaire.

A note from the author.

I am very optimistic that you will enjoy The Vacation. I hope it is a good read for you. It was fun to write. This novel originates in Hawthorne, an upscale development that is built where the Imperial Mill Village stood for nearly one hundred years. The main street was Hawthorne Street. Thus the name of the development.

For many years I was a builder in Belmont, North Carolina, translate that, Mount Bell, I am now a part time resident. Our full time residence is a motor home. We are happy to say, "Home is where we park it."

Chapter 1

The sun was still above the horizon, highlighting the homes in the neighborhood. Looking out across the common area of Hawthorne, an upscale community of Mount Bell, Sherry was thinking of her childhood, a childhood that had been spent practically on this very spot. Back then it was a four room mill house with the bathroom on the back porch. Mama, daddy, and seven kids had once lived in those four rooms. Way back then it was called the Imperial Mill Village, or simply the Mill Hill. The street in front of her house was Hawthorne. Their address was one twenty-nine. She was remembering when the streets were first paved and Christmas was near.

At Christmastime that year her 'big present' was a pair of roller skates. Oh, the thrill of playing with the other kids as they enjoyed their special toys and the thrill of being scared within an inch of her life skating down that big hill. Remembering how her feet started to weave in and out and just knowing the end of her life was near, she was scared to death. But, being the girl who would not give up, she rode those skates all the way to the bottom of the hill.

She was safe. She was eight years old and thought, if she could do that, she could conquer the world. *Hey one day I might ski down that snow covered Matterhorn we have been studying about.* She smiled as she thought that little Sherry did not know then that she would be able to travel anywhere she wanted to go. She never knew she was poor until she started college and roomed with girls who had eight, even ten changes of clothes and as many pairs of shoes. Her freshman year she had three changes of clothes and two pairs of shoes. She had been able to face that, knowing one day she would be a doctor and could afford the clothes she might not have now.

Remembering that girl in pig tails, then later with the pony tail, her thoughts followed a natural course as she remembered her dreams of travel. Before their marriage Jerry had told her of a Greek island he had once visited. It was the island he had wanted to return to with someone he loved. Coming out of her day dream, she looked over at her husband who was engrossed in a new novel. "Jerry, what is the island in the Mediterranean you liked so much?"

Jerry was caught up in a novel by his favorite author, Jack Darnell. "What did you say, dear?" Jerry said, as he put the book down and removed his reading glasses. He never missed a chance to talk to his dream girl. He still could not get over how lucky he was to find Sherry.

"I was asking, what is the name of your favorite Island?"

"Corfu. Corfu is a beautiful island. Why do you ask?"

"Will you take me there?"

"Are you kidding me? You bet your bippy, I will." He stared at his lovely wife. "Would you really like to go?"

"Yes, I think I would. Hey man of mine, we are nearing the mid-mark of our seventies. Logic tells this lady if I don't see Corfu soon, I may never see it."

"Okay we need to talk about this. Do you want to take your plane or fly commercial?" Pausing for a moment he said, "Or we could forget the friendly skies and take a ship. Something else to think about: do you want to do a structured trip with a schedule, or wing it?" Both were silent for a minute and Jerry continued.

"I know you could arrange it, but why not let someone else do it for us. Why don't you call a local travel agent and say, do it?" By this time Sherry was sitting beside her man and gave him a big hug and kiss.

Looking into her beautiful green eyes he said, "I see nothing to stop us. Would you like to take a few friends or just you and me?"

"Let me think about it the rest of the day and I will call Creative Travel Agency in the morning," Sherry returned adopting a quizzical look.

"Sounds like a plan. I'm ready to travel with my sweetie, whether in the air or we transit on the sea." Jerry said with a big smile.

"I guess I had better think about that too." Pausing a moment then Sherry came back matter of fact, "*Sweetie?* You are picking up Mary Ann's language too!" They both laughed. "Okay, I have never looked at this place called Corfu. I'm off to my computer to see where you are taking me."

As Sherry left the room, Jerry watched her go. He could not help wondering at all of God's goodness to him. There was a time in his life when, in his thinking, God played no part. But, since meeting this lady again and really getting to know her, all that had changed.

He had to smile when he thought of the simple wedding they had planned. Instead, when they had arrived at the church, the whole place had been transformed. Once he entered the church, he knew within minutes this was not going to be what they had planned. The entire front of the church had been theatrically redone to appear as the entrance of a Cathedral. Then Sherry stepped through the door and almost fainted; she stood there in shock, beautiful in her second hand wedding dress purchased at Jeri Lyn's Consignment Boutique. Immediately, the music started and their simple wedding became a flash mob and a wild musical, choreographed by his crazy crew. He smiled when he remembered Doctor T's face when the whole thing started, and then the ending when Josh and Brenda had played the piano duet of "Rock Around the Clock" at the close of the ceremony.

The smile slowly went away when he remembered how the MVA, his vigilante group, had taken the life of Sherry's first husband. Jerry had studied at Duke University with both Sherry and her husband, Brady. After graduating and completing their internship, Sherry and Brady had invested in a successful clinic in Huntersville, NC. Too soon, Brady's true colors started to come out; that fool had played footsie with the drug trade and had become a complete ass. There had been a confrontation where Brady's ego would not allow him to be reasonable and he drew a firearm on Buddy, point man for the MVA. At that time Buddy had no choice but take Brady out. The whole thing had born heavily on Jerry's mind until he had a talk with Sherry, right here at Hawthorne. Then he found that, not only was Brady a crook, but an abusive husband. Sherry had not grieved at Brady's death.

Jerry had felt all along that the sucker had gotten what he deserved, but it still bothered him that he had married the wife of someone whose death was pretty much his fault.

Thank God that had passed. It was over. And now, in their seventies, they were in heaven. Life was good.

Jerry had never married, living the life of a bachelor with his short affairs and one night stands. But he had been one driven man, driven to become the Head of Duke Medical. Then, to the surprise of the medical world, he resigned from Duke and the adventurer in him led him to become 'Doc'. He disappeared off the medical radar. The papers did not know what to make of it. 'Doc' being on the CIA Black Ops had been the ultimate thrill for a kid who was pampered as he grew up, chauffeured to school every day and the son of a man that had climbed from poverty to become a millionaire in Pittsburgh.

Jerry thought, *I did wait a long time. I still do not know why but I am sure glad I waited. Sherry was worth it. I could not have even dreamed it any better. I am glad I can give her anything money can buy. What the heck else am I gonna do with a billion dollars?*

"Honey?" Jerry realized Sherry was back by his side. He had been day dreaming of the past.

"Oh, yes sweetheart, what is it?" Queried Jerry.

"Do you mind if we take friends?"

"Of course not. Take anyone you want to and, of course, tell them the trip is your treat. Whatever makes my girl happy makes me even happier."

"I was remembering the fun I had with the girls shopping in Pittsburgh. We could do a tour, couldn't we?"

"Honey we can stop in London, Paris, Switzerland, Rome, and even go over to Sicily. We can do Corfu, go to Athens, and visit with Robert and the childhood friend you mention at times: the Cope fellow. But I think, due to the instability, Istanbul is out at present but check with your travel agent."

Sherry squeezed Jerry with all her might. "Jerry Wiley, you are the best man in the world. I could never have dreamed of a better man if I had tried. I love you."

"I love you sweetheart," he stuttered. Jerry was still embarrassed at the attention. He still turned red at the affection from this beautiful lady. *How could he have been so lucky?*

Closing her eyes, thinking, Sherry said with introspect, "His name is Tommy Cope. Lord knows he had such a sweet mama, his dad Edgar was crazy funny, and his sister was a sweetie." She paused a few seconds. "I think Tommy was either with the Diplomatic Corps or in the Air Force there in Athens. He married a local lady and made Athens his home. He took a permanent job and became a big wig at the consulate."

Pausing for a moment, "Sister Cope, now that I think of it." Sherry smiled and continued, "You know by now that all my church folk had the first names of Sister and Brother." They both laughed at that. "Anyway, one Christmas, during my time at Duke, my finances were very low and I knew I could not afford to go home. Just at the perfect time, I received a Christmas card from Sister Cope with $20 in it. I cried because the Copes were not rich themselves and could have used the money, but there it was: the twenty dollars I needed to get home to see my family at Christmas. You cannot forget things like that."

Jerry looked at his wife again in a new light. She had never told him this story. He could see the love in her eyes as they gleamed with tears. Of course, things of this financial nature were foreign to him. He had never wanted for anything in his life. He had been born into a millionaire's home. As society says, 'he was born with a silver spoon in his mouth'. He had heard the tales all his life: how his dad and mom had struggled and climbed from poverty to the status of business owner and millionaire, but he had never fully appreciated it. Somehow, this simple story told by his wife suddenly, gave him even more respect for his dad and mom. He had never really pictured them as having nothing.

"I would love to meet this mysterious fellow who left the states, fell in love, and never returned."

"You will love him. He is sorta like his dad, crazy funny. I am getting excited; there is so much to do. This is gonna be fun!" Sherry said as she headed for her computer.

Once Sherry was gone, Jerry did not pick his book back up. His mind went to the little Island of Corfu, to a staging area for one of the CIA operations. That one was to be very tricky, diplomatically. They were headed into Turkey to extract a government official that had been abducted. Due to diplomatic haggling with on and off agreements, the stay in Corfu had been months. The plans changed weekly but the delays gave him time to fall in love with the slow paced life of this beautiful Greek island.

Every weekend, from the balcony of his hotel room, he had watched the carefree fun of families as they picnicked in the city park. He watched lovers as they walked hand in hand beneath the hotel balcony, seemingly so much in love and oblivious of the world around them. It was then that he told himself, if there was ever a real love in his life, they must come here; these people know how to live and be alive.

Aroused from his thoughts by the excited sound of his wife's voice, "Hey Evelyn, do you want to go to Athens? No silly, not Athens, North Carolina. I mean like Athens, Greece; and London, Paris, Rome, and any place in between."

The conversation went on as it did most days, except this time the Mount Bell High School yearbooks didn't come out; they had bigger fish to fry, plans to make. Happily, Jerry thought: *This was really going to happen. He was finally going to return to the place that had impressed him more than any of the thousands of places he had spent time, and this time it would not be planning an extract. No life and death suspense. It would not be business; well I guess I will consider it the business of Love. What better setting for love than a Greek Island?*

Chapter 2

Sherry loved to plan. After her talk with Evelyn, there were more questions to be answered. Was this a good time of the year? How long will it take a travel agent to arrange it? The biggest decision, fly or float?

"Hey, do I smell coffee? It's not breakfast time." Jerry called from the living room.

"Yeah dude, this is talking coffee time. Wanna talk on the couch or at the bar?" Asked Sherry as she rounded the bar.

"What about the bed?" asked Jerry, in mock seriousness.

"Bed was not one of the choices dear."

"Well, okay. I'll have mine black. The bar sounds good to me. I once had a great talk with a beautiful widow there."

"So, this afternoon you are doing something different. You are a very exciting man Jerry Wiley, you usually have it black," Sherry said, laughing at her own joke; Jerry always had black coffee.

Laughing, Jerry took his stool at the bar as Sherry poured that great smelling coffee into his favorite cup. Since he first met Sherry she had ordered her coffee from the 'Holy Cow Coffee Company'. It was good coffee and made the room smell so great.

After replacing the carafe, she sat across from him and took both his hands in hers and said, "Now, tell me about the weather in Corfu as we enjoy this coffee."

After a smile and a hand squeeze, they both took the cups and, as always, smelled the aroma before sipping. "Okay, our team was there in the spring, about now, mid-April. The weather was about like Mount Bell, but I assume month after next, June will be a great time: not too hot, and the mosquitos they talked about may not be out in force yet."

"I know you have crossed the Atlantic many times. You have mentioned both by ship and plane. Would the trip itself be fun, and I mean *just the crossing* on a ship?"

"I think you know me. I always consider the journey as much an adventure as the destination. For most people there is enough entertainment aboard the commercial cruise ships to keep you occupied. Every evening there are shows, like the ship we were on for our honeymoon."

"Other than my little escapade of being kidnapped on our honeymoon and being held by a crazy man, I really did enjoy the cruise," she laughed.

"Oh yeah, that was a little exception, but there is something magical about the ocean. I'm sure you remember it from the Caribbean, though the expanse of the Atlantic is mind boggling. I am not sure how long a transatlantic crossing will be now. I assume about seven days. Remember we were only two days at the most without land in the Caribbean. A crossing now would give you six or seven sunrises and sunsets on the ocean, two of the most beautiful sights in the world when the sky is clear. The colors are fantastic every showing." Jerry paused thinking of holding Sherry while seeing an ocean in the background. To him, they were two of the wonders of the world. "Then there is always just a walk on the deck, searching the blue ocean for whales and dolphins. There have been times that a school of dolphins played, crisscrossing our bow, as if challenging the ship to a race. A beautiful sight."

"You always speak of the sea as if you love it."

"I think I do. It is like you my love: deep, mysterious, and holds the treasures of which men dream." They sat in silence for a few minutes enjoying the coffee. And Jerry continued, "It is not only the large creatures that entertain, but the small flying fishes that leap out of a wave and soar, following the contour of a wave, gracefully gliding. When I saw that, I would always think of Rudyard Kipling and the 'Road to Mandalay'. The line, 'on the road to Mandalay where the flying fishes play' always came to mind. And who could forget Sinatra and his song. So yes, sweetheart, I guess I do love the sea."

"I love to hear you talk. I am always thankful to God that life brought us together."

"As you said that sweetheart, I thought of another thing of mystery. After you have been away from port for five of six days, and you are on the deck at night enjoying the beautiful starlit canopy and you see a ship on the horizon or in the distance, there is such a feeling of kinship you would not believe. You actually feel a tug that draws you to that ship." Smiling, Jerry took Sherry's hand again and, looking into her eyes, said, "A feeling not unlike when I came here a couple years back to explain to you my part in the death of Brady; I felt a tug at my heart."

Not unusual in their lives, he dropped her hands and got up to walk to her side of the bar. He took his love in his arms and held her tight and then he gave her the deep kiss that always set his heart on fire. *This lady is the queen*, said his mind.

After the kiss and a tight hug that only her man Jerry could give, she spoke. "Then it is settled in my mind. I cannot wait to get you aboard ship again."

Without a word, they folded into each other's arms and rekindled the fire with another kiss. The sun was now going down, but something else was calling. Love was in the air at Hawthorne and the phones were turned off. Mentally, a 'Do Not Disturb' sign was put out; it was a time of love, thrills, and the anticipation of things to come.

Life was good at Hawthorne. Sherry was no longer that eight year old skating down the hill with her feet wobbling, but a grown lady ready to ski that Matterhorn.

Most of the population has no idea how wonderful life is for some of their seniors. Later, lying in bed, cuddling, as the sun set, this senior couple in their seventies were oblivious to the troubles of the world. They just knew their lives were perfect.

Spontaneity had not always been an option, but these two were making up for the times it was not possible. They understood what many did not: time will not stand still. You must take the joys and thrills when you can because you have no promise of the morrow.

Both Jerry and Sherry drifted off into a land of dreams.

Chapter 3

Jerry awoke to the smell of coffee. A smile crossed his face as he remembered the night before and Sherry's excitement. Just the thought of going back to his dream island was exciting. As always, his smile deepened when he saw Sherry standing there smiling down at him. "Okay lover boy, do you want coffee in bed or at the bar with breakfast?"

"I will take it with my beautiful wife and breakfast; may I say Mrs. Wiley, you look as lovely as a bride this beautiful morning?"

"If you are saying it, I will accept it — lie or not!"

"Well, it certainly isn't a lie, Doctor; you look gorgeous. Now give me a minute and I will join you in the kitchen."

On the bar, where they usually ate, was his favorite: a veggie omelet with cheese. Sherry was having the same with some ketchup on top. "Creative Travel doesn't open until nine. I thought we would just walk since it is only four blocks," Sherry spoke excitedly.

"*Would 'chew like company on 'or stroll?*" Jerry asked before he realized he still had a mouth full of omelet. Swallowing and clearing his throat, he corrected "Sorry, I meant 'would you like company on your stroll?" With that they both got a good laugh.

"Of course, my dear sir, and you could also protect me from the dragons and dangers along the way."

"At your service, my queen."

The rest of the mealtime was taken up with small talk about who might be free to go and who could not. Jerry could tell she was hoping for her three school mates: Evelyn, Dianne, and Mary Ann. Jerry was always reminded that he did not have the same close camaraderie with any of his school mates as Sherry did with her friends. There was no one from his childhood, mostly because he had been raised isolated from his peers.

His father had not believed in a kid going to a private school. He insisted Jerry attend public school and get to know the average citizen in this great country. He never realized how odd Jerry felt arriving at school every day in a chauffeured limousine. Jerry, being a very intelligent kid, had worked around it, handling the slurs thrown out with a smile. In fact, he had gained some friends, just not as close as this small high school in Mount Bell had produced. These girls almost seemed like family.

All the men in the girls' lives were very much Jerry's type of man. Anytime they were together they always had a great time. This extended time together would also be great. Jerry remembered how, anytime he had been overseas, it was a comfort to be in the company of friends. Sherry did not know this yet, but she would grow even closer to her friends, along with having fun. Jerry was very much in favor of traveling with a group. The danger level was low, even for couples in the areas they planned to go, but a group made it as close to guaranteed safe as one could get.

"Oh dear, honey, how long do you think we should plan this trip? We girls will have to start working on our wardrobes."

"Well I would give it a month, anyway, but do not forget there are both laundry and cleaner services aboard ship. Europe is not in the dark ages either. Laundry will be no problem."

"I know that, silly, but the wardrobe planning is a girl thing. We like it."

"And here I was gonna suggest a western approach: everyone take plaid shirts and jeans. It sure makes planning much simpler. I bet Paula out in San Antonio could give your girls some great ideas."

"Forget it, Romeo, we girls will be the talk of the ship and Corfu! I plan to be so sexy, you will be one whipped bull on your romantic Greek Island," Sherry said, giggling.

"I am turning the recorder on. Say that again, just for the record." By now Sherry was close to him and fell into his arms.

"Oh it's going to happen all right; you will need no proof at all. It is going to be proof enough with your tail dragging."

"Well what are you waiting for? Call that agent now and schedule the trip tomorrow; you have peaked my interest!" Holding each other, they were both cracking up laughing.

"Sweetheart, this is going to be so much fun, I just know it. Now turn me loose. I must get dressed for our walk to the travel agency so we can plan our romantic getaway." A kiss and she disappeared.

Jerry walked out to get the Gaston Gazette since he was already dressed. That was his practice every morning when he arose. He had never been a robe type man, and his life had been centered on, 'you must be ready.'

He sat at the bar with another cup of coffee and started looking through the paper. He always enjoyed the Gazette, even when he was Rags, a street person. He smiled thinking how fate, maybe God, had brought him here during his personal 'great depression'. It was the time in his life he was fighting his own demons. He had been AWOL from the CIA and the woods around Mount Bell had been his home/hiding place. The good citizens thought he was a bum, but they never saw him beg. Soon he was just a figure, seemingly wandering randomly around the area. He had met a lady named Susie when he entered Mount Bell. He came into town after using the trestle that crossed over the Catawba River. He preferred the railroad tracks. He seldom had to talk to anyone that way.

At the downtown crossing Susie was buying apples from the 'apple man'. She introduced herself and gave him a North Carolina Mountain Apple. She was a lovely lady, who became his only real friend in Mount Bell, and he had no idea she was Sherry's mother: a girl he had been in college with. She had lived practically on this very spot. She had fed him on her back steps many times and listened to his tales of woe, always saying, *I am praying for you and everything will be all right.* That was long ago. Now the mill houses were gone and so was Susie, Sherry's sweet mother — Sherry brought him back to the present.

"Honey, I am ready," Sherry was by his side.

"I was just off in a dream world thinking of your mother: she was the best. Funny thing I never associated her with you."

"Yes, and she never told anyone she was a friend of Rags, the street person, either. That was one thing that was always said about my mama. *If you tell Susie something in confidence, you can count on it. That information will be buried with her.* Now, I love talking about my mama, but we can do it on the sidewalk; I am ready."

"Lead on lady. I am with you and as anxious for this trip as you are." Out of the house and down the street, turning left toward Main Street, they continued to talk and plan. They waited at the light at Main Street and then crossed. Out of the corner of his eye, Jerry spotted a loose black dog running toward them from the left. The black Labrador slid to a stop about ten feet from them, barked, and turned. He looked back at them and barked again, moving his head in a circular type motion that looked to Jerry like the dog was saying, 'come on'.

"He looks just like Lassie did in the movie, 'Lassie Come Home' in the 1940's, when she went for help."

Again the dog moved toward them and barked, followed with the same actions, turned and headed up the hill.

"Let's try to follow and see if she will lead," said Sherry. "She does seem to be trying to tell us something."

As they turned, the dog ran ahead again, turned, and barked. Now that they were involved, it seemed she was saying, "hurry." So they picked up the pace. The dog led them to an open door; to an old house that at one time was the Parsonage for the Baptist Church. They followed toward the door. They both saw the legs of a man that was lying on the floor. Kneeling by the man, both doctors started checking him; his breathing was labored and his heart was erratic. The dog nuzzled in and Jerry eased her away, but the dog insisted and Jerry noticed her collar for the first time. He immediately recognized her for a medically trained dog, trained especially as a patient's companion.

Reading the collar, it said, ATTENTION: *Peanut Allergy*. Sherry saw it also and immediately said, "Fetch." The dog turned ran and immediately returned with a black bag. Jerry was calling 911. Sherry took the bag and withdrew the contents: she took one packet and opened it to retrieve the hypodermic needle; took an alcohol packet, opened it and withdrew the alcohol pad; cleansed the man's arm and gave him the injection.

She then massaged the arm a little to try to speed the serum to his blood stream. This was not a new thing to Sherry, the doctor. She had once had a patient very allergic to peanuts. She was in a familiar area of symptoms and knew the exact protocol. The dog sat very close but did not interfere until after the injection was complete; then, she went prone and crawled to her master and eased next to him. Sherry almost cried at the show of love and affection.

"The emergency crew is on the way," said Jerry interrupting her thoughts. "I assume it is a peanut allergy reaction."

"Yes, all the symptoms pointed to that. The patient seems to be coming around. Relax, my friend, we are doctors. Your handler here," Sherry was petting the dog, and nodded to her, "She came to get us and led us into your house. She is a wonder. I have given you an injection of epinephrine using the EpiPen pack your dog retrieved for me. She is one sharp handler. Please relax, the emergency medics should be here soon to give you a good checkup."

She could tell the man understood and relaxed. In halting English he said, "You doctors I thank. I am most careful, but this time I not properly read labels."

The medics arrived and Sherry explained what had happened. The EMS guys checked the patient's vitals and all was well. The patient refused a trip to the emergency room, but the EMS crew stayed for about ten minutes before agreeing. Jerry followed them outside, gave them his card, and told them to send whatever bill to him since he had called. The medic took the card and left.

The man was not a local for sure. He was dark of skin and sported a beard and loose clothing. He was slender and about seventy years of age. Sherry had, by now, gotten to know him well. Jerry came back inside and they all spent some time getting acquainted.

The first words spoken by the man after Sherry explained about the dog and the procedures they had followed, was *Allah be praised*, surprising Sherry; it was the first time she had heard that phrase other than on the news.

"Forgive an old man. I am Asam Badir Samir, recently from Istanbul, Turkey. I am new to this beautiful oasis of Mount Bell. I may have made a 'bang of impressions,' as my grandsons would say."

Speaking quietly while petting the dog Sherry said, "I am Sherry and this is my husband, Jerry Wiley; we live only a few blocks from here and were out for a walk when this intelligent beast came to get us and led us here. I am so glad we were near. You were in a very dangerous position."

"Yes that, I am sure of. And I am sure you saved my life; I will be forever grateful, Allah be praised."

"May I call you Asam?"

"Please, I am familiar that my name, it is not an easy one for Americans to pronounce. However, 'Asam' will make me happy."

"Asam, I do not mean to be forward, but are you of the Muslim faith?"

"Oh, no doctor, I am Christian. Most of my family is Muslim, however, but I know Jesus for myself." Asam continued, "I have learned that you here in this great country say 'thank the Lord' after a salvation. It is habit, I guess: 'Allah be praised,' from my lips, means the same as you saying, 'thank the Lord.' I am trying to adjust, so 'thank the Lord' you were near."

Instinct took over and Sherry hugged the man she now knew as Asam: it was automatic, a kinship. At first he was stiff, but he immediately relaxed.

Asam had invited them to the table for tea. They declined, but suggested he have some. They chatted as he made his tea in the microwave. They learned he was here to be with his son: an engineer with the IBM Corporation in Charlotte. His daughter-in-law was at school for a parent teacher conference; therefore, he was alone when he ate a candy bar that had contained peanuts.

Both doctors wanted to make sure all was well with Asam, and had placed this higher in priority than the reason they were out for the walk. Asam had been an accountant in Istanbul. After his wife's passing and his retirement, his son had sponsored him to get him into the USA.

"I tell you most of my family is Muslim," said Asam. "That includes my son; his wife is a Christian but bows to his choice. My son is not a very good Muslim but still leans to the old ways. He is good to his wife and she in turn respects him. It has been years since my son has seen a mosque."

"I know it is late, but welcome to Mount Bell. I would also like to invite you and your daughter-in-law to attend our church; it is within walking distance."

"Oh doctor, that is very honorable, but we worship here. We are Coptic in belief, and have learned a very hard lesson: sometimes it is wise to hold one's tongue in a foreign land. We are learning more and will very much consider the gracious invitation."

"Well, our new friend," said Jerry, "We will ask leave of you and be on our way. But please, no more peanuts!"

"Oh, I think you can wager, this poor soul will be very attentive from now on."

They gave him their cards and Sherry gave him directions to the church. She gave him the phone number of the pastor. They learned the black lab was simply "Blackie." They said goodbye to Asam and Blackie, then left.

Back on the sidewalk, Jerry said, "Well that was a morning eye opener. Asam would have been dead in five minutes. That is my prognosis doctor; am I close?"

"Yes, doctor: for a neophyte at this medical stuff, you are pretty quick," Sherry answered smiling, "Asam was very close to meeting his maker and I am so glad we were close by. I am taking this as a good omen. We were headed to the right place to be here at the right time."

"Then by all means, my love, lead on to this mysterious place called Creative Travel."

Chapter 4

It was only a few minutes to Creative Travel on Myrtle Street. Sherry had used this agency on a couple of occasions. The receptionist was at the copy machine, but Rebecca saw them and waved them into her office. "It is always a pleasure to see you. What can we do for you Doctor?"

"Hi Rebecca. We are going on a vacation and would appreciate your help."

"Sure, that is our aim. By the way, thanks for sending your friends Roger and Terry to see us. Now, where to on this vacation?"

"I'm sorry Rebecca but I have never introduced you to my husband: this is the best man in the world, Jerry Wiley; and honey, this is Rebecca, she heads this wild bunch."

The two exchanged pleasantries and Sherry continued, "We want to take an ocean voyage to the Mediterranean; the final destination is to be the Greek Island of Corfu."

"I have read the name and know it is one of the ports that tours from Venice frequently but, other than that, I will have to do some research. Do you mind if I call in Melanie, one of our agents?"

"Of course not." Rebecca punched a couple buttons and asked Melanie to step in. Shortly all the introductions were completed and the questions came from Melanie and Rebecca.

"Is it just the two of you?"

"Oh no, we want to take several couples with us. We are just doing the preliminaries today." Sherry said. "And, to speed things along, these are some of our ideas: there will be up to eight more travelers; the cost will be from one source; and we would like to visit several ports while in the Mediterranean. We haven't decided on a time frame, but we are guessing at least a month to six weeks. Is that enough for you to work with?"

Melanie took the lead, "Yes ma'am, that will get me started. Now when would you like to go?"

"Sometime in June would be good, we think."

Melanie swallowed, "That soon? I think we will be able to accommodate you. Let me give you a call, maybe tomorrow or day after."

"That would be great, Melanie. By that time I should know who is going; this is sort of a spur of the moment thing."

Rebecca broke in, "Spur of the moment certainly gets the juices flowing. I hope I am not being too personal or forward Doctor Jerry but it is my understanding you have your own plane. I am sure you considered it and you could make your own schedule."

"Yes Rebecca, I offered it, but this lady is a romantic and wants me on a 'slow boat' to our destination. The trip is no stranger to me. I have done it on surface and in the air. I was on that island many years ago; it is a beautiful place. We wanted the journey to be as exciting as the destination." Pausing just for a second, "I want to add one more thing: if enough suites are available aboard the ship on this short notice, I would like for every couple to have one. And also Melanie, the expense is no problem; I want this to be the journey of a lifetime."

"Then I think Creative Travel was a good choice doctor. We will be in touch as soon as we know anything. And, let me add, it was good to meet you Doctor Jerry Wiley. You are a sort of legend around here."

Jerry smiled and saluted, knowing Rebecca was referring to the times he was known as Rags: a street person here in Mount Bell. And it was definitely no secret after he had returned to marry Sherry.

"I have a lot to do," said Sherry, "But I would love to take a stroll with my love through Stowe Park, then have a cup of coffee at the new little coffee shop by the railroad tracks. I understand the coffee shop is close to the exact spot where Jessie Lee Brown was selling apples when you first arrived in this town."

"You are correct lady, and I know every step from that point to Charlotte. I walked that train track with a purpose; this small town was my destination, chosen by fate."

It was only a block from Creative Travel, back down Myrtle Street, to one entrance to the small city park. As they walked through, Sherry related again how Mr. Stowe had created this park in the 1950's: it had a miniature train as the central attraction, a dance area below a stage where the locals performed that music known as Rock and Roll. One of the performers of that day was Jim Arp, a guitar player and singer. He went on to be a lead singer and played with some of the leading groups of the time. He starred in a couple of movies and was inducted into the Rock-a-Billy Hall of Fame.

They stopped by the fountain to toss in some coins and make a wish; almost simultaneously, they started quietly singing *Three Coins in a Fountain.* Standing there, thinking, dreaming, Jerry pulled Sherry close and said, "Since just one wish can be granted, make it mine." No one else was in the park and Sherry allowed him that kiss he was hinting for. They both appreciated these times; the bond grew stronger with each passing day. Neither was in a hurry to break the magic of the moment.

Later, at the coffee shop across the street, they were having a cup of coffee: still savoring the flavor of a wonderful morning; doctors saving lives like they are trained to do; and starting the ball rolling for their magical vacation.

"Sweetheart, sometimes I forget how much time has passed; Corfu may not be the same. I hate to build something up and you be disappointed."

Stirring her coffee slowly, thinking, Sherry responded, "Jerry Wiley, if you are there it could never be a disappointment. Of course it will be different: this time I will be there. That should make all the difference."

Using an exaggerated French accent, "Ah my Sherree, you are such a romantic. I think I am falling in love with you," Jerry smiled, "I love you. Now let's head home so you can make all those calls you are dying to make."

Getting up from her chair, "I do have some calls to make, but it is more fun at present just to enjoy you. Let's do a slow walk back to Hawthorne, what do you say?"

"I'm game," Jerry returned the cups, tipped, and thanked the young lady who was smiling at the 'old' love birds. Jerry thinking, *young lady, if you only knew.*

Just a few steps into their walk home, Jerry looked thoughtfully at Sherry and said, "Sweetheart, you said something a minute ago that reminded me of the poet Robert Frost, from years back, that I think matches our lives. You said, *I will be there and* ***that will make all the difference.*** I know that you know Frost said that. I have always matched my life to his words, *I took the path less traveled by, and that has made all the difference.* Today is one of those days and I thank you."

Sherry thought, I can never out-guess this old romantic: a man who has lived on the edge, risked his life many times, and still loves a Mill Hill girl, apparently with all his heart. "No honey, I thank you for being you; that has made all the difference in my life."

It took only a few minutes to walk the two blocks home. Jerry enjoyed this. Life in Mount Bell was so different from his Pittsburgh and he was falling in love with it.

Back home, Sherry went directly to the phone to continue her excitement. Jerry only smiled and picked up his novel.

Chapter 5

"Hello Evelyn, have you talked to Don?"

"Oh yeah, he was on the lawn mower. He said, 'Honey I have told you, I have cruised. I just want to operate this farm.' I told him this farm could operate on its own and, if anything was needed, Doug was close by."

"Well?"

"Oh he reluctantly agreed. He is a pretty independent cuss at times. He said, if we go, we pay our way. I told him the invitation was come as you are; so yes, we are coming along. I know I can't wait, and he is thrilled also, I can tell."

"I know you guys have passports; I remember you telling me that. I do not know exactly when, but we are hoping for June. Is that all right?"

"Hey, you know us: we are ready to go anytime, but June sounds good."

The conversation went on for a while. Sherry had asked Evelyn to alert Dianne and Mary Ann that she would be calling. Evelyn reported that they were thrilled just thinking about it.

Jerry noticed, from his vantage point, that the year book came down out of the book case. That always meant one of two things: they had heard some juicy story or one of their classmates had died.

A conversation between the two lasted at least forty five minutes or an hour. That gave Jerry such peace. He never failed to be amazed at the comraderies of these classmates. He had never experienced that. He had not kept in contact with his classmates and, at times, he recognized a tinge of jealousy, but quickly sent it away. He was blessed to be able to share her passion towards the classmates. Even after fifty-eight years, there was a tie. Weekly they dined with Carrol, JoAnn, Evelyn, Don, Ed, Dianne, Jim, and Dean. Every meal was a rehash of high school; that even Jerry enjoyed hearing.

Of course, there was also the *Quarterly Mount Bell's Friend's meeting.* It was a dinner celebration with delicious home cooking at Cat Fish Cove. Carrol was enthusiastic in its promotion. Sherry's brother Vernon worked to entertain and help supply entertainers. Most of the 'class of '56' that were still local got together. One of the things Jerry appreciated was seeing Brenda there, the widow of Agent Muse. Remembering Bill was one of his pleasant memories.

He was also impressed by Vernon. Three tours in Vietnam as a Green Beret. He had been awarded medals but never spoke of them. He was inspired by his older brother Lefty. Lefty had been a Marine and landed on Iwo Jima. He was wounded but survived. Then there was Sherry's brother, Chief of Police Johnny.

Johnny was a standup guy who drove a '34 Ford as his chief's car. Jerry smiled when he remembered that Johnny had broken a few rules, helping 'Rags' evade the CIA and FBI, and it was in his prized '34 Ford.

Life with Sherry was amazing, exciting, and, to say the least, interesting. Through his haze of thoughts, he heard the excited voice of his lover. "That's right Mary Ann: we will go to Rome, Spain, France, and last to Jerry's dream island, Corfu."

"No, no, no," Sherry insisted. "Jerry said he was paying for it and was looking forward to some time to talk with Buck." Sherry listening, then, "Honestly I don't know the destinations, but we may know something tomorrow. We hope to go in June, so clear the calendar for a least a month."

The conversation went on for a long time before Sherry hung up. She immediately dialed Dianne.

"Hello Di! What do you think, can you and Ed go?" Jerry noticed a pause; he knew they were both excited.

"Yes the vacation is a gift to me, and Jerry said to bring you guys. He really likes Ed and cannot wait to hear more sea stories. He said tell Ed he won't have to work on this ship, all he will have to do is 'relapse'. That is some inside joke, I think."

Again it was an excited phone call. Sherry told Dianne that she would call and let her know the arrangements. Ed had let his passport expire and would have to renew it. Other than that, things seemed to be on track.

When Jerry saw Sherry headed his way, smiling, he couldn't help himself. He stood and met her. They embraced, and Sherry said, "You are a hit Jerry Wiley. This is going to be the highlight of my life, and probably the girls' too."

Holding Sherry close and enjoying the warmth of his sweetheart, he said, "I hope this is all it is built up to be. And if it is, I hope it is NOT the highlight of your life. I don't mind it being the highlight up 'til now, but of your life, I hope not."

After the kiss, "You say the sweetest things, to be an old man." They both laughed.

"Well is that all for now?"

"I think so. I cannot wait to hear from Melanie and what she's found out."

"Listening to you talking to your buddies and the excitement had me thinking about this family I married into. Of course, I always think of your older sisters, but today I thought of your brothers. I have always respected heroes —few families have one, but you have three brothers who were heroes. I like being part of your family."

"They were always heroes to me, but I never thought of them as being heroes to anyone else. They were just brothers who were good to me." All of a sudden, Sherry lit up like a light, "Speaking of heroes, that Blackie was a hero today. That was amazing how she conveyed the message that Asam was in trouble."

"Did you see the movie Lassie or Lassie Come Home?"

"I don't remember it, if I did."

"It might be a boy thing because it was a story about a boy and his dog. In the movie, Timmy, I think, was in trouble, and he said to Lassie, 'get help.' Lassie takes off like a bullet, approached a man, and takes about the same actions that Blackie did; it was honestly like watching that movie when I was twelve."

"I couldn't believe it either. My first thought was *the dog is loose*: we have a leash ordinance in town, and you seldom see a dog loose anymore," Sherry finished.

"I just hope the old man is careful; that was a very close call."

Being doctors, both Jerry and Sherry were well aware of the dangers involving the peanut allergy. Thousands are seen in emergency rooms and nearly two hundred die yearly. The average person eats peanuts and never gives them a second thought. As doctors, the thought was sobering: the man would have died if Blackie had not gotten their attention. "Honey, I seldom believe in coincidences. I believe there was a magical or spiritual connection between you and Asam," said Jerry, and he held his love close. "Sweetheart, you are blessed with a good heart."

Holding each other was a normal thing with Sherry and Jerry. It seemed they were catching-up on the time they had missed in their lives before they met.

They enjoyed soup and salad for lunch and relaxed in front of the TV to catch up on the news. Midafternoon they were surprised with the ringing of the doorbell. Sherry went to answer. Since Mary Ann's abduction, Sherry always looked through the viewer. The bell rang again, and she motioned Jerry to come over. Then she opened the door.

"May I help you?" Sherry asked.

"Pardon me, are you Doctor," the man consulted with a card that Sherry recognized as her business card, "Doctor Sherry Wiley?"

"Yes sir, I am, and this is Dr. Jerry Wiley, my husband. How can I help you?"

"Forgive me, I am Ali ibn Badir Samir, the son of Asam Badir Samir." Behind him were two young boys and a lady wearing a headscarf.

"Oh! Sure Asam, we met him this morning. Please come in."

"That will not be necessary doctor. I came to give thanks for what you did for my father because he means a lot to my wife and our sons."

"Please I insist, come in."

Reluctantly, Ali ibn Asam Badir Samir entered with his entourage.

"Please have a seat. Could I get you refreshments: anything to drink or a snack?"

"No Doctor, we will not trouble you long."

"My friend, your visit is no trouble at all. Regarding the incident this morning, what we were able to do is what we are trained to do. Did your father tell you that Blackie was the hero?"

"Of course he did mention Blackie; the boys already know he is a hero." Ali smiled for the first time, and the boys lit up like Christmas trees, nodding their heads.

Sherry related the incident of seeing Blackie running down the sidewalk, her actions, how she got their attention, and how she had convinced them to follow her to Asam. "Once we were inside the house, and I read on Blackie's collar and the wristband about the peanut allergy, I only said 'fetch'; she retrieved the bag with the antidote inside. Without the medicine, there is some concern that he wouldn't have lasted for the medics to arrive. We are just happy we could be there."

"It appears my job with IBM may become permanent. We are enjoying life here in Mount Bell. We have experienced some resistance, but overall we feel part of your town. My wife and boys have adapted American names: this is my wife Sarai and my sons Donald and Mickey, from your Disney World, I must say."

Jerry spoke for the first time, "Well it is a pleasure meeting you guys, and we are honestly glad we could help. Please give Asam our love and thoughts. We were so glad to make his acquaintance, even if the circumstances weren't ideal."

Handshakes were exchanged all around, and Ali and his family relaxed but refused the tea and water offered.

They made small talk about Istanbul where Jerry had spent some time.

Jerry shared with the family that he was taking Sherry to Corfu but did not think they would make it as far as Istanbul. Ali was not familiar with Corfu but thought his father was.

"This has been pleasant, and thank you for your hospitality. My family owes you a debt. Since my mother's passing, my father means the world to us, especially the boys. I assume my father told you he now is a Christian; to my dismay, my dear wife has forsaken her past and practices Christianity also. We have yet to come to an agreement about the boys, but, in my life, that is a small thing. I am probably closer to agnostic rather than a Christian or a follower of Islam."

As they went to the door, Sherry told Sarai she would love for them to visit again. Outside, Jerry whispered to Ali, "I was an agnostic until a couple years back; my work was my god," Jerry winked and smiled saying, "You will get over it Ali. You take care and, although I am not from Mount Bell myself, welcome to town and to our house anytime. If you find you need anything that I can help with, please call. And the best to your dad; he seems a witty fellow." Jerry finally thought he recognized just a little more tension easing.

Jerry and Sherry stood on the porch and watched until Ali and his family rounded the corner at Myrtle Street. "That was a nice thing for them to do," said Sherry, "I enjoyed the surprise visit. Wait until I tell Evelyn and Di I have a Muslim friend."

"Well let's get inside before the neighbors hear that," Jerry said, laughing as they went inside.

"I think I want some hot tea. Would you like a cup of green tea, Doctor Wiley?"

"Yes Doctor Wiley, I think that would be an excellent idea."

"Good because it is going to be *talking tea*, so get ready to tell me some of the destinations on the way to Corfu."

While the tea was steeping they talked. Jerry told her of Alicante, Spain where they could get a taste of the old world. "I know you girls are probably not into blood sports, but bull fights are popular in that area of Spain." Jerry knew Sherry's reaction even before she made a face. "Hey, I'm not asking for a date there. I just said they were popular, that is all, Doctor Wiley," Jerry said, grinning.

Sherry's favorite perfume had never changed. She had fallen in love with Chanel Number 5 in her early twenties. As Sherry poured the tea, she heard of

Toulon, France, where they could take a tour inland a short distance and get a boat load of Chanel Number 5. She would be able to see how it is created.

Now Sherry's interest was rising even more. She loved hearing Jerry talk of all the places he had been; his life had been an exciting one of travels and danger. She didn't mind hearing about it, but being kidnapped by a crazy man was enough for a life time: she did not need any more of that type of excitement.

"I guess we should go to Naples and tour Rome, maybe introduce you to the Pope."

"You know the Pope?" She asked, shocked.

Jerry smiled, and she knew he was pulling her leg. "I do know his name!" said Jerry, and Sherry slapped his shoulder playfully.

"Remember what they say about paybacks old boy!"

They finished their tea and Sherry went off to work on an Afghan Mary Ann had started for her. She was getting the hang of it. Jerry went back to his easy chair and opened his novel.

Chapter 6

The next morning, they were both up and had already had breakfast and were sitting on the front porch when the phone rang. It was Melanie. "Doctor Wiley, I have some ideas to run by you guys if you could stop by the office sometime today."

"Melanie, thank you for being so efficient. Please call me Sherry. Now about the time: what time would be convenient? We are available all day."

"I have nothing scheduled this morning, if that's good?"

"Then we will see you in a few minutes. Thanks for calling."

Jerry was ready, so they locked up and headed down the hill on the sidewalk. "What a beautiful day for a walk," Sherry commented. "I just hope we don't see a strange-acting animal."

"Yeah one a week would be sufficient," Jerry smiled. He squeezed Sherry's hand and gave her a wink. But coincidences do happen: they did see Blackie. She was across the street entering Stowe Park, but this time she was on a leash, with Asam holding it. He glanced their way, and they all waved. He had a beaming smile and a friendly southern nod of 'good morning'.

When he realized they were crossing the street with a hand signal, he told Blackie to sit. He stood waiting. As Jerry approached, both their hands went out like old friends. "I had no idea I would have this pleasure on the day," said Asam, "But this is a joy. Good morning to my two doctors, saviors, and new friends."

"Good morning Mr. Asam," said Sherry, "Does Blackie walk *you* here *often*?" They all laughed at Sherry's joke.

"Oh yes, she loves to bring me here; she has met a couple friends. But, my doctors, I have never seen you walking here in the morning. What brings two famous people out this early?" Asam asked warmly.

"We are headed to see a travel agent. We hope to visit the Mediterranean, and visit one of my favorite places in the world, Corfu. Ali says you might know of this small Greek island."

"Yes, we should talk of it one day. I do not want to delay famous people on their way to arrange a vacation."

"We will be there in plenty of time, Asam."

"Not to pry into your business, but there are places I would not go if I were you." Asam spoke seriously.

Jerry was concerned, "Before we separate this morning, quickly, what places are you referring to?"

"Dr. Wiley, I am from Turkey; I have lived in Egypt, Greece, and Syria. If our Lord will allow me, I will remain in this wonderful country for the rest of my life; I am tired of the war, killing, and turmoil. I would go no further easterly than Athens or Piraeus. It would be prudent to take in advisement the ramblings of an old man."

"I think you are a wise man, and many thanks for supporting my own thoughts. You and Blackie have a great day. And you have our address; please Asam, do come for a visit."

Breaking the surprise meeting, they headed on up the small hill to the offices of Creative Travel. "I am really glad we ran into Asam this morning. I do not believe in coincidences too much. I think we were meant to get that information," Jerry was saying as they reached the office. They were both excited and looking forward to seeing what Melanie had to say.

Melanie positioned her computer monitor so they all could see it. "This is what you are facing. The Transatlantic is no problem in June, and the ship's purser and cruise director are holding five suites until five o'clock our time. We develop a problem once we are at Barcelona, Spain.

"All the cruises are booked that hit the northern shores of the Mediterranean. Several have openings along the way where you could switch ships and continue. At some ports you would have to fly.

"We can get you on several different ships to complete your tour, but I assumed you would not want to waste one or two days to link up with the various ships. Of course there are plenty of openings for the North African shore, as you can well imagine with the unrest."

"Melanie, I perceive you have an alternative up your sleeve; let's have it," Jerry said as he winked at her.

"Yes I do. It is expensive but gloriously beautiful."

"I like gloriously beautiful; let's have it."

"You could lease a yacht," she paused for a moment to give it time to sink in. "I spent several hours last night drooling. These are super nice and have some big recommendations, one from Mr. Gates himself."

"Just how expensive, Melanie? You are scaring me," Sherry's voice went weak.

"Well Doctor, the trip could reach up to a million dollars, depending on which yacht you choose; there are several available."

"No, no Melanie. When I suggested this I had no idea of the cost. What would it cost if we waited a few months, when the cruise ships aren't booked?"

"I did not consider that since it seemed you wanted June. But, if you give me a couple hours, I can sure find out. I remember seeing plenty of openings in October. That's a good month weather-wise also, and school is back in session. I'm sure we can make October work."

"Good. Then look into that for us. I'm sorry to have pushed for June. Honestly, I hate you went to that trouble because of an old woman's silly dream."

Grinning, Jerry said, "October will not work; I'm sorry: I plan a heart attack and I want it here in the USA."

"Don't even joke about that Jerry, it could happen!"

"Bingo, ding, ding, ding! Think of what you just said, sweetheart; you are absolutely right, it could happen. It could happen to either of us at our age. Remember, you are always saying, 'Jerry, you are the boss'. How many times have you told me that?"

"But Honey, I have never seen a million dollars. I cannot think that high."

"Well sweetheart, if it makes you feel any better, I have never seen a million dollars either, but I am told I am worth that much and more. So humor me. Let's look at a yacht; my interest is peaked. Show us Melanie," and he nodded and winked.

"You are looking at the Sherakhan; she is an older yacht, but just completely refitted this year. She will take 22 to 26 passengers with all the amenities you would expect at sea. She also carries a couple of jet skis for use in port. She is the largest, at 227 feet, and the oldest.

"Note a more modern design: the Keri Lee III. She is 177 feet and will support 12 guests. It has same amenities but more toys: 4 jet skis, wind surf boards, and a laser sail boat. It is a beauty. Built in 2001 and retrofit in 2010. They say she looks like new.

"The last yacht I looked at that would fill your bill is the Tatiana. She is 147.5 feet and takes 12 guests. She only has two jet skis, but also a small outboard, along with the wind surf boards. She is the newest of the three and is also well equipped.

"Now, I'll give you these folders covering the yachts, and you can decide if you would like any of them."

"I like them all," Said Jerry "However, I am assuming that the Tatiana is the fastest, since it is the newest. Am I right?"

"Yes. She cruises at 14 knots and has a top speed of 22 knots."

"Then why don't you go ahead and get the best price you can get on her. Let's say we want the Tatiana for four weeks, with a possible extension of a couple weeks." Turning to Sherry, "Honey, how many of our friends do you have so far for the trip?" Sherry just sat there looking into space and was not answering. Jerry nudged her, "Honey?"

"Oh I'm sorry Jerry. I am lost and embarrassed; I never meant for it to get this involved, and you are saying, *go ahead.* You can't be serious honey."

"Of course I'm serious. I want to take you to Corfu, and I do not want to wait until October." Smiling, Jerry continued, "Now, how many friends do we have for sure as of now?"

"Don and Evelyn, Ed and Dianne, Buck and Mary Ann, and then you and I, which will make it eight."

"Melanie, please go ahead with that plan. I like the name Tatiana; this is going to be super. As that guy used to say on 'Hawaii Five O', book 'em." Jerry said laughing and elbowing Sherry in fun.

"Okay, then it is settled: you will depart on June fifteenth from Fort Lauderdale, Florida. I will e-mail you the details. I have never scheduled a vacation like this. You are going to have a fantastic summer one made of dreams."

"Well Melanie, it has been my dream for years. Will the Captain require a list of ports in advance, or can we just travel as the wind blows?"

"Doctor, I will have to check on that and get back to you. It would probably be a great help to have the places you want to visit listed for me to submit; that way, if there are any questions, we can get them answered."

"Of course Melanie, I should have thought of that. We will prepare a list as soon as we can. I would like to get with our guests to find out if they have a preference. It would be terrible for someone to want to visit someplace and miss the chance because they weren't asked," Jerry stated.

Rebecca came in to see how things were going. They all agreed this was the trip of a lifetime. Rough agreements were signed. Jerry wrote a check for a deposit for eight guests on the transatlantic cruise, and they departed.

From inside the office, Rebecca was watching the older couple as they left, and Melanie came in to her office. Noting Rebecca following them with her eyes she said, "They are a loving couple aren't they?"

"They certainly are. In this business I have dealt with a few wealthy folk who expected more attention than others. But these two are real. We have wealthy people in Mount Bell: some expect a lot, but that old man and his wife do not expect special treatment. During an appointment here you would never know he was worth a billion; you have to appreciate that. Negotiate the best prices you can for them. They deserve it."

"I feel the same of course. I was just going to give you the prelims on what I have. So far it looks like…" Melanie went over her plans and Rebecca gave her blessings. "I am excited for them. Doctor Jerry made me want to go to Corfu, after hearing him describe his experiences there."

Out on the sidewalk Sherry looked over at Jerry and said, "You amaze me sweetheart. There are times I think you can handle anything."

"I am going to confess something; it is something I think you know or should. I have had an exciting and fulfilling life. I have been allowed to see and do things that few men have, but winning your affections, and hearing your say *yes* when I proposed, was the crowning jewel of everything. I realize that you are the treasure, the excitement, and the thrill that I have always sought; to me you are the jewel, the priceless jewel of which I was secretly dreaming."

"Jerry Wiley, you silver tongued old man, if your boys knew what a romantic you really are, they would never believe it. They think you are 'Mr. Iron Man'; the man who would eat fire and never ask for water. But I know better. You are a lover at heart; *my lover.*"

Chapter 7

"Sweetheart," Sherry called to get Jerry's attention, "Is tonight okay with you for dinner with the gang at the Woodshed in Stanley?"

"Sure, sounds like a winner. I love their steaks; they run a very good race with the Little Red Barn down in San Antonio."

Back on the phone, "Yeah Evelyn, The Woodshed at six. You call Dianne and I will call Mary Ann. I have so much to tell you. Jerry is getting a yacht for us to use in the Mediterranean. Tell Don it also has a Jet Ski he can use to run beside the boat and act like he is mowing hay."

On the other end, Evelyn said, "Don has always resisted a cruise. Doug and Ron have tried to get him to go on a cruise. His answer was always, no way. He spent a few years on submarines, and he spent a lot of time at sea, but I think he is looking forward to this time on the surface aboard with Jerry and Ed. All of them having spent time at sea, I guess it is the boy's thing of something in common."

"I can't wait, myself. Jerry always says the journey is as much an adventure as the destination. I am even beginning to see that the planning is a lot of fun also. You wait until you see this yacht. This is going to be good. I cannot remember even seeing a yacht before."

"I have seen them pull into port at Key West when Don was stationed there, but I sure never expected to be on one. Don says the beds aboard the cruise ship will be big, but I imagine on the Yacht they will be smaller. I need him close to me anyway!"

"This brochure of the yacht says all the cabins have king size beds; I was shocked."

"Do you know how big it is?" asked Evelyn incredulously.

"The name is The Tatiana, and Jerry says it is one hundred and fifty feet long with three decks."

"I need to ask Don something." Sherry heard Evelyn call to Don and ask, *how many feet is it from the front porch to the sink in the kitchen of our house?* "Don says our house is about 45 feet from the front to the back, which would mean this yacht is three times longer than our house is deep, WOW."

The conversation continued for almost an hour, as did most of their conversations. Every conversation contained some activity, teacher, or class from their high school days.

Once the call was terminated, Sherry dialed Mary Ann. They talked a while; never as long as with Evelyn because Mary Ann was starting to have problems hearing on the phone. But the major question was answered: she and Buck would be clear to go. They were very excited and could hardly wait. Crossing the Atlantic would be new to all the ladies. And, as always, the question of wardrobe came up. "Yeah, we are going to have to think about the clothes point of view. Jerry says, if possible, we need to stick to two suitcases and one carry-on per person, just from a handling point of view. He wanted me to let everyone know that laundry and dry cleaning services were available on the cruise ship and washing/drying would be available on the boat."

"So you said tonight at the Woodshed for dinner, right?"

"Yes I am going to depend on Jerry to make it all plain. This is going to be such fun with Di and Ed coming too"

They ended the conversation, and Sherry headed to Jerry's easy chair where he was reading. Leaning down, she gave him a peck on the forehead before sitting on his lap. "Well my dear," said Jerry, "to what do I owe this attention? A beautiful lady on my lap, I warn you, could be dangerous and lead to dancing!"

"I am the wife of the great Dr. Jerry Wiley; I thrive on danger, dude!" she said, laughing. "But the reason I am here is to say you have stirred up a hornet's nest of excitement. We can hardly wait."

"If I remember correctly, my dear lady, it was thee who started this snow-ball rolling, and I have never been happier. Yeah sweetie, I am getting excited myself."

****

Sherry had arranged for them to pick up Ed and Dianne. Evelyn and Don were driving, and Mary Ann and Buck were driving down from Lenoir.

Ed and Dianne were always a joy to be around. Ed was known as the life of the party; his outgoing personality was always a joy. Dianne was more subdued when you first met her, but she added life to any party. She was also a great friend. There was never an end to conversation when the classmates got together. Ed was the only male classmate. Don had been a year ahead of them in school and a big player on the football team. The one thing Mount Bell High School could say, they had one of the best football teams: they were the Red

Raiders. Ed and Jerry had a lot in common. Neither had gotten involved in sports. There was an adventurer in each of them. Ed didn't have time to finish High School; he felt the call to sea. He had lived at a time when boys from Mount Bell either headed for the military or to Detroit to build cars. Many of them wanted to avoid the cotton mills.

Ed took to sea like a duck to water. His life at sea had been exciting, but it was on the west coast and the Pacific, thousands of miles from Mount Bell. Once, when he and Jerry were talking about their dads being strict, Ed had related to Jerry that on one cruise he had ignorantly ran up a gambling debt. He had the money back in the bank in Mount Bell. He had set up a joint account with his dad's name on the account so that, if Ed needed it, his dad would withdraw the money.

Laughing, Ed had told Jerry, *Dad would not send me the money even though it was mine.* His dad had said, "No son of mine is wasting his money on gambling!" So he had paid it from next month's pay.

At the end of his hitch, he was foot loose and fancy free and headed back across country to Mount Bell. Now he had been away from the Navy for many years; he was looking forward to a cruise on which he didn't sweat in the engine room, but he could relax like the officers he had known. Dianne had told him that they would have a stateroom. This was going to be different than sleeping in the same compartment with twenty other swabbies.

Sherry and Jerry picked the two up and headed toward Stanley. Excitement was in the air. Ed said, "Jerry, my friend, are you sure you aren't asking for too much trouble? Dianne gets wild at sea; I just want you to be forewarned." Of course, that earned him a playful slap from Dianne.

"Believe it or not, I had heard that rumor Ed. So I checked: we have a Doctor on board the cruise ship who was a front line doctor in Vietnam. He has Dianne's medical records and has already learned which sedatives to use." Jerry said laughing. That earned him his slap both from Sherry and Dianne.

"Seriously Jerry," Ed began, "this is a wonderful thing you are doing. Dianne and I have talked about a cruise but haven't gotten around to it yet. I can't wait to see the Med. I was a Pacific sailor but never in the South Pacific. The old salts say the Med and the South Pacific are beautiful twins; I am really looking forward to it."

Sherry answered for Jerry, "When I suggested this trip, he asked if I wanted friends or him. I told him I wanted both. I cannot imagine that much time without seeing you guys, and I wanted you all to enjoy it with us."

Dianne spoke, "This is going to be the highlight of our lives, I know. I could never have dreamed this. I thought the shopping trip was something, wow; this is the *cat's meow*, to use a phrase from high school."

The rest of the short trip was cruise talk. Sherry told them Jerry would be filling them all in on ports and dates over steaks; that is, he will be giving all the information they have up to now. As they pulled into Stanley, they were just behind Don and Evelyn. They pulled into the Woodshed parking lot to find Buck and Mary Ann already there waiting.

As they all headed into the side entrance, the noise level picked up. All these guys became kids again when they got together.

The maître de directed them to a private dining room where they were seated and ordered. As an appetizer, they all were having the Woodshed specialty: the marinated onion and tomato sandwich.

While the waitresses were gone, Sherry opened the meeting. "I know you all have heard most of what will be said tonight, but I wanted everyone to be together for the first meeting. First of all, we will be gone from the fifteenth of June until the seventeenth or twenty-fourth of July. Now is that okay with everyone?" Ed raised his hand.

"Yes *Brother* Ed?" Jerry said smiling, knowing a fun retort was coming.

"I was going to say the twenty-fourth sounded good, but Dianne hit me, so I ain't saying it."

"I'm with you Ed. Now, I wanted to tell everyone that, since Jerry and I have been married, the name of an island has sporadically come up: the Greek island of Corfu. He has always talked about it with such affection; the other day I just asked him would he take me there, and he said yes. Actually, his words were, *you can bet your bippy*; and that set the ball in motion. So now, after we have chatted and eaten, Jerry will give you some of the details." The room broke into applause.

Everyone enjoyed their meal. The Woodshed, located in a small town, was known far and wide for its good service and great steaks. It is a family owned business and has always taken pride in its food.

As the workers were clearing the tables, Jerry stood up to speak; the applause broke out again. "Not that I do not appreciate the welcome, but honestly, it is not necessary. We have been friends for a couple of years now, since I married Sherry. I haven't regretted a minute of it. Before I talk about the trip, there may be some things you do not know about me. I am one blessed man. I have lived the life many envy. It was not a lonely life. I have had some of the closest friends one could want." Pausing for a minute for a drink, Jerry continued. "My dad was wealthy; he enjoyed life his way. For years he was very proud of his son. I became a doctor, attained fame and what small fortune goes with that. But I left it. My father was not happy about that decision. However, we reconciled before his death and I inherited his business. There was an attorney with the company, a brilliant guy: Dallas Fletcher. My heart was not in the business so I looked at other things, and turned the business over to Dallas.

"Dallas had known for years that Wiley Industries had wider potential, so I turned him loose. While I was curing the worlds ills, setting wrongs right, Dallas was turning a multimillion dollar national business into an international business with a net worth of billions. Yes Ed, that is with a 'B'. I have never in my life been extravagant, but I have never had a jewel like Sherry. So if this trip makes her happy, I am going to enjoy spending some of the money that Dallas earned for me." The group was silent, intent on Jerry's information.

"So now we are looking at a good time together. I will not apologize for being wealthy; neither will I apologize for finally splurging to make my wife happy. She mentioned Corfu. I did fall in love with that Greek island, and I hope you will like it too. We have one hurdle yet to jump through. We will take a cruise ship to the Mediterranean but, after that, it became too complicated to make the ports we wanted. So, the folks at Creative Travel suggested a yacht. A yacht will be our home in the Med. Now, what I want to know by tomorrow noon if there is any particular place you want to visit in the Med? We are going to try Alicante and Barcelona, Spain; Toulon, France; Naples and Rome Italy; possibly Messina, Sicily, and Venice; and of course the main destination: Corfu. So please talk it over and look at the maps. If you would like to see someplace I have not mentioned, we want to go. I love you guys and I hope this is a lot of fun for us all. Now, I do not want any fussing. Sherry has envelopes for you. Inside is a copy of the yacht's layout. There is also a credit card. Our banker says they are good. Sherry intends to pay all costs for this vacation; so, starting today, if you want to do some shopping for luggage, clothes, or whatever for the cruise, she expects you to use the card. Let's all have a great time."

After the applause, Don stood up. "I am not much for public speaking, but this is sort of like winning the lottery. I have always been a little leery of surface ships," he said smiling. Everyone there knew he was a former submariner, "And Evelyn has pestered me about a cruise for a few years. Now you and Sherry have presented me and the rest, I think, with what the Godfather said, *is a deal too good to refuse.* So I just had to say, for Evelyn and me, and surely for the rest, this is unbelievable, and thank you from the heart. This is some surprise." With that, everyone stood and applauded.

As they were sitting down, Ed spoke, "What Don said goes for us as well, and that's for sure. But I do have to admit I am shocked. I didn't know a submariner could put that many words together," he said smiling. "But he did and he said it better than I could have. I am really looking forward to being on a ship where I don't have to work in the engine room!"

After everyone had enjoyed a good laugh, they continued to talk. In a few minutes, they noticed Mary Ann was standing and started to quiet down. Mary Ann nodded in Jerry's direction. "Jerry, when I was kidnapped, my life appeared to be over. You took charge and brought me home safe and sound. Ever since that time I have tried to figure a way to thank you." She had to pause as she choked a little and tears were starting to fall. "I have been unable to come up with anything that I thought would come near to showing you how much I appreciate what you did. Now this." Mary Ann pulled a handkerchief out of her purse and wiped her eyes. "I think I have always believed in God, but I have wondered about angels," pausing to pull herself together, she finished the sentence, "but I don't anymore." She sat down with tears falling freely. There wasn't a dry eye at the table. Her personality is one of caring and peace. That was all personified in that speech. Buck put his arm around her and pulled her close.

"Mary Ann, my friend," said Jerry as he rose from his seat, "In all my life I have never heard a more moving thank you. Although the thank you was not necessary, I want to tell you I am glad to have you as a friend and glad that you are safe to enjoy your life with Buck. As you know, I found my love late in life and she happened to be your friend. She had been in a kidnapping situation; therefore, she and our crew knew some of the things you and your family were going through. We had been there," Jerry paused as Mary Ann was pulling herself together after the strain of her heartfelt speech, and then Jerry continued, "Now that we all are officially agreed this is going to be a great trip, I think it is about time to allow these folk at the Woodshed to clean up so they can go home."

Outside everyone was saying their good nights; the ladies had already planned a shopping trip. The dinner had been a great success, Sherry thought. *Yes, life is good. I don't deserve this, but I am going to enjoy it. There is nothing like being this happy and blessed.*

On the way home Ed was speaking. "I joke around a lot Jerry, but this is a fantastic thing you are doing; we are tickled pink about this."

"You know Ed, I was on that island years ago as a part of the CIA. I was single but had tunnel vision for the coming operation. As days passed and the plans kept changing with the situation, the tunnel vision dissolved and I had time to watch the average Greek citizen on Corfu. Most of them would never leave that little island. The other day I was thrilled when Sherry said she wanted to go to Corfu. I have been wanting to go just to see if they had been able to hold on to that type of life. As I watched them on the weekends walking, picnicking, and just enjoying life at a slow pace, I thought how wonderful it would be to live like that; you know what I mean?"

"Yes Jerry, I think I do. In my earlier life, everything was fast paced. As the old statement goes, no one was taking time to smell the roses: working and getting the kids to all their activities, all the time remembering, when we were kids, we had found our own activities. It was a confusing life. You know, sometimes it is nice to be old; to be able to put things in perspective and live one day at a time. This cruise is going to be the greatest. I cannot wait to see your Corfu."

"I can hardly wait either Ed." Said Sherry. "You put into words just how I feel. The other day, when I mentioned this to Jerry, I was sorta thinking about that very thing. I was remembering skating down the Hawthorne hill, gaining speed, and wondering if I would live or die; my skates weaving in and out because of my wobbly legs. At the bottom of the hill, as an eight year old, I thought of traveling to see the world, and I never had. Then Jerry's island came to mind and I wanted to go."

"Well I sure am glad you thought of it; this is the best idea you ever had, especially since you included us." Dianne paused, then looking at Jerry said, "Thanks Jerry!"

As they reached their destination Jerry said, "We are just glad you can go. And by the way, I can hardly wait myself; this is going to be fun."

After Ed and Dianne were dropped off, Sherry squeezed over as close as she could to Jerry and said, "You are a hit with everyone my man, but mostly to me. I love you."

Jerry thought to himself, *it is hard to picture perfect, but this is close.* "I love you too sweetheart."

Chapter 8

While having his last morning cup of coffee, Jerry's phone rang. Caller ID said it was his friend Dallas. "Yes Mr. Fletcher, what can I do for you this fine morning?"

"Hello to you too Jerry. How are you guys doing?"

"We are doing great Dallas. This is a treat, but to what do I owe this pleasure?"

"You are suspicious Jerry, always thinking there is something behind every call." Dallas was laughing, "And of course you are right. I was sitting here thinking *I just heard of a great deal, who should I offer it to?* And I thought of you."

"I have a feeling I am about to spend some of the money you earned for me."

"That gets a little tiresome Jerry, about my brilliance, but I am learning to cope with it." Jerry could hear Dallas laughing, "I remember you saying once you would like to have a Gulfstream G650. I know of one a guy is losing unless he sells it. He is asking sixty million and change for it. The blue book is close to seventy million. I have a buyer for yours at twenty five, and you will have a Gulfstream for thirty five million. What do you think?"

"Dal, I have forgotten, how many passengers does she carry?"

"Up to eighteen passengers, and she will fly from LA to Paris in less than nine hours. And yes, Stella can fly it and, with just a few additional hours, you and Vickie can qualify for the jump seat."

"Stella wants it?"

"Are you implying that I talked to her before calling you? I am hurt Jerry, hurt I say."

"Well yes, in a word, that is exactly what I am saying, you silver-tongued devil."

"Since you put it that way, yes, I talked to her, just to get her opinion, of course."

"And that was what?"

"She wants it and refuses to fly that crate you have anymore."

"Then by all means, we need it. When is it available?"

"Stella is in the air as we speak; she loves it. Jerry, stand by; I will be right back." Jerry, smiling to himself. There is no one in the world that he trusts more in business matters than Dallas. Dallas has always had a nose for business: a second nature tells him in a matter of minutes, whether a deal is good or bad. He has been one hundred percent correct. It is uncanny. "Hey Jerry, you still there?"

"Yes Dallas, I'm here."

"Good. Stella is on the line with us; she is thirty thousand feet high."

"Hello boss. This dude is fantastic, thanks! I am gonna love this baby; she almost flies herself. Dallas said you would get it."

"Hey Stel, so you really like it?"

"Absolutely. You would even be able to fly it, it is so simple."

"Sure, I have no doubt. How long before Vickie is up to date?"

"As you know, I am sure, Dallas has set up a class for Vickie, and in a week she will be ready."

"Yes, of course I knew all about it. Dallas would never do anything without letting me know," he finished laughing. "Now if I am paying for the Av-gas, land that sucker ASAP!"

"Roger boss, but we are on the other man's dime now."

"Then, by all means, enjoy the ride. Take care. See you soon so you can give us a ride."

Dallas closed the conference call and said, "Hey Jerry, I forgot to mention that. I knew you would want Vickie to qualify and the seller is paying."

"You know I trust you *most of the time,* my friend. Now is the hangar in Gastonia still working with the Gulf Stream?"

"No change: your Gulfstream will be in Gastonia in two days. Wiley Industries is taking care of all the paper work."

"So this retirement of yours is sort of a fake. I bet you still go to work every day."

"Insightful devil, aren't you? I am only in the office three days a week." Jerry could hear the smile. "Marian tells me to go play!"

"Okay Dallas, thanks for the help; or should I just say thanks for getting us a Gulfstream? I can't wait to take her up. You know, if you and Marian ever want to use it, all you have to do is call."

"We might just do that. I finally got that lady to get a passport; she has held out for the longest."

"Give her my love. We could never ask for better friends and business associates. That is so trite and begs more, my friend. You know I love you like the brother I never had. Take care of yourself and that beautiful lady."

Rounding the bar, Sherry said, "Well, what is all the excitement about? Who was it?"

"It was Dallas. We no longer have the Lear Jet."

"Is something wrong Jerry? You sounded excited a few minutes ago."

"Oh Sweetie, I'm kidding. Dallas just called and said he has found a Gulfstream for Wiley Industries. He knew I had wanted one but was holding out for a good price. He found one and, with the Lear Jet, it is only thirty five million. That is a bargain."

"THIRTY FIVE MILLION? I will never get used to that kind of figure, darling. It boggles my mind." She paused, thinking, "But Stella loves the Lear, it is like a lover to her. She will be devastated."

"Seems she is a little fickle sweetheart. I just talked to her. She is thirty thousand feet up in our new Gulfstream and she is already in love. Honey, the Gulfstream will carry up to eighteen passengers in comfort. You will not believe it until you see it. Dallas said this one, the Six Fifty, can fly non-stop from LA to Paris in nine hours."

Looking concerned, Sherry asked, "Does this change our vacation plans? Will we fly to Corfu?"

"Oh no sweetheart, everything related to our trip remains the same. This is just a business decision and one I have wanted for awhile. Dallas just found it and grabbed it. He is a wonder."

"Well the girls and I are going shopping. Is there anything you want?"

Jerry winked. "Since you mentioned it," he was smiling and looking her up and down, admiringly.

"Jerry Wiley, you are incorrigible. We will be back for supper and I will pick something up." She gave him a peck, and he pulled her back for a serious kiss. "Forget it lover boy, I am off." She was still laughing as she walked out the door.

As Jerry sat. He picked up his novel, but was just staring at it, not reading. He was thinking of the new Gulfstream. He had an idea. *Why not?* He dialed Don.

"Is your wife gone?" Jerry questioned.

"I assume she is meeting your wife at the mall. What's up?"

Jerry told Don about the Gulfstream and his idea. "You know Ed. Give him a call and see what he thinks. I'll call Buck and see what his thoughts are. Call me back after you hear from Ed."

Jerry called Buck and there was no problem. He was thrilled. "That's great Jerry, and this is going to be a stem winder!"

The call came in from Don that all was well with Ed. So it was all set for the weekend. Jerry could hardly contain himself. "Hey Don, you know Carrol better than I. Call him and see if they want the same trial flight."

Before Sherry came back from shopping, the trial flight in the Gulfstream had been arranged. Jerry was feeling great.

Sherry came in with roast chicken, peas, gravy and biscuits. They talked a few minutes. She got out some cranberry sauce and set two places at the bar. They were both a little hungry. After pouring the tea and asking the blessing they began the meal. In a few minutes, Jerry said, "Hey baby, Friday afternoon would be a good time for a maiden flight in our new Gulfstream. Why don't you call the girls later and see if they would like to go up for our virgin flight. Why don't you include JoAnn?"

"You want the men too, right?"

"Of course, if they do not have other plans."

"That will be a great idea and maybe we can eat at that Italian place over by the Airport when we come back in."

"Why not? Sounds like a plan."

It was a good deli meal and, after they washed the dishes together, Jerry made them a small chocolate nut sundae, and they settled down for a new cowboy movie. Life was good in Hawthorne.

Chapter 9

Friday afternoon came and everyone met at the airport. Of course they were all impressed as they stood looking at the Gulfstream. Stella was gushing as she explained the practical side of 'her new bird.' Vickie stood by making comments about the technical side of the new lady.

The Gulfstream is the ONE desired by companies. It is a dependable workhorse with an exceptional history. Impressive to say the least, she has two Rolls-Royce engines. The 650 was built from scratch in 2012 and is the ultimate in executive planes. She set a speed record in 2013 and it still holds.

All the oo'ing and ah-ing was understood because this plane is impressive, and unique in this area because it is the only one stabled at Gastonia.

Stella invited everyone aboard. As they were following her, an official airport van drove up. The airport manager opened the passenger door and called to Jerry, who was walking over to see who and why someone was driving up to their hangar. "Doctor Wiley, I am glad I caught you. I just wanted you to know how excited we are to have the first Gulfstream home-based here at Gastonia." He paused to look at the group. "I was advised of your pilot's flight plan." Jerry cringed a little but continued to smile. "I hope everything is to your liking. Our goal here is to attempt as best we can to keep our tenants happy. By the way, this is Mr. Harold Russell. That is his hangar over there. It doesn't house planes but houses most of his classic auto collection. He is a good friend of mine and I wanted you to know your neighbor."

Stepping forward a little, Harold held out his hand and Jerry took it, both men had firm grasps. "It is good to meet you. I have seen your pretty pilot and mechanic around. I don't run as fast as I once did, but I still manage."

"Nice to meet you Mr. Russell. I love old cars, especially the classics. I would love to see your collection some time."

"It would be my pleasure." Jerry noticed Harold was looking over his shoulder. "Don, Ed and Carrol, I didn't know you boys hung around with rich folks?"

Don laughing, "We know you, don't we?" and everyone got a good laugh. Then the rest of the crowd came over to meet Harold.

"Doctor, I have known these boys for years. A few years back Don even gave me an old International pickup to add to my collection." Pausing to locate Vickie and Stella again, he said, "Now you ladies don't be bashful, when you see me at the hangar, come on over and I will give you a ride in a real vehicle, not like Dr. Wiley's shiny toy here."

Stella's cheeks turning a little red at the attention spoke softly, "Mr. Russell we would be honored to do that, but I do have to clarify one thing about this toy: Dr. Wiley owns it but it is really mine and Vickie's."

Everyone loved that. Jerry turned to the airport manager, Mr. Moak. "Dennis, my wife and I are taking some of our friends for a maiden voyage." Pausing for just a second he looked over at Harold, "I advise you not to let Stella drive one of your toys. She is now learning to pilot at .85 Mach, and she'll be dangerous on the ground."

"You guys have a good flight. We are hoping for a long and productive relationship. Now take care, I will say you have the prettiest pilot and crew I have ever seen!"

"Thanks Dennis. Nice meeting you Harold. I look forward to seeing those cars."

Once aboard the plane everyone was milling around. "May I have your attention: I am Vickie and will be your co-pilot; I am also the mechanic for this magnificent bird. The executive seats are for Doctors Jerry and Sherry. The rest are yours by occupying." Vickie paused while everyone found a seat and buckled in as they heard Stella winding the engines. "Now this bird is almost new, with only forty hours in the air and thirteen landings. So what we have here is class, according to seasoned flyers. Buckle up and get ready to be thrilled."

Vickie went out to direct Stella as she completed the hangar exit. She signaled the airport maintenance guy to close shop and she climbed aboard, closed and sealed the entrance hatch. Stella was moving as Vickie sat and buckled in.

Jerry smiled at Sherry, "I guess I am a materialistic man, I love what you see here. This will make overseas flights so much more comfortable for the folks who handle Wiley industries." Jerry was interrupted by his pilot.

"Ladies and gentlemen, I am Stella and I will be your pilot for the day. This is Vickie's flight for sealing her seat. This time aloft is all she needs to officially qualify her to fly this bird. She is one amazing friend and she can fly and repair this beautiful Gulfstream. Please make sure nothing is loose in the cabin. Ensure that you are buckled in. Vickie will be back for more required FAA information when we reach forty-eight thousand feet. You heard that correctly. We will be flying at forty eight thousand feet. Welcome aboard Wiley Industries Gulfstream G650."

At that moment she moved the stick forward and the Gulfstream headed down the runway. Jerry smiled at Sherry as he felt the tremendous thrust of the two Rolls Royce engines. When Stella was airborne, she smiled, looked over at Vickie and Vickie smiled ear to ear and nodded. Stella gave her full throttle and climbed at sixty degrees. It seemed to the passengers they were going straight up. While a thrill to most, and a small swath of fear for others.

Once they leveled out, Vickie unbuckled and headed back to give the safety speech. Holding the hand mike she roamed as she talked because of the layout of the G650. The layout gave the passengers a feeling of small offices, four or six seats to a section. All seats were window seats.

"We will be flying today at forty eight thousand feet. Your pilot will be holding a speed of approximately six hundred miles an hour. That is approaching the sound barrier at eighty five percent Mach one. This is like most commercial planes. If the cabin should become decompressed, your oxygen mask will fall from above." Vickie went through the safety procedures. "Your pilot says feel free to wander about, visit, and chat. The refrigerators contain drinks and the cabinets contain peanuts and snacks. We will not be serving dinner." Everyone laughed and clapped.

Everyone was thrilled. Only Jerry had been higher than forty eight thousand feet. It was a smooth flight. Sherry came back to Jerry after about an hour. "Everyone likes the idea of the little Italian restaurant for dinner. About what time do you think we will land?

"Probably in about forty five minutes sweetheart. How do you like it?"

"This is unbelievable. It is like a miniature commercial flight."

"It is, isn't it? Except there are no lines and no NSA to feel you up and bug you about what is in your pockets. I am so glad Dallas found this sucker so I am just leaning back and enjoying the idea of having it available. Some day we will fly everyone to Hawaii for dinner."

"Wow, I am glad I married a man who thinks large and can back it up." She leaned down and gave him a kiss. "That is for being you, Jerry Wiley!"

Sherry sat and they talked for a few minutes, then she said "I think I will ask the girls if they would like to go to Hawaii for dinner sometime." Then she was up again. Jerry heard the squeals of delight and heard Hawaii and WOW a couple times. Something inside him smiled. He was happy and his love was happy. For the millionth time he said to himself, *Jerry Wiley, you are one lucky dog.*

Jerry loved his station in life now. He had not married a movie star or gold digger. He had married a real woman. This real woman had real friends: no fake, no show and just real people. In his position, he had rubbed shoulders with what many would call the elite. Businessmen, politicians and the wannabe's who faked what they thought was 'class' but were as empty as a beer can at an navy beach party.

"Got a minute?" Jerry was brought back to the present by Ed. Ed was the realist of the real guys. He could make you laugh and cry. He had that mischievous smile.

"Sure Ed, anytime. What is going on?"

"I just wanted to take time to tell you that I think you are one great guy." Holding up his hand to stop Jerry's obvious response, he continued, "Don is right, I think we all won the lottery when you married our friend Sherry. I think I know you. We all know you didn't have to do this. You and Sherry could have jumped on this magnificent plane and flown to *you know where* by yourselves, had a romantic time, and been back to Gastonia without us even knowing. That is until Sherry phoned Di, Evelyn, or JoAnn to tell them how you seduced her with your charm and money." Ed paused smiling at his friend, "But you included us. I just wanted to thank you. You are one stand up dude."

Jerry was impressed but not surprised at Ed's grasp of the present. "Ed, I would bet that you even understand a little more about me. When you came over I was sitting here thinking about 'peers.' My business friends ask among themselves, what was on Jerry's mind? He could have married one of many young models or actresses and he married a doctor from Podunk, North Carolina. They cannot believe it because they do not understand it," pausing ever so slightly and smiling, "But you do, don't you Ed?"

"Yes my friend, I believe I do. In layman's terms, you are a real person, so your heart sought out a real person. I don't know if y'all were taught any poems by Edgar Guest up in Pittsburgh or not, but he had a way of saying things that got to the heart of the matter. In one poem he said, *It takes a heap of living in a house to make a home, but it ain't home to you though it be the palace of a king,*" Jerry joined in for the final line, "*Until your heart is wrapped around everything.*" They both laughed.

"Yeah Ed, I was forced to learn that poem also, even up in Pittsburgh."

"Well that's how I see it: you had everything in the world but what you needed was someone your heart was wrapped around. You just happened to find that in Podunk, NC."

"So there is a poetic side to Edward?"

"Yes and I sure am glad you married Sherry and took the rest of us to raise."

"Took who to raise?" It was Sherry standing over Ed's shoulder.

"Oh Honey, Ed and I were in a very deep philosophic discussion. It would be hard to explain before we land. I'll explain it all later when we have more time," said Jerry, laughing as Ed was getting out of Sherry's seat.

"Your attention please, this is your pilot speaking: please return to your seats and buckle up; secure any loose objects. We expect a smooth landing. The temp on deck is a warm eighty five degrees with a slight breeze."

Everyone was looking around. Is this a joke? When they left the airport it was a nice seventy one degrees. Sherry looked at Jerry who was trying to keep a straight face. "Where are we Jerry? What have you cooked up?"

Jerry held his hand up, signing to wait. "Do not interrupt your pilot; I am sure she is not through yet."

"We will be landing at the Circle R Ranch in San Antonio, Texas. My orders are to refuel and be ready to take off within two or three days. I am sorry if there is any inconvenience. If so, please take it up with management. Your luggage will be handled by Circle R cowboys and cowgirls. Ladies, please don't tell me your man did not tell you this. Please don't tell me that he packed your suit case. So hold on to your Stetsons cowboys, 'cause we're coming in for a landing. Enjoy your stay." Stella and Vickie were also enjoying the surprise.

Questions were flying; Sherry was breaking a big smile. "Jerry Wiley, you know this is onc of my favorite places in the world. I can't wait to see everyone on the River Walk, and the boys at the Alamo. Jerry, you are precious."

It didn't take but a few minutes for the men to explain they had packed what they thought would be needed. Jerry had told them that all toiletries would be stocked at the Triple R Ranch. The girls could use their credit cards to buy at least one outfit.

Plans were, after everyone got settled in their rooms, that the Triple R Ranch bus would give them a quick tour of downtown San Antonio. They would then return and enjoy the evening entertainment at the ranch, opening with a chuck wagon dinner, some square dancing, and entertainment by none other than *The Sons of The Pioneers.*

There was yet one more surprise for Sherry. Paula and John were going to be at the dance tonight. John had a Ranch near the Triple R and Paula was a cowgirl poet. Sunny of the Pioneers wanted Paula to recite a real Texas poem. Sunny was the oldest of *The Sons of the Pioneers,* and he was from Asheville, North Carolina. Sherry had met Paula on the internet and had introduced Jerry to her on their last trip to San Antonio.

Stella's second landing was perfect. The excitement was high and the men were proud of themselves for pulling this off. This was going to be fun.

Chapter 10

The Triple R was an active ranch; cattle roamed around the landing strip and out back of the ranch house. The house had been laid out like the one on the television series Dallas, only much larger. It served as sort of a fancy Bed and Breakfast. There was also a large bunkhouse with plenty of room for visitors who wanted a Dude Ranch vacation.

Mr. Romano met them personally, in standard western working attire. Whether it was showmanship or standard practice, he had ridden up on a beautiful Palomino horse. He dismounted and had his horse, Trigger, greet the new arrivals. "Please meet the king of horses, Trigger." On command, Trigger dropped to one knee and lowered his head. Then, with another hand signal, the horse stood and trotted off to the barn.

"I am Rollo Romano. Welcome to the Triple R ranch. I understand you will be with us at least two nights. We are so glad you chose to come to Texas, in particular San Antonio, one of the most famous of Texas towns. Yes, we know it is a city, but we still like to think of it as a town." He shook hands. They stood under a gazebo area for a few moments and he explained the evening schedule.

Two cowboys had the luggage on a small four wheel buggy that was hooked to a huge, neatly decorated goat; they were headed for the ranch house. Stella and Vickie had been directed into a shady hangar area. The Gulfstream had been put to bed. All the newcomers were escorted into the ranch house and given their room keys with directions.

Within fifteen minutes everyone was milling around the small but well provided buffet, stocked with finger foods, decorative small sandwiches, and barrels of drinks.

"I can't believe this. Carrol has never been able to keep a secret, and of course this whole thing is amazing," said JoAnn. Then, looking over at Jerry, "You are good, bro; you are good." JoAnn said smiling.

Dianne spoke up, "Wow, and the rooms are fantastic. I think I am back in the old west. I expect to see John Wayne walk through one of those doors that have stainless steel door knobs made from horse shoes. What a trick."

"What about the vanity fixtures in the bathroom that look like old water pumps? Yep, this place is fantastic," added Ed.

"Yeah, I was looking at the Sears catalog, until I realized it wasn't there to read," Don said, as Evelyn hit him playfully.

As the bus pulled up Jerry said, "Okay everyone, let's take a bus ride and get a preview of tomorrow's activities."

Everyone seemed to be on a high. They were all excited. Just a little over three hours ago they were boarding the plane and expecting to fly around a little and return to eat Italian near the airport. And here they were, settled in a luxury Bed and Breakfast, eleven hundred miles away; a surreal feeling. The guys were beaming. They were now headed to see the Alamo, every American boy's dream.

The driver was a very good tour guide. Everyone could hear and understand. They loved the Spanish accent, it added to the trip. The Triple R is close to the community of Somerset. Ed was getting a kick out of reading the names of the towns on the road signs. "I know you took a wrong turn somewhere in the sky Stella. That sign said Charlotte ten miles and we just passed one that said Castroville. We are five miles from Cuba!"

"Oh but sir," came the driver's voice over the speaker, "Most folk assume that Castroville is somehow Hispanic, but a man named Henri Castro emigrated here from France with family and friends of German heritage. They settled along the Medina River. Castroville has a hardware store that is the center of the town. They have carried farm and ranch supplies from the turn of the century."

"Okay cowboy," called Ed in mock anger, "What about Charlotte? I know that is in North Carolina."

"Yes sir, we do hear that a lot, however, your Charlotte cannot hold a light to our Charlotte. All the women are beautiful senoritas and our men can all ride a wild bull; some can even talk a lot of bull. To top that, we will even reach 2,000 souls in our Charlotte next year; *how y'all like dat?*" The driver said, laughing after putting on an exaggerated southeast accent. Bringing the whole bus to a laughing roar.

"Please look below as we cross the next bridge. We will be crossing the famous San Antonio River Walk, also known as the Paseo del Rio. I understand tomorrow you plan to enjoy it. It is a wonder and we Texans are proud of it.

"I will be making a left onto South Alamo St. We will pass our most sacred shrine on your right. The Mission San Antonio de Valero is referred to worldwide simply as *The Alamo*."

As they passed the Alamo everyone looked in awe at a place in history that, until now, had only been a historical place in a school book. "Now my friends, some of your distant families in the southeast went through a terrible time with the Civil War, when members of their families were on opposing sides: some with the Yankees, some with the Rebels. Something many do not know, nor consider, is that I, for instance, had family on both sides of the cause that the Alamo represents. Some of my relatives did not want to leave the care of the Mexican government. Most of them, however, wanted to see a free land called

Texas. So we Mexicans that were referred to as Texicans by many, fought with our new friends. We all know the eventual results after the battle. Santa Anna, with thousands of soldiers, and the defenders, numbering around one hundred twenty five, fought a bloody battle for thirteen days. I lost family on both sides, but I am so proud of the Texicans who stood firm."

The bus was now quiet as it rolled north on Alamo Street. Breaking the silence, Carrol said, "We just passed an old hotel called the Crockett. Did you see it?"

"Sir, that too is a very famous landmark. She stands seven stories, with about one hundred forty rooms and suites. It was built in the early nineteen hundreds. I will be heading this bus back to the ranch. I hope you have enjoyed the ride. We will be back in time for you to freshen up and get prepared to feast and dance to the music of *The Sons of The Pioneers.*

Jerry held up his hand for attention. "While we enjoy the ride, I just wanted to tell you all how much this means to Sherry and me. I am learning to enjoy your fellowship and just the plain fun of conversations that have no connection to business. Tomorrow after breakfast we will retrace our steps into San Antonio, walk the river and actually walk through the Alamo where some of my heroes gave their lives. I have walked through there at least ten times and each time it has given me goose bumps. I hope it has the same effect on you."

"Oh yes," Sherry spoke up, "Mr. Romano says they have interdenominational church services Sunday mornings. Whoever wants to attend can and we will leave afterwards for some serious shopping. I am told our driver knows the best places to shop."

Back at the ranch, everyone headed to their rooms for the last real surprise of the trip.

Chapter 11

In their rooms each couple found western outfits to wear for the night's festivities. Jerry had asked the men to get sizes for skirts, blouses and boots for the girls. He had asked Vickie and Stella their sizes. When everyone met in the lobby they were admiring each other. They were all thrilled and they could smell the meat roasting on a giant rotisserie. The Triple R cowboys had been roasting a half steer since very early this morning.

The serving was efficient with two lines. They joined a line with the other guests and many locals from the area. Triple R Barbeques were well known in the area and with the famous *Sons of The Pioneers* being the entertainment had brought the attendance to its maximum. Mr. Romano had retuned thanks over the meal in the beginning so once they were seated everyone started eating.

"I hear you guys are from North Carolina. Would you let another Tar Heel join you?" They all turned at the sound of the very friendly voice. The source of the voice was obviously one of the band members. They made room and as the man took a seat he continued, "I'm Sunny from Asheville, where y'all from?"

Don spoke, "We are from down around the Gastonia area. Aren't you with *The Sons of The Pioneers*?"

"Yeah, I am proud to say I am, they tolerate me because I am so old and purty," bringing a rising laugh from everyone.

The meal was fantastic and the conversation even better. They all got to know Sunny and all about what *The Sons of The Pioneers* were doing these days. There was a loud run on the drums to announce the local lead in band as the dancing area was cleared. The MC came on strong, "Ladies and Gentlemen, Cowboys and Cowgirls, put your hands together for the King and Queen of the dance floor, Rancher John and his pretty lady Pauline, with John's favorite, the Texas Two Step."

Sherry turned to Jerry, "You beat all, you knew this didn't you?"

"Well is it okay?"

"Okay? It's wonderful! Girls, that is our friend Paula, Jerry didn't tell me a thing about this."

As the music started Ed and Dianne were the first to head for the dance floor. They were an item on the local dance floors back home. They were followed by Buck and Mary Ann. After a couple of songs everyone was on the floor having a great time. After a few dances John and Paula made it over to the group and they were introduced. Jerry had already invited them on the cruise but John said it was time for the cows to be dropping calves and they could not get away. Paula had said, "Nothing gets in the way of ranching; we both have learned and accepted that."

The Sons of The Pioneers were introduced and they sang a couple of songs. The jokes were hilarious and the music better. After about fifteen minutes Sunny took the mike. "Folks we have some surprises for you. I know I look and act like a Texan, but I was born a Tar Heel from North Carolina. I want you to welcome Carrol T from Mount Bell, North Carolina." Carrol was shocked, but had no choice when the two cow hands escorted him to the stage as the crowd stood and applauded. He was taken to a spot beside Sunny and was handed a guitar. "That is a Gibson. I think you said that was your axe of choice, so strap that sucker on and join the famous *Sons of the Pioneers* in singing *Tumbling Tumbleweed*!" The band started and Carrol had no choice but join in. After about ten bars he was now part of the band. He was back home at Catfish Cove and happy as he could be. JoAnn was grinning from ear to ear seeing Carrol up there performing with a world famous band. Her childhood hero Roy Rogers had been a member of this group. She leaned over to Evelyn, "Won't be no living with that boy after this!"

The group sang *Blue Prairie* followed by *Whoopie Ti Yi Yo.* After the song one of the group said, "Hey Sunny, didn't you write that one?"

"Yeah, yeah I did. I heard it a couple times then I wrote it." The house came down with laughs and applause. Then they broke into Sunny's trade mark song, *Ma Don't Allow no Guitar Playing Around Here.* Sunny was famous for playing twenty-two instruments. In this song he played seven of them.

"Folks, I'm slap tard, so while I rest up please give a warm welcome to our Dancing Queen and local poet Paula as she gives us her latest poem, *Wanna Be Cowgirl.*" To a rousing applause Paula took the mike. The band started playing *Don't Fence Me In* very quietly.

Paula spoke quietly, "This is sort of an autobiography of this Texas lady who has always been a *Wanna Be Cowgirl.*"

Wanna Be Cowgirl

Her shirt is shiny to match her boots

True country people are not her roots.

Can't ride a horse, doesn't know how

Never had the experience of milking a cow.

Tight, tight jeans and a little name belt

A silver buckle and a hat made of felt

A howling coyote dangling from her ears,

She drives an' dreams, as sunset nears

Doesn't own a ranch, but wishes she did

Had these thoughts since she was a kid.

Driving her truck and pretending to be

She's a 'wanna be cowgirl', don't you see?

Someday a cowboy will make her his wife

Then she can have a real cowgirl's life.

The babies start to come, she must grow up

Give up her jeans and the pick-up truck.

Trade the shiny shirt for a little housedress,

Get busy cooking and clean up the mess.

She'll save the belt to prove her size

As she gets larger around the thighs.

Now she is minding her grandchildren, telling this story

She's a 'Wanna Be Cowgirl' in all her glory.

Paula finished to a standing ovation and the *Sons of the Pioneers* then sang *Cool Water.* When she returned to the table everyone was hugging and telling her how good she was. Paula is easily embarrassed and John said, "All right now, you are gonna have her face so red she can't get around our Bulls without making them charge at 'er."

The evening was fabulous. Everyone was worn out from excitement and dancing. They said goodbye to John and Paula. Inside in the Lobby they noticed a crowd gathered around the piano and could hear some short runs on the piano.

"What is going on over at the piano, some late entertainment?" Don asked one of the cowboys standing by.

"Nah, but folks are standing around to see if a new hit song is born. Our neighbor Paula gave Sunny her latest cowboy poem, and he's setting it to music. We have seen this before, he's good. And like most show men he likes to show off too, that helps, shucks, that helps even roping cows," he said laughing.

Just then there was a heavy introduction run on the piano, and Sunny's voice came out strong with the words:

Here lies a cowboy *who has roped his last steer*

Uttered his last cuss word, drank his last beer.

He was a kindhearted man, that's what I heard,

Helped his fellowman, you could depend on his word.

Once he bought some land and a few longhorn cattle

Trying to make a living turned out to be a battle.

The rain wouldn't come, the air was hot and dry

As the buzzards circled over, flying in the sky.

Here lies a cowboy *who has pitched his last bale,*

He was full of optimism, did not intend to fail.

The mortgage came due, no money for the bill

Then his expectation, became hard to fill.

Here lies a cowboy who rode his last horse,

His wife had got fed up and filed for divorce.

When he meets St. Peter he will tell him a yarn,

Wearing his old boots, which are quite worn.

An imprint in his pocket of a little round tin,

Well! For a cowboy to chaw tobbacy ain't no sin.

Cowboys *are a dime a dozen, but no one can take his place,*

Riding into heaven to meet his maker face to face.

Sunny repeated the last two lines several times and everyone joined in. He did one more long run on the keys then spun around on the piano stool. The rendition had been notes and narrative, something Sunny could do well. "Folks, what do you think? That was ***Here Lies a Cowboy****, by Sunny and Paula.* I think with a little polish that will show up in Branson. Now I am tard, I am somewhere in my seventies, but (singing) *I Wish I was Eighteen Again*". The crowd gave a lot of applause and Texas whistles. He gave a bow, tendered a big smile and headed for his room, giving a lot of *thank you's and handshakes* to the well-wishers as he left. The rest of the crowd slowly faded into the night for some well-deserved rest.

Chapter 12

The next day, after a Texas-style breakfast at the Triple R, the bus loaded and they headed back into San Antonio. Then the group was dropped off across the street from the Alamo and headed down to the Riverwalk. The Riverwalk is one story below street level. This entrance across from the Alamo is a work of art consisting of water falls, cascades and narrow ponds with fish and ducks. Sherry had already suggested they take the river tour boats first thing so everyone could have a chance to see if there was something special that caught their eye and they wanted to do or see up close.

Everything is festive. The walk is lined with bistros, restaurants, cafes, strolling musicians and sidewalk shows. The river is narrow and has swans, ducks and cranes swimming among the tour boats. The boat handlers are experts at maneuvering the turns required. One could get the idea that they were in Venice.

Jerry suggested they split up and meet back in two hours and exit the Riverwalk where they had entered. The result was two groups, the men were together leaving the ladies to enjoy the souvenir and dress shops.

Everyone was in awe and having a great time. Jerry suggested coffee and they all agreed. Ed said, "I think I will have one of those fancy looking sweet rolls." They were at the Marriot Coffee shop. Once Ed took one, the others decided he had a great idea.

They sat around for about half an hour enjoying the coffee. Everyone laughed when Don told them he had called Doug to tell him to keep an eye on the farm because they were in San Antonio. Doug had not believed him. It took some explaining. The same with Buck and Mary Ann; they had received the same reactions from their family.

Carrol looked over at Jerry and spoke, "I want to tell you, my friend, that was the highlight of my amateur musical life, I actually played and sang with *The Sons of the Pioneers!* I don't know how you did it, but I will never forget it, that's for sure."

"Fact is Carrol, I had nothing to do with that, that was strictly Sunny's doing, but I want to tell you we all got a kick out of you for the first fifteen or twenty seconds on stage. I have never seen such a bewildered look. But when the band started, you were right there and we were all behind you! *You done good.*"

"Yeah at first I thought JoAnn was going to have to run up and give you mouth to mouth," laughed Ed, "I knew Sunny wasn't going to."

"I will admit, I was scared to death, but those guys are real and they are good too."

After the rolls and coffee were finished, they walked around the Riverwalk. They stopped to watch and listen to the strolling Mexican Band as they played. Each member of the group was dressed in fancy Mexican attire. It was all quite a treat. They spent a lot of time just sitting at different locations to enjoy the scenery and simply people watch.

The conversation came around to the Alamo. All of them knew the famous folk who defended the Alamo until their deaths. There were thousands of troops with President General Antonio López de Santa Anna and less than one-hundred-fifty defenders toward the end. They were all drawn to the statement of their bus driver that he had family on both sides of the war, something none of them had ever considered.

Buck mentioned that we remember Bowie, Crockett and Travis but he was anxious to see the names of others and where they were from.

Carrol broke in, "If I remember right many of the men there were from out of state who came to help defend Texas. I am interested too, in seeing the inside of the Alamo."

Jerry told them of Brackettville, on down toward the Texas-Mexican border where there is a replica built by

John Wayne and others to film the movie *The Alamo*. There is a village built to replicate the small village of San Antonio as it was when the battle took place.

As they were talking the girls walked up — everyone carrying shopping bags. They laughed and talked awhile then headed across the street to the Alamo. They all paused at the huge monument street-side honoring the defenders of the Alamo.

They took the rest of the afternoon wandering through and around the Alamo. They all paused before the name of Micajah Autry and the six men from North Carolina who died defending the Mission.

It was a solemn time and they were disappointed that taking pictures was not allowed inside the Alamo Mission itself, but they *mostly* respected the rule. It was sort of a religious experience knowing so many men died there. Most of the defenders had lived in Texas less than two years. While many had just recently rode or walked to Texas and gave their lives delaying an army that was later defeated because of this short delay.

The ride back to the Triple R was not as boisterous as coming in, but this group was now supporters of San Antonio, Texas. This had been a momentous day.

Sunday before church services on the ranch, Paula and John arrived. They usually attended services at the small Rock Church near their home that was a Texas

Historical Place; but this was a special occasion. After church Paula and the girls took the bus shopping. The men took a Triple R van to John's Ranch and he showed them around. John was very patient with the tender feet guys, explaining the finer points of protecting his herd. Not the least were the newly coined 'Bloat blocks.' They were sort of like a salt lick, but more of a '*Rolaid*' for cows. The clover was big this year and the gas caused by the delicious clover caused bloating that sometimes is deadly for a cow. So the blocks saved the rancher a lot of work and helped his herd.

"John, I don't see any brands. On 'Rawhide', Rowdy Yates and the boys always branded the cattle," commented Ed.

"Ed that is too much work for us old guys. The government wants us to ear tag 'em. Still we older Texans would rather see the brand, but like I said that is work, and the tags also help trace disease problems. I do have a Brand, registered with the state. It is 'J' 'O' Not Connected. Like this," John took a stick and drew his brand in the dirt.

Then John introduced them to the *cubes*, kind of like a 'doggie' treat for a cow, it actually contained a lot of nutrients. Everyone got a chance to feed one of the cubes to a cow of their choice. The guys were having a good time. The only one of the crowd still living in the country in North Carolina was Don, but he no longer had livestock.

John took them over to his stock tank, and since it needed some water he demonstrated how he added water to the tank from the well. The 'stock tank' was actually a small pond with a dam. He explained about Paula's love for all animals and always fed the rabbits and the turtles in the pond, "Actually I think they understand her. She talks to them like children and she has a way of communicating that amazes me."

After a lot more discussing they loaded back in the van. They all heard it, it was a long way off, but it was unmistakably a siren. John asked the driver to stop. "**If** they make it this far you are about to see a real live Coyote. That is most likely a border patrol chasing a stolen truck or van. The drivers are known in these parts as Coyotes. He will have a load of illegals who have crossed the border south of us. If we are lucky he will wreck before he gets here. When the Coyote is being chased he will not stop until he wrecks. Then those onboard that can still run, will scatter into the wilderness. They may catch one or two but the rest will get away." The siren was getting nearer. John explained that he or one of the ranchers along this road must repair a fence at least once a month because of the Coyotes.

Now they saw the dust trail. Everyone was staring at the unpaved road. Sure enough there it was, and on the back of the pickup must have been 6 or 8 men holding on for dear life and the cab was full. The truck barreled past. "Lord help me, he is going too fast, he ain't gonna make the next turn and we just fixed that fence. I declare I think I'm gonna put a steel barrier with some concrete up there."

About the time John finished talking the truck left the road. The screams of the guys in the back could be heard above the roaring engine that had lost its muffler. The driver handled the wreck like a NASCAR driver straightening the truck as it took out John's fence. The truck had lost two tires, but plowed on into the field. Some of the men had been thrown clear and were running the same direction the truck was taking. The truck finally stopped when it hit a washout, and everyone still on the truck bailed out and ran in all directions. Then the Border patrol slid to a stop at the road's edge. This one was not a SUV with four wheel drive and stopped at the road to watch the illegals scatter. He had his mike in his hand.

"That's Tommy one of our local boys who has made good. He is probably trying to get a helicopter, but none of these guys will be caught and I have a fence to repair." John asked the driver to drive on up to the Border Patrol car.

Tommy was looking at the van, then smiled as he recognized the Triple R brand on the front of the van. John waved through the window and Tommy smiled and walked over. "Tommy dadgummit if you are gonna let 'em go, don't chase 'em and they won't tear up my fences!" he said laughing.

"Sorry John, same spot as last time, huh?"

"Yep, I have some friends here from North Carolina. We were just out looking at the cows." John introduced everyone. Tommy had to interrupt them a couple times to answer the radio.

"Now you guys can see firsthand our problem in South Texas. Tell everyone you know about this. We need all the exposure we can get, seems like no one in DC knows, cares or believes it. By the way John, you buying the Triple R?"

"Not this week," laughed John, "Just showing some of Romano's guests around."

Tommy said good day and headed back to the cruiser to answer another call. He went off in a cloud.

"I better get you guys back to the Tripe R and get this fence fixed."

"Hold it John, we ain't helpless," said Jerry, "We got time and nothing else to do, what do we need?"

"Oh we got the fixings over in the shed by the stock pond, but you boys are on vacation."

No one would hear of anything but fixing the fence. "Besides Imma feel like John Wayne repairing the fences them rustlers busted, then Imma load my six shooter and go after 'em," said Ed in a mock John Wayne voice, bringing a good laugh at a time it was needed, especially for John.

It was not a lot of work for the number of men working, Don was very familiar with this work and they soon had the fence fixed. John explained that a tow truck will come and move the wreck. "The truck will be stolen, always is. The tow truck will use the gates and make sure no cows get out. Everyone around here knows to close every gate they open."

Actually it had been a very exciting day. They were a little tired, but what a day. It was story telling time when they got back to the ranch. The girls were already back. John told Paula about the latest Coyote incident. "So you guys got to see firsthand one of our problems. That is one of the good and bad things, good you got to see it, but bad that it happened, again," she said in disgust. "It seems to be a plague that no one can stop. We understand why they want to come to Texas and don't blame them for wanting it, but something needs to be done to control the problem."

Mr. Romano came out and invited John and Paula to stay for supper and they agreed. John was free, since the fence was repaired. *The Sons of the Pioneers* were not leaving until in the morning. Some of them had their wives, but musicians like to jam, and that was the evening after a good meal. Sunny introduced his newest song, 'Here Lies a Cowboy' written by Paula. He even coaxed her to help with the recitation. It was just a lot of fun.

Carrol had been fitted with a guitar. Don, Ed and Buck joined in on 'Cool Water'. John and Paula showed their *stuff* doing some clogging and tap dancing. The finale was Vickie. No one but Stella had ever heard her sing, but when those vocal cords took hold of 'How Great Thou Art', everyone was mesmerized. That was a voice for Carnegie Hall.

Jerry announced, "Sherry informs me that in the morning after one of the Triple R's great feeds, would be a good time to head back to Gastonia. But before we disperse I want to thank everyone. I mean everyone here at the Triple R, including John and Paula for taking us in as family, treating us like royalty and giving us a great weekend. Thanks."

Cheers, amens and applause erupted as they dispersed and headed for their rooms. What a day!!

As they left Jerry noticed that the 'Trail Boss' of *The Sons of The Pioneers* along with Sunny had cornered Vickie. It looked like a very serious conversation. A thought ran through Jerry's mind, *I could be looking for a mechanic soon.*

Chapter 13

The North Carolina tourists were fed Texas style and given a great send off. There was so much excitement

and conversation that the two hour flight seemed only minutes. The flight was smooth and the weather was perfect. Everyone had a window seat and enjoyed the city of Gastonia as the plane lost altitude to land. Stella received permission from FAA to do a circle that allowed everyone to see their homes from the sky; that was an extra kick. It was around noon, and arrangements were made by the ladies to meet and get prepared for the cruise. JoAnn said, "I hope you girls hold out, I couldn't handle weeks of excitement like the couple days we've had." Turning to their hosts, "Thank you from Carrol and me for taking us along for a wonderful trip. We had a fantastic time, but I'll have to trim Carrol's wing feathers after his stint with *The Sons of The Pioneers*." she was saying as she hugged them.

Everyone dispersed to their respective homes; Sherry and Jerry were on their way to Mount Bell. Jerry looked over at Sherry, "Did you notice that management from *The Sons of The Pioneers* was talking to Vickie last night?"

"As a matter of fact I did. Did you have any idea that girl could sing like that?"

"None whatsoever. I do know that most of her family sings. I have heard her mother could have been professional, but I was blown away by the strength and power of that voice. I looked and did not see my mechanic. I saw unleashed talent. I sure would hate to lose her, but if that is what she wants and this is a foot in the door, she sure has my blessings."

"I guess we think alike good sir, I believe that is a carbon copy of my thoughts. She is a sweet lady and a good worker. She deserves a break and the world needs to hear that voice."

Back home Jerry had phone calls to make and Sherry was attending to the business of the neglected house because she had not planned to be gone two or three days. It was nearing five o'clock and Sherry sat down beside Jerry who was back to his novel. He smiled as he marked his page and put the book down, "And to what do I owe this lovely interruption?" he ended with a quick peck.

"What do you say to a hot dog and a milkshake or a Blizzard?" She smiled knowing that his weakness was a Tropical Blizzard at the local Dairy Queen.

"I really had my mind on some Pennsylvania summer sausage, but I can forego that for a Tropical Blizzard."

After a few years, they still had not mastered the *'she said supper he said dinner'* thing. So in honor of their differences he had coined the word 'Supner.' But today it was dinner and would be a sandwich and a Dairy Queen Blizzard.

The Dairy Queen was one of the oldest establishments in Mount Bell. The tables were still the 1950's style booths. The two of them loved sitting across from each other. It was a thrill rolling their minds back to when they were sixteen, pretending they had known each other back then.

The only people who can know the feelings of seniors in love are, seniors in love. They had both agreed on that. Along with the attention to the *Old Lovers*, Jerry had long ago learned to nod and smile at the folks who stared at them. It seemed that every year some new wild story was dreamed up of Rags and his infamous time in the woods and on the streets of Mount Bell. Most of them folksy, a few very wild; but both of these seniors had learned you cannot control what folks think.

A young reporter from the Gazette had heard some of the stories and had asked for an interview. He, Rags and his wife had agreed it was probably one of the best ways to calm the inquisitive minds. Ms. Turbyfil was very good. They had enjoyed the in-depth thoughts of the reporter as well as her humor.

She had written a good piece with their pictures. The good had outweighed the bad, so it worked out well. However now word was getting out that a billionaire lived in the Hawthorne section of Mount Bell.

Both of them had agreed that a very good security system was definitely needed. The attraction to the underworld to milk the very wealthy families of money was real. The tactics varied from threats of releasing uncomplimentary pictures or improprieties to the tabloids, up to and including kidnapping and ransom.

Jerry was always alert to his surroundings, a practice that had become second nature over the years in his varied professions. Tonight it was locals and the famous local old couple. They enjoyed it.

The excitement of the cruise was never far away, "I think tomorrow I will head down to Jeri Lyn's to see if she has snagged some great stuff I could wear on the cruise. A couple of the girls are going with me, I think."

Jerry just smiled, he knew better than to suggest anything different. He was still amazed that a lady who could fly to Paris or London and shop for anything she desired, would go to a consignment store. It was never the money, it was knowing his Sherry was real. He could tell a little change since she learned how rich she was, but not enough to change the wonder of a 'Mill Hill Girl' as she would say.

They spent a wonderfully quiet evening together, watching a movie on television while enjoying cuddling like teens in love. They both were thinking, *I hope this feeling is never lost.*

The evening ended with them both falling asleep reading, awaking at different times and heading for bed. A solid night's sleep was unusual at their age, but that is what they had, the trip had worn them out.

The next day at Jeri Lyn's in East Mount Bell. The girls had a great time. Jeri showed them some great items that her friend Shirl had dropped off. Many still had the tags still hanging. "Shirl is a regular," Said Jeri, "And you can always count on comfort and quality."

Everyone found one outfit and Sherry also found a pair of sandals she could not live without. Then on to the mall to finish a day of shopping.

Shopping was the priority about every other day until everyone had what they wanted and all was being packed. On the day before the flight to Fort Lauderdale, Jerry drove over to the hangar, partly to get out of Sherry's way and at the same time check on Vickie and Stella's plans while they were gone. He knew Dallas and Marian were flying to South Dakota sometime during the period they were gone, but sometimes the corporation had a flight scheduled.

He arrived at the hangar condos. Both girls had a flat in the well-insulated hangars. Air traffic was light at Gastonia, but still irritating if you were trying to watch TV or sleep if you did not have the insulation protection. He rang the bell at Stella's condo. It took a while but the door slowly opened. Stella smiled but he could tell she had been crying. "Oh hello Boss, come on in, but the place is a wreck. Vickie was inside she stood and Jerry found a seat as the girls sat. Vickie had also been crying.

"Okay ladies, it's obvious I interrupted a cry fest, what is going on? ...... Wait, I am sorry, it is a habit of mine. This is none of my business, but if I can, I sure want to help some of my favorite people."

"There is really nothing anyone can do Boss. We have a friend who is in trouble……" Stella was stammering a little bit.

"Oh go ahead Stella, it is embarrassing but I am sure Jerry has dealt with some of this stuff in his life. If he has time to listen, tell him."

"Of course I have time. I'm here to get out of Sherry's way."

"I hate to lay this on you when you guys are headed for a great vacation."

"Look sweetie, compartmentalization is my middle name, let's hear it."

Chapter 14

Using some tissues Stella tried to dry her eyes and clean her face a little, "Boss, Vickie moved in here at about the same time as our good friend Connie moved to Gastonia a few months ago. She is a single mother and Carla is her sweet thirteen year old daughter. Being new in school here and very pretty, some of the guys started hitting on her for dates. The girls she met seemed a little jealous, but still gave her some pretty good advice. Steer clear of Billy Bob the local rich kid. Well she thought it was jealousy so one day walking home from school, up pulls Billy Bob in his gold

Corvette, offers her a ride home. Billy Bob did not take her home but took her to one of the local BBQ joints and bought the best sandwich they had. They talked and joked and he took her home. Telling her she was the most beautiful girl he had ever seen, and that he could spend his life with her on the French Riviera. No touching no kissing."

Vickie chimed in because Stella was choking up. "This happened for a couple of days. In the mean time she was being told he was a shark, but he had been the gentleman, so how could he be a shark. She just assumed the girls at school were jealous. Except for one girl, her new friend Jane, who only said, *please believe me I know, I dated him a couple times. Drop him, he is no good.* By the way Billy Bob is eighteen Carla is still thirteen."

Back to Stella, "So Monday night, he calls her, *hey darling how are you. Are you dressed for bed yet?* She answered yes. Then he gave her a line a mile long about never seeing a naked woman, and if they were going be married he wanted to see what he was getting. He told her he knew she would be beautiful. *Take everything off and stand in front of a mirror and use your cell phone and let me see.* By now she was hooked, marriage and all. The next night he wanted to see more and more pictures from her cell. So she kept sending them, about ten pictures all together. Last night the hook came. In a text he expected sex Wednesday night. All kinds of kinky sex he had in the text. She said *I am a virgin Billy Bob I thought we were going to wait.* Then it was, I will pick you up Wednesday. Your mom will be in church, but you will be sick. And we will have a ball. She texted him back that she would not do that. Her mama trusted her.

"His return text was, *your mama will love these pictures. I will send them to her and all the guys and they will send them to everyone they know. You are going to be famous, so be ready Wednesday at seven thirty. See you then lover.* Of course she was devastated, ruined. It so happened the next day her friend Jane came to visit, essentially to warn Carla of what had happened to her. Jane had known that her dad would practically kill her if he found out. She had complied and after that Billy Bob dropped her like a hot brick. Then Carla told Jane that it was too late and they cried together."

Vickie looked at Jerry, "What do you think?"

Thoughtfully Jerry spoke, "First, how do you guys know this?"

"Oh I am sorry," said Stella, "Carla was out walking trying to clear her head. They only live a couple miles from here. She likes planes and has visited many times, we are sorta friends to her as well as to her mom."

"Fair enough, how well does Connie get along with Carla?"

"I think they have a good relationship."

"Could she handle the facts?" asked Jerry very sincerely.

"Both Girls agreed that they thought she would be hurt and upset at first but after a little while could accept it."

"Good, call both ladies and if they are available, have them come over. And let me handle it from there."

"Oh, do you happen to have the boy's name or phone number?"

Vickie handed him a piece of paper with that information on it, "I have it. I was going to invite him over and beat his head and Corvette in with a big wrench."

"I think I know just the folks who can handle this." He took out his phone and hit speed dial. "Josh my man, how is the young married couple doing?" Pause listening, "I have a name and phone number, I want a copy of everything on his phone, pictures, numbers, and texts." Listening again…. "You are kidding, that is illegal? It cannot be, NSA does it all the time without our permission. Jerry gave the name and number. How soon?"

"That soon? Good, you know Stella's e-mail, send the contents to her computer, compressed. Oh, since you are working, there will be a few nude shots of young girls, blur or delete the bodies, but leave the faces for now. This is one sorry dude and we are going to take him down a few notches."

"Josh can have that in an hour. I am going to make a couple calls." Jerry called the team to tell them they needed a meeting of a couple principals. He explained the situation succinctly. They would run the *event* because he would not be around. He was going to be sailing the high seas. Buddy and Sticky could make it, at ten.

Connie and Carla were on their way over. They knew nothing of what was planned. Just that their friends' boss was here and would like to meet them.

The girls arrived and were introduced to Jerry. They asked a couple questions about his company. And that was his lead in. "I was a rich kid, but thank God I was not a spoiled rich kid. There are too many of those. But I became a doctor, then I worked for the CIA. I also ran Wiley Industries for a spell as the CEO. What I am going to tell you now, and this is serious and very secretive. I once ran an organization, the best in the world. WE were the best at solving problems. No one was better." Jerry reached into his pocket and took out his FBI badge and handed it to Connie. "That was given to me and my team by the Director himself. There are only sixteen of these in existence."

"Wow you worked for the FBI and the CIA?" Asked Carla.

"That's right. Only a few months ago we solved a kidnapping and brought the girl home to her boyfriend and solved many disappearances in the doing, Stella knows, because she was there. She even flew the seventy year old girl back to her seventy two year old boyfriend," they all laughed.

"He is telling the truth. The man was holding the lady in a big fancy house. The first plan was to let me drive a Hummer thru the front door with the team in it; but the Boss is a kill-joy and changed the plans. But it worked anyway."

The girls were engrossed in the story. "Now as to why you are really here." Just then Stella's computer barked, 'You've got mail'. "Stella would you check that and see if it is what I need."

While Stella was checking the mail, Jerry continued, "We have run across a sorry dude in Gastonia who has been holding girls for ransom, mentally. He plays up to them, gets their pictures — some in compromising positons and I am sure he has Photoshop and can make any photo an embarrassing photo for his needs.

"I think I have the contents of his phone on Stella's computer now. Do I Stella?"

"Yes Boss I think you do."

Then let's all look. Carla was shocked and scared, she had seen at least five of her new friends. Three of them were among those who were telling her to leave Billy Bob alone. Fortunately all that was shown were faces.

"Is that you Carla?"

"Yes that is Carla," said Jerry very calmly, "That is why you are here. According to the text messages I have read, he has a date with Carla next Wednesday night. Am I right Carla?"

"Yes sir, you are."

"But we will be in church Wednesday Night sweetheart."

"There is the rub Connie. He had made some pictures that will embarrass your daughter and you. He asked for the date on Wednesday and Carla at first in the text, said she would not do it. But he is a smooth talker Connie, have you ever been in love?—Sometimes we do irrational things. So against her better judgement she finally agreed. Now, what we need, is for you, Carla to pretend to keep the date. You only have to meet him at the door and step outside and the team will do the rest. I assure you, you and the girls in

Gastonia will never, ever be troubled again by this sorry excuse for a boy, who thinks he is a man. Now, can I get you guys to do that for us? It would be a gift to many girls and women."

"Doctor are you going to kill the boy for pictures?" asked Connie.

Very calmly Jerry said, "Do you date Connie?"

"Yes at times. But what has that to do with this?"

"Seriously how would you feel if one of your dates took an innocent picture and transposed that onto some lewd porno shot and then threaten to show his friends and even put it on facebook if you did not do everything he asked?"

"I would kill…… I mean …."

"I know exactly what you mean Connie and I understand, but no, we will not really harm the kid. However you can bet the team will have him thinking he is going to be taken to these girls' fathers and brothers and that he will eventually disappear from the face of this earth in a vat of acid, or something to that effect. The boy is not a good person Connie. You can be proud of this girl. With all the pressure she has been under by the 'big man on campus,' the rich playboy with a new Corvette and promises of marriage and trips to the south of France, she has not folded. Some of the girls have been used and discarded like trash. You have a fine daughter here, and you have a lot in which to take pride. I am going out to look at the plane. I will be back in a few minutes. Just so you will know, this kid is going down. I do not want to force your cooperation, but it will help. I will not feel bad at either of you, if you say no, but with or without it, we are going to shatter his rich playboy life." Jerry nodded to all and left.

Outside he called Sticky and told him what the situation was and he was going to miss him on the cruise but he knew they were too busy. They both got a good laugh. "Do whatever needs to be done, I wouldn't feel bad if the windshield and a driver's side window on that 'vette were destroyed, giving him something to explain to his dad. Take care. I will see you at my house at ten, okay?"

"I can't wait to play again. See you later," said Sticky seriously.

Back inside, the girls were all hugging and crying. Connie turned to Jerry, "Thank you doctor. Carla has told me everything, and yes, you bet, we both will do anything we can to put this creep in his place."

"I don't have to touch him do I?" said Carla through tears.

"You might have to take his hand and walk a few feet from the door, but after that someone else will have him so fast he will not see it coming. Then you and the girls are free as birds. I have no doubt this will be an elaborate rouse. I just talked to Sticky, John Moore, he will be here and since I cannot be here I asked him to do something for me. Oh by the way Carla, do you like that 'vette?"

"No, I hate it, he has been in it."

"Good, because I asked the team to do me a favor, smash that windshield and a window while he is watching. When he sees that, he will know his trouble is just starting. One last thing, you probably wonder how we got that data off Billy Bob's phone without him knowing. We can do that and more. My team circumvented many laws, but always for good. Be assured that our man will wipe out his entire phone memory, and then for insurance the phone will disappear. So you can tell the girls that all data has been erased from his phone, plus that particular iphone is gone."

"Let me say, you cannot imagine the hell these guys will put the young man through. We know it will take a mental sledge hammer to take that 'privileged' idea out of his mind, but if there is any humanity in him they can do it. If they do not reach that deep and help him out of the hole he has dug for himself, believe me he will wish he had. Presently he faces twenty to fifty years in prison just from what we know. No telling what would come up on a thorough investigation. So if there is a brain in his head, he is no threat. If he becomes a threat that we do not know about, you will have a number to call and we will take care of it. We take our mandate seriously."

"Doctor," it was Connie, "You said John Moore that is not the North Carolina DOT guy is it?"

"Yes, the same, Sticky has been on board since the crew was put together. Why do you ask?"

"I was just surprised, I had a friend who had a problem with the DOT about a drive way and went to Mr. Moore years ago and he solved her problem. She said he was a stand up guy."

"That's a fact, now I am going to leave you. Someone will contact you. It will be a guy named Tuck, Buddy or Sticky. They will let you know what is to be expected. I think all will go well, I trust these guys with my life, and I always have. I am not exaggerating, I think they are the best in the world." Jerry departed after verifying addresses and phone numbers.

Connie and Carla stayed for soda and sandwiches. They demanded to hear Stella and Vickie's tale of Mary Ann's kidnapping and the team's rescue. After the story they were all looking forward to Wednesday night and Billy Bob's time for horror.

Chapter 15

Monday June fifteenth finally arrived. All the couples had arranged for a family member to get them to the airport at around eleven thirty. Sticky had volunteered to drive Jerry and Sherry to the airport during the meeting the night before. The meeting was relatively short, but the facts and acts were roughed out concerning the *Event* and Billy Bob.

The bags were at the door and ready to leave before nine AM when Jerry's phone rang. He did not recognize the incoming number.

"Hello, Jerry Wiley here, what can I do for you?"

"Dr. Wiley, I apologize for the call, but my father insists I call. This is Ali ibn Badir Samir. I would like to talk to you about a huge problem of mine. It would be best if we talked in person, if at all possible."

"No problem Ali, but we are due to leave in an hour or so. Are you home?"

"Yes sir, but if this is inconvenient it can wait."

"Come on over and let's talk. Bring your dad if you like."

"If it wasn't important, I would not think of interrupting your plans. I will be there shortly." The call was disconnected.

Jerry explained what had transpired on the phone. Sherry immediately started brewing some green tea. In five minutes Ali arrived alone. Greetings were said and Jerry led him to the bar. Sherry made tea for the three of them.

"Thank you so much Doctors, let me say up front, if what I ask in anyway makes you uncomfortable I will understand. I am well aware of the feeling in this country and the world concerning the crazy murdering terrorists who are extreme Islamists. I abhor and detest violence and the infamy these radicals have caused my people," Ali concluded.

"I, we, judge a man by his testimony, and his life. Unless I have reason not to, I take a man at his word. We met your father only briefly but he won our hearts. You were kind enough to bring your family to thank us, which was unnecessary, but very thoughtful. I respect you and am ready to listen, if my position is clear to you."

Ali explained that the day before on Sunday that Homeland Security had paid them a visit. The visit was not confrontational and it was official, but informal. IBM is satisfied with my work, but since being in North

Carolina I have met no one outside business associates to speak as a… a reference. They wanted a name of someone from the community who could vouch for my character. As you can see, I am asking you to say you trust me. That is a big stretch for anyone in this country under the present religious tension between Christians and Muslims," Ali paused to see if he could read Jerry's face. He saw no negative in the eyes, so he continued, "I informed them there was a couple of doctors who might vouch for me. I told them before giving the names I wanted to get their permission for such a heavy subject. That is the situation *in a nut shell* as I have heard said here in America."

"First of all Ali, I really do not know you, that is a fact. You don't know this of course, but I am proud to say I have served this country in many capacities, some I cannot tell; but I love this country. It is well known I was once a CIA agent. I swore an unending oath to protect this country against all enemies, domestic and foreign. I do not take that oath lightly."

"I understand doctor, I explained that to my father," rising to leave. "I appreciate your time and wish you a safe trip, maybe………" Ali was interrupted by Jerry.

"Please sit back down Ali, I have more to say." Ali sat waiting, "I am a man of my word. I have always kept my word. Are you a man of your word Ali?"

"Yes doctor, I am."

"Then because I am short of time, and you seem to be honest, do you swear on your father's honor and yours, that you will never harm my country, that your work in America will be to support your family and the effort for the betterment of humanity? Take a moment and think about that."

"Doctor I do not have to pause to think. I am seeking citizenship in the USA. I want my father to live here, because he has seen enough death for two lives. I will support this country with my life, I swear by all that is good, by Allah and by your God. I plan to be an American and will stand with you against all enemies domestic and foreign. I will also stand against any man of Islam who commits acts of violence," Ali choked up on the last line, and tears were apparent.

"Fair enough my friend. Please give our names and number to anyone inquiring and we will take care of it. Oh, and tell your dad we will think of him and his love for Corfu when we arrive. Upon our return we must get together. I do not want this support to be only business. We would love to have dinner and visit. I am sure we could learn a lot from you guys." Jerry took the proffered hand. It was a firm handshake. He and Sherry were walking Ali to the door.

"Oh, Dr. Sherry, you and your friends will be traveling in many areas where the Muslim faith is practiced. I think no harm will come to you. It is my prayer, but take this card," Ali handed Sherry a card the size of a business card, "My wife was given this by her Coptic Pope and she wanted you to have it. It is a well-protected symbol, a secret. If you are ever in trouble and see this sign, be assured the person holding it will be of no danger. Just nod your head yes, that is all you need. My father says this knowledge is known to the trusted Coptics alone. No one other than a Coptic would know it. There is nothing else on the card and should never be. Thank you."

We will guard it my friend, please give our best to your dad, wife and family. We will see you when we get back. You do eat steak don't you?"

"Yes, sir."

"Then we must share some of the best in the South when we return. Now you take care."

As Ali left he looked toward the top of the hill. He gave what looked like a slight hand sign then turned down the hill. The car drove off.

After Ali left they talked. Sherry was not surprised and did agree with Jerry's decision. Jerry had a couple of last minute things to do. Just as he finished, Sticky pulled up out front. Sherry was on the porch with the suitcases. As they were loading, she said to Jerry and indirectly to Sticky, "Ali would probably be a handsome man, but the shaggy beard hides the real man. Is it some Muslim thing?" It appeared to be rhetorical so no one answered—Sticky did smile slightly. They were headed for the airport in no time. The rest of the vacationing party was there when they pulled up. Jerry made a mental note to call Homeland Security to check on the situation with Ali.

"Boy am I glad to see you Jerry, I thought I was going to have to manage this herd!" Ed said as he grabbed Jerry's hand and they shared a bear hug.

Stella was ready with the flight plan filed. She and Vickie helped load the luggage and get everyone aboard. Everyone was all present and accounted for. The Rolls Royce Engines were fired up and they were off. Fort Lauderdale is just a short flight.

In a little over an hour Stella took the 650 in with a school book landing at Fort Lauderdale-Hollywood International Airport. Stella taxied to a private gate where a ship's VIP shuttle was waiting. The weather was gorgeous, clear skies and a light breeze. It was balmy.

A short ride to the Port of Authority and on to the Silver Sea's berthing area, their home for the next week. There is no way Jerry and Sherry can ever escape special treatment, so the Wiley Party was immediately escorted aboard given ID cards. The ID cards were linked to one account and worked as a credit card to that account.

They were directed to a nice lounge area overlooking the beautiful Atlantic in the distance. Everyone chose the ship's special coffee and it was delicious. They had been informed that the suites would be ready in thirty minutes with their luggage inside. The ID card was also the digital room key.

The ship was beautifully built with tons of mahogany it seemed. The wood designs were all hand carved. In a few minutes the ship's cruise director arrived to spend a few minutes talking about the ship. He introduced a mate who would go over the abandon ship procedures, an international requirement on all cruise ships. The talk was succinct and very plain. Their abandon ship station was three decks down on the port side.

The cruise director asked if anyone had a talent they would share on the Friday night talent night and said if so, give him a call. His number was on the ID card also. He wished them a good voyage and suggested they try the frozen yogurt. "We have some of the best," he said before taking his leave.

Most everyone took the advice about the yogurt and took a bowl to go with their coffee. Jerry had been given a buzzer to tell him when their suites were available. "I've got to tell you, this is a little plusher than a submarine," Don said as he hugged Evelyn. "Honey, I might have been a little hasty refusing to take a cruise. I have a feeling I am going to like this." Evelyn smiled up at him. Then the buzzer sounded.

"Okay Don, now you can really thank her for talking you into this," said Mary Ann as Buck pulled her close.

"Yeah, come on Dianne, I know you want to thank me for talking you into this," Ed said as he squeezed his girl and they all headed for the elevator. The whole crowd was now just relaxing and realizing the vacation was finally starting.

Their suite gave a commanding view of the piers around and even the blue waters of the Atlantic just past the inter-coastal water way. Leaving port is always an exciting time, like entering a new world heading into the unknown, considering the vastness of the ocean. To some this will not be apparent until a few days out. The ships horn sounded, and the command, '*All ashore that is going ashore. You have five minutes to depart the ship.*'

Below they could see the port crews loosening the lines and the ships crews hauling in the lines to store them. There were whistle signals and horn blasts that directed the crews and tugs. Efficiently in five minutes the landing walk was loosened and swung into the ship and secured. Two toots on the tug's horn and they could see rather than feel the ship slowly moving away from the pier. They were headed to Europe over the same ocean that Christopher Columbus and his three tiny ships had sailed to discover this great land. What a good feeling.

They began to feel the head winds and they could not contain themselves. It seemed so natural to wave at those on the pier and along the channel. The excitement was real, the ship was under way. Two toots of the tugboat and a big blast of the ship's horn and they were on their own and underway. The next time the ship would stop they would be in Barcelona, Spain.

Jerry sort of herded everyone out of the wind and said, "This cruise is for everyone. Your time is yours to be alone or to share. There is no set schedule except dinner if you want to join for a meal together. Our time is seven PM at dining room one table two. Sherry and I will eat there at least tonight and get the feel if we want to do it free time or semi-formal. To be honest, I think I am ready for a nap after relaxing on the balcony for a while. Please enjoy this cruise, we intend to."

There was a few minutes of chit chat and they all went to their staterooms.

Sherry set the dead bolt, took her husband by the arm and swung him around into her arms. They shared a long hug and kiss, "I love you Jerry Wiley, I have been thinking a lot about what Mary Ann said awhile back, she hinted that you might just be an angel and you know what? I'm about to agree with her." Another kiss, then on to the balcony where Jerry sat down and eased his love down on his lap.

"Speaking of angels, I married one. Now I want an angel kiss." For an hour they sat watching Florida falling away in the west. There wasn't much talk, just touching both body and lips. "I think I am ready to go inside and take that nap. If you like, sit here and enjoy one of the most beautiful natural movies in the world, the living Ocean."

Sherry stood to let Jerry get up, where of course there was another kiss. "I will come inside in a few minutes, you are so right, this is a wonderful movie." Jerry stepped inside leaving a smiling wife enjoying one of his favorite things in life, smelling the fresh salt air.

Chapter 16

Monday evening everyone was dressed casual for dinner and sat at the same table. The menu was a choice of steak, Alaskan pink salmon or duck. The salad was delicious fresh veggies. There was a band playing very quietly as dinner was served. The waiters introduced themselves and were very efficient.

After dinner they all decided to see the evening show in the forward theater. The first night's show was a Swedish dance group and band. They were amazing and must have had a super choreographer. The moves were unique and some the crowd had never seen. Applause was nearly constant. It was a great evening of entertainment.

After the show they all congregated on the port side with a clear view of the moon riding low and reflecting on the black waves. They again enjoyed coffee and frozen yogurt. This was a time to give opinions of the suites and dinner. Everyone gave the ship five stars.

Buck and Mary Ann were all loved up, "Mary Ann and I have decided this is going to be our second honeymoon."

"I'm with you Buck," said Sherry, "We had a great honeymoon the first time, but I ended up kidnapped, so this one is going to be it, and I am already enjoying it."

"Hear, hear," said Don, "I also declare this to be a fifty-eighth honeymoon for my beauty and me. I don't think two can have too many honeymoons." The group applauded.

Ed was holding Dianne close when he said, "I must say there is nothing like being able to enjoy a cruise. Dianne and I have made a couple cruises, and they have been fun, but they were interior cabins and very small, more like the navy ships, but this? No one could be prouder of those sailors below than I, who are making this a historic cruise for an Old Swabbie. I've got to tell you, I love all this attention to detail for the passengers."

The beauty of the rolling ocean is entrancing. The smell of the fresh salt air seems as clean as a summer's shower. After an hour of conversation and fellowship Buck and Mary Ann along with Ed and Dianne decided to do some midnight dancing. As they headed off toward the elevators the remaining two couples said good night and headed for their staterooms, the end of a lovely day.

The next morning Jerry met Don at the coffee shop getting coffee for their wives back in the staterooms, "Jerry this is great, we cannot thank you enough. I am learning that those surface sailors that I felt sorry for, actually had it made, being able to see the sunrise at sea. In a submarine we seldom got to see that."

Jerry finishing filling his cups and said, "Actually Don, I never thought of that. I know you guys stayed down most of the time. Funny the simple things you miss, the sunrise and sunset at sea have a beauty that cannot be duplicated." They talked until they separated for their suites, but agreed to meet at the omelet shop in an hour.

Coffee on the balcony overlooking the deep blue Atlantic was so relaxing. The slow easy movement of the ship was in itself a soothing action to the soul. "I can hardly believe it has started sweetheart. This is such a good feeling and so romantic. I am glad you decided to cruise us over, rather than fly."

Jerry smiled his sneaky smile, "Of course dear, I had my reasons; I knew a few days at sea were much more romantic than a seven hour flight. We get our minds on the future so much at times we forget the present and its importance," they were standing up and leaning over the balcony rail holding their cups. Jerry took hers, placed both on the balcony table and took her in his arms. "I have this sexy senior lady, and I do not wish to waste the present. You look lovely this morning Mrs. Wiley," they kissed for all the ocean to see. They held each other tight, two people merged. Coming out of his haze he looked down at her, "We are meeting Don and Evelyn in twenty-five minutes at the omelet chef's station. I hope that is okay."

"Of course, I'll be ready in a few minutes. I'm still trying to digest life with superman, and honey that is not flippant, I mean it. Being married to you is amazing."

Jerry watching her as she was getting dressed said, "But you have it just a little wrong my dear, it is I who is married to a *Wonder Woman*. Everyone, well most everyone, thinks a wealthy person is different than the rest of the world, but we are not. Seeing you now, is worth all the wealth in the world. If I didn't have a penny, sweetheart, I would feel like a millionaire when I hold you. Always remember, you are the prize beyond price my dear. Now let's go have breakfast. "

Don and Evelyn were already standing looking at the menu of omelets. There was no line and the chef was smiling and waiting for the orders. Don chose the ham and cheese. Evelyn has a penchant for hot food, she chose the *Western Omelet on Fire*. "That's my girl," said Don.

"I normally get the veggie omelet but today I want the ham and cheese with mushrooms. Sherry wants the veggie with extra tomato." Jerry gave their order.

As with everything else aboard a cruise ship, the chef is a showman. It was entertaining just watching him make and cook the breakfast. He rolled and flipped the omelet with the ease and flair of a Ringling Brothers' juggler. They found a seat overlooking the ocean, Sherry blessed the food and they enjoyed their first breakfast at sea.

As they were finishing, the rest of the crew walked up. They had enjoyed breakfast in the ships dining room. They exchanged reports and learned that Ed and Diane won the Rhumba Contest last night and the prize was a trip on the ship's helicopter where they could skim the ocean, then take some pictures of the ship from above. That excited everyone. "The skipper said we would have a chance to take pictures of friends on deck waving as the bird hovered."

"I slacked off on Buck, I didn't want to take a chance on winning. The helicopter idea sorta scares me," said Mary Ann and everyone laughed.

"A likely story Mary Ann," said Ed, "I thought you could come up with a better story than that."

"Well it was the best I could do in the time frame I had, smart aleck!" That got a big laugh.

As they talked the girls decided on a swim and a leisure time in the hot tub. The guys were going to play miniature golf and Ed wanted to climb the rock climbing wall on the aft deck. There was a concert in the afternoon that some wanted to hear, so they all agreed to drop in for that.

The day was beautiful and a great day for just making an adventure of scoping out all the amenities of the ship. After the guys finished an hour of miniature golf, they started making their way aft, checking out the ships facilities.

Once they got back to the climbing wall everyone had to give it a try. It was a lot of fun with the young passengers cheering the old men on climbing. They all made it and were proud of themselves. For being the oldest passengers to climb all the way to the top today, they all won ten dollars in tokens to use in the ships casino. Walking off Buck and Don indicated they were not going to try their luck so Jerry and Ed took their tokens.

Since the evening meal was late, they decided to have lunch at the forward buffet at one o'clock. They headed back to the staterooms.

The girls were dressed and ready to look the ship over, so after thirty minutes they headed out to explore again.

****

The Event concerning Billy Bob.

Meanwhile back in Gastonia, Stella had agreed to let the team use her condo for a briefing and a sort of headquarters communications office. They were also going to use the hangar area but it was going to be blacked off by heavy curtains. Stella and Vickie were going to move the Gulfstream out for the show.

The basic simple plan was to pick Billy Bob up, blindfold him and tape his mouth, drive him around for a half hour or so, then drive the rented van into the hangar and shut the hangar door. A filming area was to be set up with cotton mill warehouse stuff set around. Maybe a junk car. Looking around Billy Bob would only see what the team wanted him to see. They would have a South Carolina radio station playing pretty loud. But no planes were scheduled to land or take off that time of day.

The only players this time would be Josh, Megan, Stephen and Jennifer besides Tuck, Buddy, Sticky and J Leon. Everyone would wear jumpsuits and ski masks. The visible weapons would be real.

They planned to do a professional video of a confession, however forced that did not matter to them. J Leon and Josh were setting up the electronics for the recording while the girls and Stephen did the lighting. Jennifer was going to ask the questions from a prepared script using the information taken from Billy Bob's phone and from Carla's input. Her voice would be electronically altered so it could never be traced.

Basically the plan was to scare Billy Bob within an inch of his life and leave him with enough knowledge of what he faced legally if he ever broke a vow he was going to make. If they felt compelled to release the information to the justice system, when the cops came to arrest him, he would already have a broken arm or leg and be missing most of the thirty thousand dollar caps in his mouth.

Everything was ironed out and all jobs assigned. They said goodbye until around 4PM on Wednesday.

Chapter 17

Everyone had enjoyed the walk around the ship and ate lunch, then to the afternoon concert. It was a small band backing up a pianist who was magnificent. The runs and fill-ins were unbelievable. Evelyn who was no slouch on the piano herself was duly impressed and was heard several times as a quiet cry of surprise slipped out. “I want to do that,” she whispered.

The lady went from Bach to Beethoven. She even threw in a little Jerry Lee Lewis in between. She did her impression of Liberace and Elton Jon. She did a little Victor Borge comedy with the moving piano. All in all it was a great concert. She was scheduled in another ship’s theatre on Thursday and they all planned to be there.

After the concert they went their separate ways until dinner. Dinner had been coconut chicken or orange crusted lamb. The salad was a perfect chef salad with giant shrimp. The waiters had put on a show of folding table napkins into animals and balancing silverware. It seemed the ship was blessed with talent and showmen.

Following dinner they took a walk on deck under a blanket of beautiful stars. "Look, a falling star," it was Mary Ann pointing. The deck of a ship at night is a magic place. Looking out over a vast ocean that is shimmering with the reflections of the stars and moon. The sailor/passenger starts to realize they are thousands of miles from land. There are no neighbors, no lights of the city, just a vast expanse of space. This ship against the elements. The reality occurs to some; *we are trusting this skipper to know where the Rock of Gibraltar is located in relation to their course.*

That in itself is a shocking realization that you no longer control your destiny, this time you are not driving.

The evening's main theater featured a world famous juggler and a country western singing group that filled in between acts. It was much more entertaining than any of the men had expected. It was a ball and they enjoyed it.

Tuesday seemed to end too soon. They all liked the yogurt and migrated to the snack bar where the yogurt machine was located. They finished the evening with some good tales and stories of their childhood. Ed had told Jerry how he saved Sherry's brother Johnny from falling in a well, when both families had lived in the country.

Buck yawned, and Don said, "Same here Buck."

"What? You guys are not dancing to the Midnight Band?" asked Ed. Everyone declined, "Well we won't either," he laughed as they all headed to their suites.

Inside their stateroom, Don led Evelyn out onto the balcony. They sat holding hands and looking out across the vast darkness. "Sweetheart I spent many days below the surface of this ocean away from you. I just wanted you to know there wasn't an hour I did not think of you. I never thought much of having you with me aboard a ship looking at the ocean. I am so glad you insisted on taking up Jerry and Sherry's offer."

"Honey, I just knew we would enjoy it. Doug can handle everything back at the farm, and it is time we really get to enjoy our lives in the autumn of our years, as the saying goes."

"I know you are right Ev, it was just sort of a stubborn streak in this old Submariner. I guess I hated to find out what it was like on the surface. But I want to tell you I was up and out here on the balcony early enough to see the sunrise and it was amazing. You know I love beauty. Just a bloom or a butterfly can keep my attention, but this morning was a real eye opener. There is nothing like a sunrise over the open sea. I am going to do it again in the morning."

"I saw you out here Don, I wanted to come out but I did not want to interrupt. I have seen that look. It is the same look you get looking at one of your orchids. But let me tell you something old Submariner, I will be with you in the morning."

Don squeezed her over to him, as close as they could get in separate chairs, and said, "Jerry thinks he has the best ……. little does he know."

Evelyn whispered into his ear, "Why don't we go inside and explore further, this world of the surface sailor, Submariner?"

Don said not a word as they stood, kissed, opened the balcony doors and walked inside, ready to explore like young kids.

****

While in the next suite over, Buck and Mary Ann were getting ready for bed after watching a movie on TV. "Let's step outside darling," Buck, dressed only in his night shirt, said that very casually to Mary Ann. Mary Ann had already gotten undressed and wore only her night gown. To Buck she looked like a queen.

"Like I am?"

"Of course, who is going to see us? This balcony is as private as our house on top of the mountain.

"You got it my man, I am all yours."

They sat on the balcony watching the stars and moon reflect and glitter on the waves. The canopy of stars along with a beautiful moon caused a slight shutter in Mary Ann's soul. This was a beauty to be shared, and they were a couple of lovers, ignoring their age, who could appreciate the romantic element. The beauty of this situation was not lost to them. They were still newlyweds; in their seventies, they still sometimes felt like teen agers again. This was one of those times.

"Sweetheart, I have tried to tell you how much you mean to me. I won't go over the whole thing again, but when you were kidnapped I thought my world had ended. I cried, I prayed, I almost cursed the situation, because there was nothing I could do. When you were returned to me I felt like I was God's favorite person in the world with Him bringing you back to me. Now tonight as I look out over this ocean and realize that you are back, you are really here with me, I can only say, Sweetheart I love you more than life itself. You are the beauty of the world to me." Buck paused for a long time, no one said anything, just looking across the vast expanse of ocean. They both turned, their eyes locked and he said, "Mary Ann, I love you more than words can tell. You are life to me. You are the Christmas gift I dreamed of. Sweetheart you are the most beautiful creature in this world and I love you."

They stood, leaning on the balcony rail, they kissed. They silently enjoyed the thrill of each other. "Buck you big wonderful lug, I am glad you are in my life. You have filled a void I thought never could be filled. When I was gone, and I thought I would never see you again my heart was broken. The only way I could see a reason to live was to think that one day, some way, God would work it out; and He did. WE are both very lucky my love, very lucky." The sentence was ended with a period, the period was a kiss. Buck opened the Balcony door picked Mary Ann up like she was a flower and took her to bed. It wasn't long until they were both in heaven. The ocean breeze was gently moving the drapes as the balcony door was easing itself shut.

The sun was up before either of them stirred again. When they did they were still in each other's arms. They smiled, then laughed. "I feel as giddy as a young girl," Mary Ann said after she kissed Buck and started to get up.

Buck lay there while she used the facilities first, smiling to himself. *For a couple of seventy year old newlyweds, this ain't bad.* The smile got bigger.

Chapter 18

Wednesday Morning everyone met topside at the miniature golf course. Breakfast this morning had been a different time and place for each couple. The ship supplied so many different venues of food; the passengers enjoyed the many choices and wanted to experience them all. The several chefs could come up with many delicious entrées. Ships also have fruit and ice carving artists that can enhance every eating experience. Everyone enjoys the carved watermelon. The ability to use the natural greens and shades of red to form waterfalls, trees and birds amazes the patrons.

From the vantage point of the small golf course the group enjoyed almost a three hundred-sixty degree view of the beautiful Atlantic. They all paused to look in the direction some passengers were pointing. Everyone's attention went to another ship that had appeared on the horizon. It is a feeling that only a sailor knows. The kinship felt by just the sight of a ship, m entally telling the observer they are not alone. There are more humans on the sea. Although at sea up to twenty miles separates passing ships, a kinship is felt for an hour or so until the ship fades, headed for an unknown port with a mysterious cargo.

There is a strange mental phenomenon that sometimes occurs. Imaginations start applying puffy white canvas sails on the passing ship. Imaginations of warships and pirates edge into minds of some sea farers. For a few minutes some minds engage in fantasies from movies and books they have read.

Ed was one of those individuals, holding his golf club high as his saber and pointing in the direction of the disappearing ship, "Avast ye lubbers, we shoulda gave chase, fired a shot cross't her bow and took 'er fer a prize! 'Ave ye no desire for gold and jewels?"

Everyone was laughing at his performance when Di poked him a little with her golf club and added fuel to the fire with her own pirate accent, "Ah ha Blackbeard me matey, thou toldest me last night ye already had yer treasure!"

Ed smiled, and blushed a little, "Yeah baby, there was that!" With that the crowd howled with laughter. From then on for the rest of the golf game no one was seriously playing, just having a great time enjoying the fresh smell of the salt air.

They wandered over the ship, in and out of the many shops on the Mezzanine Deck. Some of them picked small souvenirs but knowing the vacation was just starting mostly they just shopped without buying.

They found a light buffet for lunch and the rest of the afternoon finished pleasantly. They started getting dressed for dinner. Tonight at eight o'clock the entire party would join the Captain at his table; the menu was Texas steak and Maine lobster.

Jerry was dressed and alone on the balcony, he looked at his watch. A little after seven the ship would change time zones tonight but for now they were still on Eastern Standard Time, *The Event should be starting about now back in Gastonia, Good luck guys, sorry I am missing this but I know it will come off beautifully,* he thought with all confidence. His mind was still back in Gastonia when he realized his beautiful wife was standing at his side.

"Back to the present, S'gar (Esgar)," Sherry said using the name from his past. The name he had legally adopted as head of the Modern Vigilante Association, his MVA. "I know you are thinking of your boys, I am too. You trained and taught them well, they are about to do society a great favor, and I for one am very glad."

Smiling as he closed the compartment in his mind, he looked down into the green eyes of his love, "I can't hide a thing from your intuitive mind, can I?"

"Do you want to?"

"Never, I am learning to share, let's head toward the mess decks." After a kiss, where Jerry was careful not to disturb even a hair of Sherry's perfection, they headed out.

There was lots of chit chat as they loaded the elevator. It is always exciting to have an invitation from the Ship's Captain. Not everyone has that opportunity. Of course, the ship's cruise director presents a list to the skipper who approves the guest list. Guests are usually someone in society such as a politician or movie star. Jerry being a former CEO and still a big part of Wiley Industries was targeted from the beginning. There are Skippers that always leave one evening for the average passenger. After all, they are the ones that pay the majority of his salary, and it is a wise man who recognizes that.

The Maître de escorted them directly to the Captain's table where they were seated and drink orders were taken. Immediately after the drink orders the Captain's Chef was introduced and his assistant took their orders for their choice of steak and cooking instructions. It was apparent he wrote nothing down. Upon the arrival of the Captain they all stood, the Captain nodded and motioned they all should be seated.

"What a pleasure this is to eat with the party of the famous Jerry Wiley. My purser does do a little background on my guests, and I must admit, Rags,"

Jerry smiled as everyone laughed, "Or Jerry, you are the most colorful since Red Skelton. I am honored."

"Thanks Skipper, we are the ones honored. For a man who won the Navy Cross and skippered a battle ship at the young age of twenty nine, you have done pretty well yourself."

"Touché my new friend, I see we are not the only ones who check backgrounds," the Skipper bowed in Jerry's direction. "Now, I hope all is well on your cruise thus far. We do have an excellent staff and I am very proud of our ship's reputation. It is a pleasure to be at the helm, and much different than a warship, rather than a duty, this one is a pleasure to be at the helm."

The Skipper took the time to speak to each guest and learn something of their lives. He was very impressed with Don's Submarine days. He was surprised that both Ed and Buck were familiar with the ships power plants.

The meal was delicious. Tonight was special. After coffee and the Chef's special cheese cake, the Captain was escorting his guests to the main ball room for the Mid Atlantic Dance. The ladies were all decked out and ready to show off their dresses and their foot work. Jerry glanced at his watch. It was now about nine thirty and no word.

****

Earlier in the evening the *Event* was set in motion. Tuck and Buddy, leaving nothing to chance, had surreptitiously placed one of J Leon's special bugs on Billy Bob's 'vette. They were all in place and the van was parked across the street with J Leon monitoring the progress of the 'vette. He held up three fingers to the window under the curtain for all to see.

The 'vette came to a quick stop at the curb. He slid out the driver's side and was smoothing his hair back. He was whistling as he approached the door and then rang the bell. He rang it the second time, trying to see thru the high door window. The door opened. "Hey baby is mama at church?"

Stepping outside and closing the door she turned and said, "Can we just get this over with?"

"Oh Sweetie it ain't over until Billy Bob says it's over." As he turned he saw a form beside his precious 'vette, "Hey…." That was as far as he got. Two dark figures in ski masks were on either side and a van pulled quickly up into the driveway.

One of the figures, not too gently, pressed the neck muscles and Billy Bob released Carla's hand. One of the figures slapped a flesh colored tape with a cute mouth drawn on it over Billy Bob's mouth. "Now young lady you go back in the house, this won't take long. Do not call the police. We are going to introduce Brother Billy Bob to the real world. I think he may even want to find Jesus before tonight is over. Note the man beside that pretty Corvette over there, why I think that is a sledge hammer." Just then, Sticky, also wearing a ski mask in the semi darkness, smashed the windshield, then both headlights that were still on. "Yep, my guess was right. It was a sledge and he sure knows how to turn head lights off." The street was deserted as Billy Bob was escorted into the van with tears falling freely. He did not see the tow truck drive up and load the Corvette. There would be no paperwork on this tow job. The driver was prepaid to drop it in the mall parking lot.

"Now, son you're probably wondering what this is all about," Sticky said as he taped Billy Bob's eyes shut. "We are pretty thorough boy. This is about the eighth girl that we know of." Billy Bob's hands were tie-wrapped behind his back and he was laid on the floor. Billy Bob kicked but Sticky was ready for it and crotch slapped him, "Do that again and I might remove your equipment. I'm thinking about doing that anyway before we do you. I think your dad deserves to see that, don't you?" Pausing just a little he continued, "Sure you do. Dad would be proud of his macho son who shames and scares girls into sex. You would apologize to them if we let you, wouldn't you?"

This type of talk went on for about fifteen minutes. "I don't know," said Tuck, "We really don't need a confession, we have the phone records and the pictures we could just put him in the barrel of acid and get it over with; I hate scum that would do my cousin that way."

"You are probably right," said Buddy as a matter of fact, "But the boss lady wants the confession first."

"Seems like a waste to me. I have an order for five hundred gallons of acid going to Hong Kong. We figure his weight and remove that much acid from a drum. It won't be opened for six months, we strip his clothes it won't even color the acid." The two were talking as if Billy Bob wasn't there. The total ride was about thirty minutes. They had made a circle down New Hope Road then back to the Airport. Billy Bob felt the van come to a stop and heard a garage door going down. He was not too gently taken from the van and placed on a stool of some kind. He felt heat. He could tell some lights were on.

"Hold still, I am removing the tape from your eyes." Billy Bob felt some skin go with the tape. "Sorry about that, I didn't mean to hurt you." Sticky said sarcastically.

He could only see bright lights but he could hear voices behind and beside the lights. Now a lady's voice that sounded strange, "Billy Bob, you are not on trial here, this is not legal. But we do not like what you have been doing to young girls and that is much worse than stretching some laws. You have belittled, shamed and caused grievous pain and suffering. We are busy people and don't have time for this, but here we are. Our organization knows your life. We have gone into your phone and retrieved everything there. It has been printed and duplicated. It is in hard copy and digital."

Another voice, "You are eighteen years old. You have had sex with girls as young as twelve, forced sex, legally rape. We have added the charges up, if you were to go to trial with a sorry lawyer, you are facing at minimum two hunded years in a Federal Penitentiary. With a good lawyer like your daddy would have gotten if he had been given a chance, you would have faced at least eighty-three years. Some of these sentences are mandatory. If you had wanted to, you could have learned this at North Carolina statute 14-27 thru 14-208. But since this isn't going to trial this is information for you only."

A voice he had heard in the van spoke up, "I am going to remove your mouth cover. You are to speak only when spoken to. If you yell, there is no one near to hear, but I will smack you and tape your mouth and we are out of here. Do you understand?" Billy Bob nodded. The tape was ripped off, not too gently.

A voice explained that he was going to make a video confession, also it was explained this was not for court, but could be. It was for the newspaper and TV. "Now are you ready to make that confession?"

"I…. if I do, what happens to me?"

"That is not set in stone, but right now the vote is you disappear. We have seen very vulgar pictures you forced girls to make and read your threats to little girls about showing their pictures on facebook if they did not have sex with you, and that is saying it nicely since we are in mixed company here. For that alone, I would just like to shoot you. However, I am only one voice. We have many people here ready to listen to your confession. We understand it was so many girls you probably do not know all their names, so we are going to help you there. We will give you a name and you will tell the lights what naughty things you have done. Understand this is not debatable. You talk now or you never talk again. It is that serious. When it is over, we decide what we do. Do you understand?"

"Are you going to kill me anyway?"

"I did not say I was going to kill you. Boss, I didn't exactly say that. He probably thought he heard that."

"I understand, go on." Said another voice from behind the lights.

It took about an hour, but thru tears Billy Bob confessed to all the crimes. Everyone knew it was partially from fear and some from remorse, but it was done. There appeared to be a group meeting further away. The radio had been turned up. He heard what was planned for him to hear, of course part of the program.

Loudly Tuck said, “No way, you cannot trust the fool. He will end up breaking the rules and go to trial, I say we just finish the creep.”

In a little while he heard Megan’s voice, “Well I know he does not deserve any compassion, but I think he should be given one more chance.”

More noise, then the voices were back near. And Megan spoke, “You have been a wretched person, but I have decided to give you a chance. Some are afraid you might be stupid. If you are, the pictures and confession go to the local news media, your family, and the Federal Prosecutor. We will dump your next cell phone, and give them that also. Our organization will monitor you for a year. Be advised if we see or hear of any story you tell, concerning some mysterious group picking you up and forcing you to do things, you best look out, because the team will be back. I would think about the consequences.”

"If you approach any underage girl again, if our monitors find you speaking to any of the girls you have wronged, I claim the right to come for you. In this organization I have that right. Keep in mind one of these girls was my cousin, do you understand my position?" It was obviously a male voice he had heard before.

"Yyyes Sir."

"I will add this. The only words you are to say to any of these girls if you find yourself in a position and you must say something, all you say is *I am sorry for hurting you. It will never happen again. I have to go*. Do you think you can do that?"

"Yes Ssir."

The van was loaded again and again Billy Bob was blindfolded and his mouth taped. The door was heard to raise and they drove off. They took the same circuitous route and back to the Mall Parking lot. The *Event* had taken longer than they had planned but it was over. Billy Bob was let out near a dark section of the access ramp onto I-85. He was told to count to one hundred then remove the blindfold and mouth cover. He was told his car was in the Mall parking lot about a half mile from where he was. He was pushed up next to the fence in the dark and the van left with its lights off.

Back at the airport all was back to normal and the Gulfstream was back inside. Connie was called and told that all was well. There was never going to be a problem with Billy Bob, but if on the outside, it ever happened again, all they had to do was call. Once everyone was accounted for J Leon sent the message to the Silver Seas' communications center. It read, "To Doctor Jerry Wiley stop Billy Bob has religion stop Enjoy your vacation stop.

****

It was eleven thirty and Jerry saw the communications officer approach the Captain. The Captain indicated Jerry with a nod, and the communications officer brought an envelope over to him. They exchanged pleasantries as he gave Jerry the message, Jerry thanked him. The officer clicked his heels, did an about face and left.

Jerry opened the envelope and reading the short note gave a big smile and a wink to Sherry. The rest of the group noticed the exchange and were wondering what would make Jerry smile that broadly.

Later after the dance Jerry invited everyone to their suite for an explanation. Once there he told them the whole story, then showed them the note.

Chapter 19

Thursday morning everyone slept late except Buck and Mary Ann. They had decided to have a leisure breakfast in the ship's dining room. Sitting at the table they discussed the talk of last night and the kid's situation in Gastonia.

"The world needs more Jerry Wileys," said Mary Ann, "I cannot imagine the mental anguish the girls went through. I hope they scared the S… sucker out of fifty years of growth, he deserves it."

"I certainly agree darling. Can you imagine the stories hidden in Jerry's mind and life? He really is incredible, and you my dear are living proof of that."

They also talked about the generosity of the team, and the hundred thousand dollars that had mysteriously appeared in Mary Ann's bank account. When she had called the bank and found it was not a mistake, she almost fainted. The next thing she did was call Sherry. Sherry talked to Jerry in the back ground and he said that he had heard that some guy in Florida had wanted her to have it." She could get no more out of Sherry. Dusty later told her the team had taken money out of the safe. It was all from high paying clients and no way to trace the money to a rightful owner. Jerry's team had distributed it to what families they could trace, that had lost loved ones. "Dusty told me that he had learned one thing in that operation and that was *Jerry Wiley thinks of others, he is one unselfish guy.*"

Later that morning everyone met up and leisurely walked the ship, taking in the various shops. Cruise ships have a big thing about photos. The ship's photographers are constantly roaming, taking pictures and they show up in the picture gallery. The pictures are posted prominently, and copies are for sale as souvenirs. Some of the couples liked their pictures and purchased them.

They laughed at the pictures of the guys climbing, they had not realized that they were being photographed. In a few minutes pictures were discovered of the dance floor featuring the girls and the fun tables were turned. It was all in a day of carefree cruising.

The band was playing as they passed the Panorama Lounge and no one was on the shiny marble dance floor. On a whim Jerry turned to Ed, "Hey mate, do you and Di mind showing us two neophytes a few dance steps? We are not dancers."

"I am so glad you asked, I am itching to dance." Everyone knew that was about Ed's second name.

As the band played, Sherry and Jerry who knew only the basic two step type dance and that only with each other began to dance. It was a fun time and they kept it up with Di taking Jerry aside and Ed showing Sherry the basic moves. The whole group joined the fun and it continued until the band announced one last number. Jerry and Sherry were going to try together. They did well with a few stutters by Jerry. But all in all they finished the whole song as a dance, Jerry said later *I usually just stand there on the dance floor, move a little and get some sugar.*

During the day Jerry fielded questions from every one about the *Event* back in Gastonia. They were all fascinated. But for the present Jerry was not going any further than Mary Ann's story and the latest *Event* in Gastonia.

The last days of the cruise were even more relaxed with the couples picking their way about the ship. Most evening meals were together but best of all, the couples were taking the time to enjoy one another. When you are in your seventies the partner looks much different. Life is gauged much differently. It is about quality, and it is truly about love, not just sex, but seniors know that in reality life is one trip thru, not a rehearsal, this is it. When you are listed as a senior citizen, petty things remain petty. The senior learns hard truths, friends drop off the map and the eyes you look into may darken or your eyes may darken. At the age of this group, happiness, love and companionship rated up there with sex, *well almost*, they all had agreed, because as Don had said, "We are not dead yet!"

The day before the cruise ended the big announcement over the ship's speakers was, "Attention, This is the Captain speaking, for all who want to see the Rock of Gibraltar, It will be in sight in approx. fifteen minutes and can be viewed for almost two hours. I suggest pictures. This is the most notable Rock or Island in the world."

That announcement stirred excitement. Since Jerry and Sherry's patio had a clear view to port, they invited every one over. They were able to get pictures of every couple with Gibraltar in the background. The Captain gave some of the highlights of the Rock's history as they passed. The Rock is Crown property and is 1350 feet high, mostly limestone and in WWII was never captured by the Germans.

It wasn't long until the group began to see the difference in color of the Mediterranean and the Atlantic, and also it was not quite as rough. The color was an amazing blue and it met all the hype of the beauty of the Med.

The last night of the cruise the Captain had the weather decks cleared. It was a huge dance floor, and the three bands aboard would provide the music alternately for dancing on into the night. There were cookers out for a big BBQ. Some were steaming crabs and lobster, hamburgers, hotdogs and several varieties of steaks and ribs. The Captain was on stage that evening to kick things off and announced, "This is my version of a Mediterranean Luau. It has been such a pleasure having you aboard, a few of you will continue with us, but to those departing tomorrow, enjoy the most beautiful Sea in the world. Some of the most precious folk in the world enjoy this Sea. We are proud of it. Now, let's all enjoy the evening. We will dock in Barcelona at ten o'clock in the morning by the ships time. Thank you for choosing the Silver Cloud. God bless you all." Applause of the hundreds of passengers rose and echoed over the beautiful Mediterranean, as the night's festivities began.

On some of the first songs Jerry and Sherry tried out their new dance talents and were really enjoying them but found their physical stamina was not equal to their minds. So they sat out a couple of songs. During that time they noticed the Captain headed toward them. Sure enough he was coming to talk.

"Doctor, I came to personally say what a pleasure it was to serve you on the trans-Atlantic. I don't get to do this often enough, but I get messages from my crew concerning passengers, negative and positive. I encourage it. The crew has loved your party and they were shocked at the lack of demands for service. I just wanted you all to know, the entire Silver Cloud thanks you."

"Skipper we are just proud to be here, but thank you for the compliment. This is a good bunch. We have all loved it."

"One more thing, I understand you have chosen the Yacht Tatiana for your Mediterranean stay. An excellent choice. Captain Sam Solomon was once my Executive Officer. You could not have chosen better. Your crew will be furnished with special tags for your luggage and we will send it directly to the Tatiana, if that meets with your approval."

"It certainly does Captain, and many thanks for all you and the crew have done." The Captain saluted and left.

"What a nice guy," said Mary Ann from the adjacent table, "I like that guy."

"Hear, hear," came the cheer from the group and the night continued. They danced until they were exhausted. Couple by couple they straggled to their suites. There was no problem going to sleep. Reveille came after the sun arrived. Jerry brought orange juice and coffee back to the room. After getting dressed and tagging the luggage, they headed for the omelet bar for the last morning. Everyone had the same idea. Now they were all anxious to see what the yacht would be like.

It was eight thirty when the coast line became easily observed. Everyone wanted to see Spain, the mystical country of matadors and lovely ladies. Barcelona is the fourth fastest growing city in Europe. Population is over five million taking in the suburbs. They were reading the statistics of the city, when Jerry said, "Not to scare you but they have rail service from here to Madrid that travels at over a hundred ninety miles an hour." Jerry read.

"You are kidding," said Ed, "That boggles with my mind, I want you to know, I hope the rail crossings are really blocked well, and cars and pedestrians are given a lot of warning. I'd sure hate to be driving across those tracks and see that sucker coming."

As they neared the port all reading stopped, it had been a week since their feet were on ground. Everyone was anxious to go ashore. As they stood at the rail watching the Skipper do a trick with the cooperation of the tugs, Jerry's phone rang. It was a satellite phone versus the cell.

"Yes, may I help you?"

"I tried your room Doctor Wiley, I am sorry to bother you on the Satellite phone, if there is extra charges the ship will cover them."

"The phone bill is no problem what can I do for you?"

"Doctor," said the voice, the Skipper says you and your party may depart the forward gangway in twenty minutes. There will be vans to take you to your destination. Courtesy of the Silver Cloud."

"Thank you very much and give the skipper our thanks along with the appreciation for a superb cruise."

Jerry repeated the information just as the ship's personnel came for their luggage. They all returned to their suites for one last sweep to make sure nothing was left and then headed for the forward gangway. It was a beautiful day in Barcelona.

Chapter 20

A new country and more excitement. The streets were crowded and the sidewalks bustling. The Tatiana was berthed on down the waterfront away from the huge cruise ships. The pier was wide enough for the vans to discharge the passengers and their luggage at the yacht's gangway. The yacht's crew took charge immediately, moving the luggage aboard.

The captain was tall, dark and athletic in appearance. He was a handsome man, the striking image of a ship's captain. Standing at the quarterdeck he called, "Welcome aboard the Tatiana (Tah-she-anna) ladies and gentleman, I am Captain Solomon, we have been looking forward to sharing our Mediterranean highlights with you."

The party was shown their berthing spaces. The yacht has three decks, with the master suite on the upper deck, and the others were on the third deck. All were roomy and comfortable. Since the Tatiana was set to accommodate fourteen passengers there would be more room for all.

The skipper informed them his crew would be serving them lunch, then informed them, "There would also be an evening meal, unless they chose to eat in Barcelona. One of our crew, Susa Muhammad, will be your driver at each port. A service of the Tatiana. This afternoon and in the early evening he will show you Barcelona as few folks see it. He will let us know if you plan to have dinner with us or in our lovely city. An evening meal is included in your contract, here or in a local restaurant Susa will point out to you."

Captain Solomon was amiable and everyone liked him from the start. Lunch was delicious and as they finished a local dessert, the van arrived at the gangway and their afternoon tour began. Susa was a clean shaven dark skinned man, handsome in a rough sort of way. He spoke in halting English, but understandable.

It was a treat for everyone to see the back streets and local housing areas of Barcelona. Susa did not sugar coat the areas of the city that were dangerous to get lost in, but clarified the areas were very few for such a city.

"This Poble Espanyol, is a Spanish village. Please take an hour to wander through it. It contains likenesses of squares, towers, churches and a village — things famous throughout our beloved Spain. It was built in 1929. We call it an open air museum. You will find artists and craftsmen of all colors. This will give you a taste of Spain."

The Poble Espanyol indeed was a sight, and of course everyone also recognized it was a tourist attraction, enjoyed it and treated it as such. They did sample some of the local pastries, then returned to the van.

Susa pointed out one of the three restaurants where they could dine at the expense of the Tatiana. Everyone wanted to eat ashore, so Susa notified the Captain of their decision.

After driving through the main city Susa announced they were approaching a very special place for you Americans. "Just ahead you will see a tall tower. It stands near two hundred feet in height, with a statue of America's discoverer, Christopher Columbus standing atop."

Of course it was a very ornate monument and was built in 1888. Everyone disembarked and walked around reading the plaques that were in several languages. Susa was with them, "We of Spain claim Mr. Columbus as a citizen. He was born in Genoa but moved eventually to Spain. We are proud to claim him as a son."

"There is a special place we must go, but the sight is most beautiful at dusk, so we will head for your dinner engagement then see the final sight after you have eaten."

At the restaurant they were presented with dishes they could not pronounce: Zarzuela Exquisite, a mixture of fish and other seafood served in a decorative circular pattern and Escalivada Typical, a dish of eggplant and roasted red peppers bathed in a sauce of olive oil and garlic.

"That one is out," spoke up Buck drawing an amen from Ed.

The waiter in perfect English added, "The Escudella I carn d'olla, this is a stew of pork, beef and chicken. It also has vegetables, rice, noodles and butifarra which is a Catalan sausage."

Jerry said, "Most of you will like the last item, it is a very delicious stew. And if you like a mixture of seafood, try the Zarzuela Exquisite. You will not be disappointed with either."

Only Don ordered the seafood, everyone else had the stew. At the end, they all agreed it was delicious. Several of the group had to taste Don's fish, and agreed it was good.

The meal ended with the desert of the house, Mel I mato. Not until after it was eaten and the plates cleared did anyone ask what it was. They then learned that it consisted of curd cottage cheese with honey. After all, Barcelona is the seat of the famous Mediterranean diet. They all enjoyed a last cup of coffee, then headed for Susa and the van.

"Your last stop is 'Mirador de l'Acalde' the most photographed spot of most tours." As Susa spoke the van turned out onto a balcony, a terraced area with a magnificent view of the harbor area and the Med. With just a little searching everyone saw the Silver Cloud then their eyes followed the water line and came to their new home, the Tatiana.

Pictures were taken, and at the end Susa took a picture of them all together with the Med in the back ground, and then they headed back to the pier. It was the close of a most beautiful day.

The skipper met them at the gangway and pointed them to the bar area. Relaxed they were served their choice of fresh juices and nuts.

"In about an hour the Tatiana will get under way. Our heading will be for your next port of choice, Cannes, France. We hope you will enjoy breakfast on the upper deck at your leisure. The cook will serve from six AM until ten at which time we should be ready to tie up at the pier. I suggest you enjoy the Tatiana for a few hours at the pier. Use the wave runners and power boat to get a feel of the harbor and beach. Feel free to take the bathing suits and enjoy the beaches in the south of France. Do you have any questions?"

"Yes Captain, how does the Tatiana handle the port authorities and customs?"

"I am glad you asked Doctor, The Tatiana is a familiar site at these ports. They are expecting us to tie up at ten o'clock. The authorities will have a custom's official come aboard to check your passports and do a cursory check of our ship. It normally takes less than fifteen minutes. Anyone else?" After pausing a minute, "Now afford yourselves of our refrigerator and snacks. If you need anything just ask any of the crew or pick up any phone and dial one. Someone will be with you to assist. Once again, you have given me a list of some wonderful ports. I think the choices are the top of most lists. But one thing you do not know, Mount Etna in Sicily is due to erupt in a fortnight. I want you to see that. It is a wonder to behold and something not everyone gets to see. We will talk this over and may have to change the order of ports to see this, but we will take in all ports you have requested. Now tour the Tatiana and enjoy the harbor sites."

The Tatiana is billed as a super yacht, and she lived up to her name. She has ample exterior exposure for enjoying the perfect water and weather of the beautiful Mediterranean. It seems that everyone heads to the topmost deck, for the best views.

"Don, if the Navy had been anything like this I would have given them twenty," Ed said as he stood beside Don looking at the harbor and the glistening lights off the water. Night was settling in now, and you could hear music coming from the many bands along the water front. Music and sea coasts just seem to blend together and mentally create the perfect atmosphere.

The feeling also has a hint of *you need someone* and without any plodding or instructions each man sought out his lady to squeeze in the Mediterranean moon light. It was magical, a time for love.

Before the huge V-twelve four thousand M93 engines were fired up, everyone was in their assigned cabins. Each cabin had a king-size bed and a beautiful view. The air was filled with excitement and the first night on a super yacht seemed to spell love. The Tatiana had some very happy passengers.

Chapter 21

Cannes, France; the yacht was approaching the city of dreams. Jerry was getting coffee for their cabin and Buck walked up. "Oh Hi Jerry, we slept in this morning, I guess y'all did too."

"Yes I love the movement of the yacht. It just put us out of it."

Looking thoughtfully Buck said, "I really don't know diddly about human races Jerry. Being from the North Carolina Mountains where we have white and black. We are not completely ignorant, 'cause we do have television," he smiled and continued, "I really like old

Susa, but with a last name of Muhammad, isn't it sorta strange he would be working for a Captain Solomon?"

"Buck, I have been in this area a lot, except in Israel and the Arab league, and it isn't that uncommon."

"Well I am glad to hear that, because he is one likeable dude. I guess we had better get this coffee back to the ladies hot, sorry to detain you." Both the guys headed for their cabins.

Sitting in their yacht robes on the lounge chairs watching the beautiful blue of the Med, Jerry laughingly told Sherry about Buck and the names, "And I guess it does sound sorta strange, a Jewish Captain hiring an Arab sounding name."

"Since you mentioned it, Susa seems strangely familiar. I had several Muslim patients in Huntersville, I keep telling myself that I am probably mixing the situations up, and it has been awhile. Also he doesn't match the patients, because they had very good command of the English language. At times Susa does, and then at other times, he struggles over words."

"I have noticed that my dear, but I have also noted in my travels that some people are theatrical, they want to appear, well foreign, to tourists. Would you like for me to ask the Captain about him?"

"Oh no, Jerry, don't do that, this whole vacation has been a dream come true. I am just being silly. Speaking about Huntersville patients, I do not know if you were nervous with your *first real patient*, but I was. " Sherry paused smiling as she sipped the delicious coffee. "My receptionist announced my first patient, a Tony Z. Darnell. This guy waltzed into my office, I mean actually waltzed in. He sat opposite me and I asked his problem."

"Tis my ticker Doc. It goes crazy when I see a good looking woman. I cannot control it. Like now, I didn't know I was picking a beautiful doctor, but I did. Now it is going crazy, go ahead check it!"

"I thought he was weird, but I did check and it was beating at about 150 a minute. Finally I did get him to be serious, and learned his regular doctor had retired and he needed regular care. He had suffered with heart problems in the past. He was a technical specialist, but his hobby was dancing. I found out he was a well-known professional dancer. He absolutely refused to give up the dancing, so we worked out medications and he continues until now, I guess. Oh, and the other odd thing was he drove a 1954 Buick convertible, pristine, an absolutely beautiful car. I came to enjoy his visits, he was real underneath the facade."

"Well my first patient was a crotchety old man, he never had a good word to say about anything or anyone. He thought I was too young to be a real doctor so he found someone else, and I was very glad."

The announcement of 'Breakfast on the upper deck' was made, so they got dressed and joined the others.

Cannes was an hour away. The Captain joined them. "I am sure you will enjoy Cannes. The motto here is 'Life is a Festival', and you, as Americans, have most likely heard of the Cannes Film Festival. It is one of the most well-known festivals. Before the tour however, as I suggested you should make use of the Tatiana's toys, the wave runners and the runabout."

"Skipper, Buck and I thought we had over slept this morning. The sun was a little early, but the coffee is delicious. The harbor tour on the wave-runners is a good idea."

"Very good Doctor, Susa will give the driven tour this afternoon into the evening if you wish. Now the chef will take your orders."

The breakfast was very good, not the variety aboard the cruise ship, but this chef was good.

After breakfast they checked out the 'toys'. Ed and Di, Buck and Mary Ann on the Wave runners and Don at the controls of the small power boat with Evelyn, Jerry and Sherry. They had a blast, it was a feeling of freedom. The Chef had packed a snack for everyone and it was aboard the boat in a neat compartmented ice chest.

After about an hour of touring the harbor area Don led them toward the beach area. He found a clear spot and they all beached and tied up. They alternated staying at the 'toys', while touring the beach area. Beaches always give a feeling of freedom and festival. It was no different here at Cannes.

They spread blankets, relaxed in the sun and enjoyed their snack. This chef had prepared a great lunch, not just snacks. They took an hour after the meal just to lie in the sun and nap or think. Sherry thinking, *the beach was one great idea.*

Buck looked over at Ed, "I never expected to be lying on the beach at Cannes, France with a beautiful lady, but I am."

"Ditto to that my friend, I sure am glad I had a friend like Sherry when I was growing up! You know, if she had played her cards right years ago, she could have probably hooked me." Ed said in mock seriousness.

Don overheard and responded, "I am glad the girl didn't know anything about cards, if she had, *we might* be down at the Broke-off now." Then they all laughed.

The Broke-off was a local swimming hole in the Catawba River at Mount Bell. It was a huge hunk of concrete left when the railroad trestle went down in a flood in the 1920's. It was surrounded by deep water and made a great swimming hole. But as Don intimated, it wasn't Cannes or the Mediterranean. "Well I am hurt Don, hurt I tell you, the Broke-off is a great place."

"I have to agree with Ed," chipped in Jerry, "I watched some boys having a great time, diving, playing tag and just lying in the sun, the same sun we are under. And in their way, they were as happy as we are now. Guys, that was a strange time in my life. Those same four boys Buddy, Tuck, Sticky and J Leon, named me Rags and it stuck. Now those same boys are just like my sons," pausing just briefly, "But this is grown up fun and I must admit, it is better to lay on a beach in Cannes with a beautiful lady!" and as he finished, he leaned over to kiss a smiling Sherry.

Once they decided to head back to the Tatiana, they switched positions, with Don and Evelyn, and Sherry and Jerry on the wave runners. There was a little horsing around, but they headed back to the Tatiana.

Back at the yacht, they all enjoyed some juice, then showers in anticipation of the afternoon and evening in Cannes, France.

The tour was great. First on the schedule. The girls had heard the Promenade of La Croisette. The In place to be. But after a while they knew it was not for them. This was for the rich and famous the Bugatti and Rolls drivers were in abundance just as Susa had hinted. There is something about driving around in such a world renowned city. It wasn't quite as exciting as thinking of it. The traffic was very busy and heavy. Susa handled it like the pro that he must be. No hand gestures, just a smile when boxed in by some harried drivers. Still, seeing all the history and ancient buildings caused the minds to wander back to times before cars, trucks and busses.

Susa suggested a sidewalk café in Le Suquet, after their short beach front escapade. There was room to park the latest rented van, giving them plenty of time for coffee and French pastries. Susa informed them, "Le Suquet, she is the old city, plenty places to pictures take. Great old architecture. Many folk just enjoy the stroll."

"Honey you go with the crowd, I just want to sit here and relax, have some more coffee. This is France to me."

Sherry smiled, "Okay, but everyone will mark you as a kill joy."

"Maybe not, possibly Susa and I can come up with a surprise. You will probably pass this way again, and I might feel like strolling with you." Sherry turned and caught up with the group. After a few minutes he spoke to Susa.

"Pardon me Susa, but if my memory serves me correctly, Grasse is close by, could we make it to the perfume factory before it closes?"

"Oh Doctor, I am sure we can 'make it' as you say, it is only a few kilometers or about six miles from this point. If you will excuse me I need to check the van for oil and petrol," Jerry nodded and Susa busied himself in the engine compartment.

Jerry couldn't help but feel Susa did not want to talk. He had the feeling the van was just an excuse. But he also realized that many folks in the service industry were not thrilled to 'serve' the elite of America. There had always been a small under current, caused by ignorant Americans who felt they were above these hard working Europeans.

He enjoyed just sitting here sipping this delicious coffee. For about thirty minutes he had a table to himself. Susa had checked the oil three times, cleaned the windows, and with a small whisk broom, had swept the van that did not need it.

The group had decided to cut short this walk, and were back at the van in less than an hour. After hearing Jerry's idea all the ladies agreed *head for Grasse.*

They reached the perfume factory in time for one more tour. The process was amazing. The workers pressed a variety of flower petals into wax to be absorbed. In their coolers were thousands of exotic flowers with a variety of scents. The process of distilling the odors caught everyone's attention. It was amazing how many dozens of flowers it took to make an ounce of perfume.

The factory store of course was the last stop on the tour. At that point everyone wanted some of their favorite perfume. Jerry knew Grasse put out a good bit of Chanel Number Five, Sherry's favorite, so of course he bought several ounces. Evelyn's favorite was White Shoulders, Don had to buy some. Before they left, everyone had bought perfume, and headed back to the yacht. Susa had called back to say the passengers would enjoy dinner on the Tatiana. They were driving back a little after dark and Cannes was beautiful in the evening. Everyone was happy with their short time in Cannes. This was some vacation!

Chapter 22

The Tuesday evening meal was superb, starting with a special Chef's Salad. Mediterranean tea and coffee were served with the meal. The fresh baked bread was a surprise and smelled just as delicious as it was. Main course was Turkish coffee, rubbed brisket, and the surrounding veggies were delicious with a hint of cinnamon. It also was top of the line cuisine. Everyone was talking about the cook who also filled in as a seaman when coming into or leaving port. The Tatiana certainly had a handy crew.

Later that evening they said good bye to Cannes and watched the lights disappear in the distance. Their hundred forty-seven foot luxury sea taxi headed for the port of Pisa at a speed of nineteen knots, about twenty-two miles per hour.

Susa doubled as a disc-jockey playing music they recognized as back home, but old. It seems the Captain had done a little research. With Ed and Di's urging Jerry and Sherry continued their dancing lessons. The teachers were pretty good. By the end of the evening the students were a lot more at ease. Everyone had enjoyed the evening. They all had taken the time to enjoy the Mediterranean at night. "Is every night this beautiful?" asked Mary Ann.

Jerry answered, "My experience is more of these than others. My memory is just what you see, absolutely perfect. We will have to ask the skipper to stop one night so we can all go swimming. You must experience the clear beauty of the Mediterranean yourself, swimming in it at night."

Everyone was a little surprised at the passion of Jerry's statement. He could tell by their looks. "Let me tell you a little story, while over here on assignment one evening my boss, an old man of thirty seven challenged me to a race. I was six years his junior and an expert swimmer. Well that old man took me to a deserted beach. He pointed to a buoy about a quarter mile out. I am going to whip your young rear end agent. Let's go."

"He ran and dove in and I walked down knowing this was no contest. When I reached the water I realized this dude could swim. He was already about a hundred feet out. Try as could, I could not catch the dude, but I also found myself slacking off enjoying the beauty of this sea. He beat me to the buoy by a little over a hundred feet. The lead I had given him.

"Hanging onto the buoy he said to me, *Now Jerry I brought you here because you are the one man with me who appreciates beauty. Now that you have seen your feet at night in this clear water and even at times saw the bottom at thirty feet. Is this beauty or not?* I couldn't argue. It was the most beautiful water I had ever encountered, even more beautiful than the Gulf of Mexico."

"The Captain tells me tomorrow before we reach Florence we should see some schools of flying fish. I am anxious to see that," said Buck.

Ed injected, “I think you are onto something with the night swim Jerry, I am looking forward to that.”

The rest of the evening was spent just admiring the sea and listening to the tapes Susa had put on the speakers. As the evening wore on the couples excused themselves until Jerry was sitting admiring his wife alone. Then he said, “Darling, I think this vacation has been one of your best ideas since our marriage. You make the perfect hostess and your guests are happy. That is very easy to see.”

“I am not being snowed by the smooth talking Jerry Wiley, I know we are all happy, but you are the financier of the vacation, not me.”

“You are beautiful in the moonlight my dear, but you are wrong. It is your demeanor. May I remind you’re your finances are the same as mine.”

“But I could never do this,” protested Sherry.

“May I remind you?...... That you are financing this vacation,” Standing by the rail overlooking the moonlighted Sea, Jerry took her in his arms and kissed her deep and passionately. “It is a lady named Sherry that makes this vacation a winner, and a winner it is Sweetheart.” After a few more minutes they too called it a night as the Tatiana plowed thru the blue Mediterranean toward Pisa, Italy.

The Yacht Tatiana was not due until noon on Wednesday of their second week of this great vacation. The talk was excited as they spoke of seeing the leaning tower. They had opted to take the train to Florence where they could actually see the original statue of David by Michelangelo.

After they docked in Pisa, the group took a van delivered to the pier and Susa started the tour. He had maps and they headed for the leaning tower, after they drove around and found a parking spot for photographs. After that Susa drove them around Pisa then back to the Tatiana for dinner.

The next day they headed directly for the train station. They all boarded for Florence and their main objective, the Academia Museum of Florence to see Michelangelo's David. They were all surprised at the local travelers using the railroad and the comfortable feel of the train.

Florence had been the home of David since the fifteen hundreds. The Marble nude is over fourteen feet tall. On the way many jokes were conjured of the huge nude, but once viewed and the art of it realized, they stood quiet before it. Michelangelo's work could not be denied. It was a perfect work of art.

They also learned that Michelangelo did not die a pauper as many had heard, but had died a recluse. And in life had lived as a pauper. He was involved and wrapped up in his talent, not the value of it. He seemed to live for his work.

They also toured Florence with a local group, Susa had waited at the train station. On the return to the train station the talk was of the detail and size of the statue of David and how someone in the fifteen hundreds with archaic tools could produce such a master piece. They took their time in the museum. Susa had arranged for a local tour group and the entire trip was exciting.

First stop was Brunelleschi's Dome. His work of genius is an engineering marvel, and is an undisputed high point of Florence.

Viewing all rough stone work of Florence was very interesting, but at sunset they reached the Piazzale Michelangelo. From this location the colors of the sunset were spectacular. They actually hated to head back to the train after their sunset dinner.

They were tired and most of them napped on the train back to Pisa. From the train station they headed for the yacht where the Captain had juice and snacks available, but only Jerry and Ed took him up on it. Everyone else headed for their cabins.

The Captain told them they were still on schedule, tomorrow they would tie up late afternoon Friday at

Ostia, then Saturday a van trip to Rome. "I know you are tired, would you like to delay the Rome trip a day?"

"Let me suggest this Captain," Jerry said, "Yes we are tired, I am in no rush. Why don't you slow the Tatiana down a little? Take our time, can you enter the Ostia port late Friday evening, and let us sleep at the pier until mid-morning Saturday?"

"Certainly doctor, did you have something else in mind?"

"Yes Captain, we would like to kill the engines for an hour or so after dark tomorrow evening before Ostia and take a swim at night in your beautiful sea, does that sound feasible?" asked Jerry.

"Of course it does Doctor."

"We would like to offer you and the crew, not on duty of course, a chance to join us, we would like that."

"I am sure some of the crew would jump at that chance my friend, and thanks for the invitation."

"Okay we will plan that, now, by your leave, I think I will hit the rack." Ed nodded his agreement and they headed to their cabins.

They had planned a staggered breakfast, sleeping late with a leisure day at sea. Friday morning at sea, the Wiley party had a super breakfast. Ed and Dianne were the last to arrive, "Ah, Ed my friend you and the pretty lady must have danced for a while after we parted, last night."

Both were smiling, "You could say that, now where is the coffee?" asked Ed.

The Tatiana had a slow roll to her at the slower speed. It was a pleasant feeling. After breakfast everyone was in shorts or bathing suits to enjoy the Mediterranean Sea and sun. The Skipper suggested they move in closer to shore and everyone get a look at the Italian coastline up close and personal, using the Tatiana's toys, the Wave Runners. "Skipper that sounds like a winner."

"Coffee and cappuccino toasts from everyone; hear, hear, three cheers for the Skipper." Everyone responded. Corrections were made by the watch and soon they were doing five knots and the Wave Runners were launched.

It was a free flow time, lots of fun, adult kids as they went in and out of the little dotted islands. Ed and Don seeing who could jump the highest over the small wakes.

The girls even took some solo time. A couple needed a short 5 minute course, and soon everyone had enjoyed the exhilarating feeling of flying over the beautiful blue water of this sea. After a few hours the Wave Runners were returned to their berths. Everyone had a bath and they enjoyed a late lunch. After lunch some were covered with suntan lotion to enjoy more sun while some napped back in the cabins. This had been a welcome break and an interesting time to see the coastline. Areas not listed on tour maps, just Italy. It was more of a USA North East coast, with some small beaches and a lot of rough, craggy expanses.

As darkness approached the Chef suggested surf and turf as a late dinner after their swim. Everyone was excited.

The swim was as exciting as Jerry had explained. The Skipper taking no chances had stationed Susa with floats to cast if needed. Everyone learned quickly that Jerry and Buck were underwater ducks. Jerry had wanted this underwater action so everyone could see how clear the water was even at night. Jerry and Buck went down 15-20 feet and the ones swimming above could see them. It was a fun time, those who could not swim well were using life jackets from the Tatiana. The whole evolution took only about an hour and a half and they all had worked up an appetite for the coming Chef's special.

Everyone bathed and dressed casual for dinner. In their short time in the Mediterranean the Wiley tour had learned most people on the sea make stews and soups from seafood. But tonight it was beef from Spain and brazino, a member of the sea bass family. Locally in Italy it is called spigola

This spigola was grilled and served on a bed of sliced oranges and parsley. Several of the party had to learn that in many parts of the world, the head stays on.

The fish was absolutely delicious and the Spanish steak, very tender. The Chef had explained the Tatiana always uses the same ranch for its beef. It is grass and grain fed, and is always young beef. As far as meals go, this had been the best. The Chef was complimented many times.

Chapter 23

After such an active evening they all slept late again. As they had slept the Tatiana had pulled into the Port at Lido di Ostia, The crew was given orders in soft voices. The Skipper had met the Port authorities. The maneuver had not disturbed any of the passengers.

The group had agreed on a ten AM breakfast for Saturday and everyone was up for it. After all, Rome was special. The name alone said history and conjured up names from ancient history such as Paul the Apostle, Constantine, Julius Caesar and Augustus. The excitement would not allow anyone to sleep late. The talk was a mile a minute and a buzz. For the first time everyone, without exception, had one of the chef's special sweet rolls, coffee or cappuccinos.

The group would leave the Tatiana for a Saturday overnight in Rome. Everyone wanted to visit the Vatican of course. They were scheduled to return to the Tatiana late Sunday night and get underway soon after returning aboard.

A small bus was supplied today, each couple carried a suitcase and an overnight make-up kit for the ladies. As the trip progresses some asked Susa of his family back ground. "I am surprised that my bland background family, could of interest be to you and your exciting lives."

"Whoa there," said Don, "most of us here are from a cotton mill back ground. We are enjoying this country and adventure at the generosity of a wonderful couple. What you see here is not the way we live our daily lives. Now back to my question, where are you originally from my friend?"

"I did not mean to you to be insulting sir, I am originally from Turkey. My name Susa, is taken from a town in the Iran. To be sure, Susa is one of the most old cities in our big world. It is two days walk from the River Euphrates."

"Wow have you ever been there?" asked Dianne.

"For sure one time as a child my parents carried me there on pilgrimage, for me to see."

They did learn a little more about Susa, but he seemed embarrassed or private about some areas. The talk subsided as they neared Rome.

The trip to Rome was about an hour, the traffic had been a little heavy. As they entered the city Susa said, "Rome is not a place familiar, so the Captain gives me a list and the GPS. We head for his first point."

They arrived at the Piazza Navona, one of Rome's large squares. Susa discharged his passengers to pick them up on the far end of the square. "Those buildings look like they are constructed of Marble," Ed commented and pointed to the white spired buildings.

"They probably are," said Don, "They used a lot of marble when this was built, but I think you were just a baby then."

"All the world needs is one more smart aleck," laughed Ed. "We have been running short of them."

"Not on this trip," said Evelyn, getting the biggest laugh.

They all admired and commented on the craftsman ship, and the date of 86 AD chiseled into a monument. The center piece of this square was in the beauty and workmanship of the three fountains that graced the Piazza Navona.

They only glimpsed inside the Piazza's Stadium. It was huge. "The Romans didn't do too much that was small, did they?" asked Buck, it was a rhetorical question.

Back in the van, Susa announced the next stop was to be a museum, the Castel Saint'Angelo. Susa had picked up enough brochures of the places they were going to visit at a tourist shop while they walked the Piazza.

They opted not to stop at the museum, only do a drive-by. "Guys, I think we underestimated the time in Rome. How about two nights here? I can call the Skipper. We agreed this was an open cruise," then turning to Susa, "What do you think my man?"

"It could be a wise decision, since you do not have the driver expert here also."

Jerry called the Captains personal number, after many rings he got no answer, nor recording. "My friend Susa, I cannot raise the Captain, do you have another number for the yacht?"

"The Captain furnished me with a local phone, I will call the first mate." In a minute, Susa handed the phone to Jerry.

"....and we are not sure of his condition." Jerry had taken the phone mid-sentence.

"Excuse me, this is Doctor Wiley, is this the first mate?"

"It is Doctor, as I was saying to Susa, the Captain became violently ill, he is in the local hospital and we are not sure of his condition."

"I am so sorry to hear that, and hope it is nothing very serious. I am calling to say we will be in Rome an extra night and will return to the Tatiana on Monday evening."

"That will be excellent Doctor. We will expect your return then. I will expect Susa back here to spend the night once he gets you settled in the hotel."

"I had planned to put him up in the hotel, but if you insist of course he will return."

"Thank you Doctor, now could I speak back with Susa?" Jerry handed the phone to Susa, thinking the mate sounded terribly strained. I guess he would with the possibility of losing a charter mid-stream.

For the rest of the day Susa also seemed a little on edge. But Jerry was not going to let this ruin their vacation. They could find something to do in Italy for a day or so until the Skipper recovered.

Susa drove them by the Castel Saint 'Angelo. The brochure read it was originally a mausoleum, then a prison and now a museum. The film *Angels and Demons* was filmed here.

They drove slowly by the Roman Forum Ruins, highlighted by several tall marble columns. The last stop of the day was the Spanish Steps—one hundred thirty five very wide steps leading down to the Spanish Square. Reading the information that the Spanish Steps were built with French money brought a big laugh. "I am surprised it wasn't USA money," said Mary Ann.

Susa dropped them off at the Hotel Bernini Bristol in the heart of Rome and then he headed back to the Tatiana. The hotel was indeed in the heart of the Eternal City. A luxury hotel with roof top dining. They all met on the roof at eight for a delicious and beautiful meal.

After dinner everyone wanted to walk around the area for a little while. They had walked only a short distance when Don started singing *Three Coins in A Fountain* and the men all joined in as they approached the *Trevi Fountain*. Before the song ended everyone was singing and they all threw coins in the fountain.

Sherry leaned close to Jerry and looking up said, "My wish was granted some time ago when you asked me to marry you. Since then my heart has worn a valentine."

They kissed to everyone's applause, then every couple joined in, love was in the air.

"I think Mary Ann and I must needs get back to the hotel, I think she is tired." Buck said matter of fact, that bringing cat calls and comic comments.

"As a matter of fact Buck, Sherry is a little tired also," Jerry commented smiling.

"Okay, I'm tired too," said Dianne and Ed gave a thumbs up.

"Okay I will make it unanimous," said Evelyn, "Don looks tired too," giving everyone a chance to continue a raucous laugh as they turned and headed back to the Bristol.

Arrangement had been made for one more night in the same rooms. They were to meet at nine thirty. Everyone was having a private breakfast in their rooms.

The first day and evening in Rome had not been tiring. It was a relaxed day. Everyone had a good view of Rome at night, and love was in the air. Standing at the window holding each other, Jerry said, "My wish was granted also Doctor Wiley, my dream came true in the form of a beautiful lady from Mount Bell. I can never tell you how much I love you lady, there are not enough words."

"I really do like to hear you try, let's start with a kiss, and go from there."

Rome is truly the Eternal City, filled with love, At least it is tonight, Jerry thought.

Sunday morning at nine-thirty everyone was ready when Susa arrived. After everyone was in the van, Jerry asked Susa to hold it for a few minutes. Buck quoted some scripture and Sherry led a prayer of thanks and asked for blessings on the day's trip and improved health for the Captain, then they were off.

It was a full day taking in the city from another angle. They stopped at the Arch of Constantine to admire the artwork and take pictures. Then on to Capitol Hill and after that the famous Catacombs. This was the longest trip of the day they spent almost three hours there. They had a great guide who made the tour very interesting.

They all wanted pizza, "You cannot be in Italy and not have spaghetti and pizza," laughed Ed, "That would be like going to Philadelphia and not having a Philly cheese steak sub!"

The pizzas were delicious. The hotel concierge had given Ed the address of the oldest, most famous pizza oven in Rome. The smell and taste were superb. Susa had found a good parking spot near and came back to join them.

"Susa my friend, I haven't asked, but how is the Captain?" asked Jerry.

"Doctor, I am sorry to say I did not get to the yacht last night. The new Captain called and asked me to wait at the train station for some supplies, but they never arrived. I slept in the van and am sorry for my appearance. I cleaned up a little at the train station."

"So you have no word. That is strange."

"I thought so also Doctor Wiley, so I called the First Mate. He said to continue my job with you and return to the ship with you tomorrow evening. He only heard the Captain was holding his own, so he is no worse."

"I guess that news is as good as we are going to get. Some of the group want to spend some time walking around the neighborhood. Will you and the van be okay as things are?"

"Of course Doctor, please take the times you require. I am fine."

They really had a great time just walking. Ed met a man who recognized him as an American tourist. The gentleman, Luigi, had lived in Virginia, USA for a few years. He was anxious to talk. Ed brought him over and they all chatted for a half hour. He remembered grits and eggs for breakfast, and missed them. Ed mentioned that he was looking for some good spaghetti.

Luigi smiled, "Would you all join me for dinner?"

"We could not do that, Luigi, that is a very generous offer, but we could not accept," said Sherry.

"Oh please, one moment." Luigi took out the world famous cell phone and made a call. Speaking in Italian shortly he smiled broadly and hung up

"My wife says she will be very disappointed if you do not stay. At one time we had a very large family, my wife misses cooking her famous spaghetti, eight or ten is not big crowd she says thirty is a crowd."

"Luigi, do you have the room? Please, we do not want to put you out."

"Plenty of room and a large table. Can you be here at seven this evening?"

"Of course, this is such a nice surprise." Jerry took the address, repeated it and also got his phone number. Luigi walked off smiling, and even did a little shuffle dance.

Now everyone was surprised and also excited to actually be in a local home and eat some real Italian spaghetti. They headed to the Pantheon, then to the last scheduled stop, the Colosseum. The Colosseum is the most famous amphitheater in the Roman World.

They all wanted to go back to the hotel to rest a little and freshen up before their unscheduled dinner.

At seven they were met at a quaint cottage by Luigi who introduced his bubbly wife Rosa. They were led through the modest home to a beautiful grapevine covered patio with a huge wooden table having wine jugs for candle holders. There were pots of pasta and sauce. There was one large pot with the pasta and sauce mixed. A gallon jug of red wine was on each end of the table. The smell of fresh baked bread drew eyes to baskets of garlic bread. A feast fit for kings. Along with the wine were sweet tea and bottled water.

Luigi asked to say grace, after crossing himself, he spoke in English, thanking God for such a blessing of having these wonderful people for dinner. Then he said, "Please serve yourself as our kids used to do."

With parmesan cheese and other condiments available the Wiley group enjoyed a real home cooked meal. The spaghetti was truly real Italian and delicious.

The evening ended and Jerry was the last to leave. Hugging both of them he again thanked them. He gave them his card and urged them, if they ever made it back to the USA, to call. He wanted to return the favor.

They returned to the hotel for the last night there. Again, they would all have a private breakfast and meet Susa at nine-thirty for the last day ashore at the Vatican.

When they were both in bed, and relaxed Sherry asked, "Okay Romeo, how much did you leave Rosa for that superb meal?"

"They are wonderful giving people, someone I would like to be like. They are loving folk also, we were fortunate our paths crossed."

"So?"

"Okay, okay, was five hundred enough?"

"I think God will bless you Jerry Wiley, you are one of the good guys." The conversation was interrupted by a long sweet kiss, "Now we can enjoy a good night's rest, knowing we are richer for meeting Luigi and Rosa. It is amazing how God allows us to meet good folk. Good night sweetheart."

"Good night Honey."

Chapter 24

Monday morning everyone had their overnight bags ready when the van arrived. Susa was friendly as usual, but still a little withdrawn he asked, "Have your plans begun to vary any Doctor, or do we still continue over to the Vatican?"

"Ah, to the Vatican my friend maybe the Pope will invite us in for a chat," answered Jerry cheerfully. "By the way my good man, have you heard anything concerning our Captain, or his condition?"

"No sir, I talked to the First Mate early this day, the situation remains the same on the Tatiana."

Everyone was still talking about Luigi and Rosa and their hospitality. As they pulled away from the Bristol a scooter almost ran into them. Looking in the mirror Susa said, "Doctor I think the scooter is following us, he made a one-eighty and is now close behind. The passenger is waving a package."

The scooter moved up in traffic beside the van, and to their relief everyone could see it was Luigi driving and Rosa holding on and waving the cloth sack. As soon as he could find a spot Susa pulled over. Luigi parked right in front and was at the side of the van as the sliding door opened.

"Forgive us please, Doctor after you leave our casa last night, Rosa is cleaning up, and she screams loud to wake the neighbors, when she finds your gift. Then she declares: We must do something special for them."

"So for my special new friends from America, I have baked some mini zepoles and two chocolate amaretti cakes."

"That is very sweet, Rosa, but the meal was worth everything we left and more."

The gifts were accepted and the smell was heavenly inside the van. There were napkins and every one had to try the small mini zepoles. They were similar to the French beignet but with a little tougher dough. Lips were covered with confectioners' sugar as they bragged on the taste and said their goodbyes. The chocolate would be shared later.

"Can I pick good folks or what?" asked Ed smiling as he cleaned the sugar off his mustache.

Everyone agreed, even Susa chimed in at the taste of the pastry, as he threaded his way out of the heart of the Eternal City. Destination the heart of the Catholic Church.

The Vatican had van and bus parking, Susa was staying with the van. The group was met by a tour guide who after introductions gave them a quick overview of the Vatican.

"We are the smallest independent state in the world both in area and population The Vatican is one hundred ten acres with a population of less than a thousand. Today you are scheduled to see the world famous Vatican Museum, the Sistine Chapel, the Vatican Gardens and the largest church in the world, Saint Peter's Basilica. The church took one hundred years to build." Everyone noticed that they were perused for their dress. They had all been informed of the dress code: all shoulders and knees covered, no sleeveless dresses or mini-skirts, no shorts and no hats. The standard is strictly enforced.

The tour was fantastic. Midway thru, for lunch, they chose the Ristorante dei Musei Vaticani. The Vatican provided two more restaurants but tourists at the hotel gave them very negative reviews. There is also a snack bar and a sort of cafeteria. The group varied in their choices, but lasagna and pizza won out by the majority.

They all agreed concerning Rome and the Vatican that no words, books or pictures can ever describe the real thing. Of this group, none were of the Catholic faith, but there was a good feeling, wandering thru so much religious history. As Christians it is always good to know you have brothers and sisters of other persuasions with different concepts of Christ Jesus, but still worship and believe.

The lunch did not come up to Rosa's preparations, but it was still good. Then off to the gardens and the Basilica.

Impressed and tired at the end of the day they were glad to climb aboard the van. Saying goodbye to the Vatican the van headed toward the port and the yacht Tatiana. After about half an hour Jerry asked Susa, "Do you remember a restaurant a few miles from port that had a huge statue of a plump chef out front?"

"Yes sir, The Ravioli, I remember the odd type name."

"Why don't we all have one last meal ashore there?"

"Very well doctor, I think you have made a good choice."

The meal was very good, and the group came back to life, at least for the present. Everyone was going to be glad to find their berth aboard the Tatiana that was for sure.

Aboard the Tatiana all was quiet, the First Mate was on watch, and greeted them rather coolly. Jerry asked to see the Captain. But First Mate, who had always been very congenial, said the Skipper was tired and asked not to be disturbed.

"Then please request the Captain, when he arises, not to leave port until we have talked. This group is also tired and ready for some sleep."

"Doctor, I will convey your message and concerns to the Captain. I trust you will have a good night's rest."

Jerry was the last of his group to leave the deck and enter his stateroom. Sherry was already climbing into bed and he immediately undressed and followed. Within minutes they both were deep in sleep.

At midnight, the First Mate woke his relief. Once the relief had refreshed himself he reported to the bridge. He was receiving his turnover instructions when the new Captain appeared on the bridge.

"First Mate, please prepare the vessel to get underway in thirty minutes, set a course for the Straits of Messina."

"Captain, Doctor Wiley asked that we not leave port until he had discussed the rest of the cruise, since Captain Solomon is sick."

"Mate, who is the Skipper here?"

"You, of course sir."

"Then please follow your orders, I will deal with our guests when they awake in the morning. Further if the good Doctor should come to the bridge and ask about the engines you are to say, you are only running a normal in port test, is that clear?"

"Aye, aye, sir," the First Mate replied with a sharp salute.

At approx. oh one hundred on Tuesday morning the Tatiana was easing out into the Mediterranean and headed south toward the Straits of Messina. Once the course was set, the First Mate turned the helm over to his relief, the ship's chief engineer, and slowly headed for his quarters dreading the confrontation he knew was coming in the morning.

Susa was waiting for him outside his quarters, the mate motioned him to remain silent, then invited him into his berth. Once inside Susa asked, "What is going on Matey?"

"My dear friend, we have been hijacked, the Captain Jamal Rahim is an Islamic terrorist, high on the most wanted list."

"Then why don't we throw him over board for God's sake?"

"Here is what hurts my friend, he showed us pictures on his phone of every man-jack aboard and his family. Each family is being held at this time, and if we do not cooperate, everyone will be killed, most likely beheaded. I have a beautiful wife and three children. How about you?"

"I gave false information to the skipper when I came aboard and he knew it. It is very complicated but not illegal."

"I have a feeling Captain Jamal Rahim knows that my friend, but I am not positive."

"Okay, what is the reason behind this?"

"I am assuming it is money. This Dr. Wiley is a billionaire and I am assuming ransom is the motive. But please may I remind you of the families of your shipmates and I implore you not to do something really stupid, please?"

"Of course my friend, now what happened to Captain Solomon?"

"He is in chains at this moment, in good health I am assuming and sharing his quarters with Captain Jamal Rahim. Now we will talk more as time goes on, so let's both get some sleep." They shook hands, knowing they were both in trouble. Susa headed to his own berth.

Chapter 25

Jerry awoke at about three AM. He knew they were underway, but he still went to the small balcony window to confirm what he knew. With his right hand he reached under into his left arm pit and pressed a small embedded button that immediately sent a signal via satellite to five offices. Buddy, Tuck, Sticky, J Leon and Wiley Industries. The meaning was, *I am in possible danger.* Then he chided himself, *I should have followed my intuitions when a very healthy Captain was immediately incapacitated. I sure hope he is okay. This is a burden many folk do not know of, the dangers involved at being very wealthy.*

He stood looking out, then lay back down. Sleep was impossible, so he got dressed and eased out the suite's door. He wandered a little and then went to the bridge and found the Chief Engineering Officer at the helm. "Good morning Chief, got any hot coffee?"

"Oh Good morning Doctor Wiley, couldn't sleep huh? Hot coffee in that pot, take a clean cup and help yourself," the Chief said smiling.

With a cup of hot coffee in his hand, he sat with the chief whose eyes never left the scope and gauges. "So Chief, how is Captain Solomon, or are you not allowed to say?"

Jerry noticed a quick look of surprise, but the Chief recovered quickly, "I hear he is holding his own, we are all pulling for him of course."

"And what port is next on the new captain's agenda, I see we are headed south southeast?"

"Doctor, my course settings are for the Straits of Messina. We will not be at the Straits before my watch ends. Captain Jamal Rahim will bring you all up to date at the morning briefing. How was your time in Rome?"

"We had a great time. Susa was a good guide. By the way, is Susa a long time shipmate, or did he just come aboard for this cruise?"

"This is his first cruise with the Tatiana, I understand he came highly recommended from other ships in the Med."

Pretending to watch the sea for a few minutes, then Jerry asked, "What is Susa's job aboard when the Tatiana is underway?"

"He is an able-bodied Seaman, you probably know that is a catch-all phrase. He was mostly hired because of his driving skills and knowledge of most ports. In fact he was hired specifically to be your driver."

"He has done an amazing job of that also. He handles the traffic, autos, trucks bikes and scooters with ease and without the Italian tendency to yell and shake their fists," saying that Jerry smiled big.

"You nailed that Doctor. The one thing you can count on in an Italian car is horn, mouth and some profanity, and in all seriousness, none of it is serious in most cases."

They both laughed, "And you nailed that one my friend, I believe it is a sport."

They passed an hour or so just watching the sea and talking in general about the Mediterranean and its ports. The chief told Jerry of his wife and three children awaiting him, emphasizing that they were back in Spain awaiting his return. Yawning, Jerry said, "I think I will rejoin my wife Chief, I hope your remaining watch is uneventful."

"Thank you Doctor. It has been a pleasure getting to know you. Life is strange, me getting to know you on one of my mid-watches. I hope you get a couple hours of sleep," the Chief said as Jerry headed for his stateroom.

As Jerry opened the door he noticed a piece of paper just inside the door. He picked it up and went to the suite's head, he closed the door and turned on the light. It was a scrawled note: ***We are hijacked, Captain Solomon is chained in his cabin with the new Captain. Joe the seaman is one of the Hijackers. The rest of the crewmen's families are in danger if we do not cooperate. You have a friend among the crew it is best for now that you not know me. Please burn this note. God help us all.***

Jerry turned off the light and quietly found his satellite phone. He text'd his old crew, maybe one of them would get the message, he had only one bar off and on. He repeated the note as close as he could especially that the crew's families were in danger. After hitting send he deleted the message and awaited an answer. He set the phone on vibrate and slipped it into his pocket.

His mind went tactical. It must be about money. My priority is to convince the hijackers that they only need me. Let's get the vacation party off the boat, that is the first objective. Then a silent prayer, ***I do not understand this God, but my girl is convinced that all things work together for good to those that love the Lord. I haven't been even close to good, Sir, but as YOU know very well she is as close to an angel as there is here on earth, and she does love you. All I ask is please protect her and her friends, give each of them, peace over the next few days.***

There in the dark Jerry thought, I know if you boys got the messages and signal, we here have some surprises the hijackers do not know about. On the other hand, maybe it is time to learn to trust in God as my girl does.

The next morning they had a breakfast of bacon eggs and grits. They had bacon and other pork on the cruise and Captain Solomon had said to the question, "I am a business man, whatever my guests request within reason, they get." There was plenty of coffee and the new Captain still had not been within sight. Everyone was concerned about Captain Solomon, when suddenly he walked onto the mess deck where they were eating, closely followed by a man they had not seen and assumed he was the 'replacement Captain'.

Everyone started to rise in respect for the Captain but he motioned them to remain. Then he spoke, "Please forgive me but I have been under the weather as you Americans are known to say. Captain Jamal Rahim has filled in well for me. He has agreed to accompany us on the cruise. Doctor Wiley, at your leisure please come to my at-sea cabin on the Bridge, and we will discuss the coming ports. Earlier I mentioned Etna and an eruption that is tonight and we will slow the Tatiana down to coincide with the eruption which will be this evening around twenty-one hundred, or nine PM to you landlubbers," laughed the Captain. "I have seen this once, the crew will be looking forward to the sights since none of them have witnessed it before. Now continue your morning and enjoy the day at sea. By the way, I am feeling fit and 'in the pink' to steal an American saying.

Nothing seemed askew now since everyone had seen the Captain. Jerry waited about an hour, then headed for the bridge. He knocked, "Request permission to enter," using the USN terms for entering the Captain's area.

"Enter," was the only command.

Inside both Captains were seated, and indicated he should take the only unoccupied seat. Then Jerry spoke trying to give as timid an appearance as possible, "Is there a problem, Captain?"

Captain Jamal Rahim spoke, "Only one slight inconvenience Doctor. I am going to take charge of this vessel for a few days. Extending your vacation should not be much of a problem for a man of your wealth."

Looking at Captain Solomon, "What is this Captain Solomon, some joke?"

"Far from it my friend, Captain Jamal here tells me you are going to give him a large amount of money, in exchange he is going to allow me, my crew, their families, you and your friends to live."

Jerry looked very worried, and was silent for a long two minutes as he looked from one Captain to the other. "Since I have never been involved in a kidnapping for ransom, I have been schooled on the matter of course, being wealthy; I was told it was a hazard that comes from wealth. Of course I never thought to be the center of a ***situation***. So tell me how you plan to make this happen."

Again it was Captain Jamal Rahim who spoke, "It is very simple Doctor. All we are asking is twenty-five million American dollars in cash," at that Jerry appeared very nervous, "Come on Doctor that is only a drop in your bucket. We know a Mr. Dallas Fletcher is authorized to pay a ransom by your secret arrangements." At that Jerry tried his best to look deflated, it was actually true, but it involved more. "All you have to do is call him, isn't that correct?"

"Www-well yes it is, but under the present conditions I am not about to call him. What assurance do I have that everyone will not be killed if Dallas can raise that kind of cash in your time frame? You must know we do not keep even fifty thousand dollars in cash, near at hand."

"First of all you have my word, what else would you expect?"

"I am first of all a business man, Captain, I have learned not every man's word can be trusted, so if I err, it will be on the side of safety. Before I will call Dallas I expect this boat to pull into port and discharge everyone in my party except me. I am all you need to get the ransom."

"That will not happen Doctor. We will just eliminate everyone on the boat, and send a message. Upon receipt of said message, the families of Captain Solomon and his Crew will also be eliminated. At this very moment every crewman's family is being held by my people."

"Then my friend you may as well try to send that message," Captain Solomon's face immediately was pale, Jerry continued, "Because as you must know I am a black belt and even at my age and in these close quarters, can kill you before you can raise that pistol you are holding. If you need the money, it would be very ill advised to kill so many people without receiving even one American dollar. I assume you are that wise."

"If I were to agree with your insane demand, when do you plan to enlighten your party?"

"First of all I need to know where we are headed and when will we arrive?"

"That is no problem, we are headed for Toronto and we should arrive tomorrow afternoon around eighteen hundred."

"Fine until then we will ride the status quo. I will inform my wife and once the party is safely in a hotel, she can inform them. And then I will call Dallas, is that fair enough?"

"I will allow you this concession, but not one thing more. Keep in mind there is no place in the world that your wife can be, that I cannot reach. If you try to fool me in any way I will find her, bring you two together and behead her in your presence, before beheading you, as you say, is that fair enough?"

"Let's hope it doesn't come to that. Now Captain Solomon, you can be assured if all goes according to the stipulations made here, your family and those of your crew are in no danger from my actions."

"Thank you for that assurance Captain. I have found you to be a man of your word," spoke Captain Solomon.

"I must say to you Captain Jamal, I have no idea how long it takes, nor even how it is done, to put together that much cash. And I certainly do not know how to get it thru customs and deliver it."

"You can trust me to inform you of the method and procedures once the money is 'put together' as you say."

"If that is all, gentlemen, I will return to my friends." Both Captains nodded and Jerry departed. On deck Ed had just told a joke and everyone was laughing. Jerry got his cup and drew a cup of the chef's delicious coffee. Of course his mind was rolling over possibilities. But getting this group of wonderful friends off the boat without a casualty, was the first priority.

Sherry had learned her husband, and she detected something, but could not know what. "Is everything all right Honey?"

"Yes, only one small change. We will pull into Toronto tomorrow evening for a couple of days, then on to Corfu. I think everyone will like Toronto. It lies in the boot heel of Italy."

The rest of the day was spent relaxing in and out of the staterooms. Everyone was wondering about seeing a volcano erupt. They had a delicious evening meal and was relaxing on deck when the Captain announced they had entered the Straits of Messina. They noticed that several other yachts along with a couple cruise ships were slowly entering the straits. The volcano eruption was a big deal. It was a money maker for visitor viewings. Very few people are injured during an eruption. Hundreds of years of eruptions have taught the Sicilians from building any permanent structures close enough to receive damage.

Captain Solomon had proven his title of Captain, because they had a ring side seat for the amazing sight. There was an obvious roar, and even the sea gave a reaction. At first they saw something like a red flame, then immediately the lava went hundreds of feet into the air. Red hot going up, it faded from bright red to dark on the way to earth. Then the lava spilled over the volcano's rim in all its flaming red glory. What an amazing site it was, the bright red molten rock flowing down the mountain side crushing some trees and setting the ones that survived immediately to flames, before turning to black.

Nature's show lasted nearly thirty minutes. The view burned into the crews mind was the red hot lava slowly easing down the mountain, turning from bright red to orange to a cooler color then fading to black.

As Mount Etna settled down to a slight rumble, Captain Solomon told the observers, "Now inside that crater is a lake of molten rock near 2000 degrees Fahrenheit." This group knew they had just witnessed what few people ever get to see. A beautiful, but dangerous natural phenomenon. It was now Tuesday evening.

Wednesday morning breakfast as usual, everyone was still excitedly discussing Etna, what a trip this was continuing to be. Everyone was thrilled to be enjoying the life of the rich and famous, even if it was temporary.

Chapter 26

Within minutes of getting signals from Jerry's emergency GPS signal, phones were ringing. In a few more minutes there was a five way conference call. Attorney Dallas Fletcher in Pittsburgh, Buddy, J Leon, Sticky and Tuck. Dallas spoke, "I received the signal, give me your impressions, let's go alphabetically as we usually do, Buddy?"

"I am in the dark, all I know is according to schedule they should be on the Tatiana in the Med. I know they have completed Rome from our source, what do you know J?"

"They are at present steaming south-southeast, nearing the straits of Messina, which is the waters between Sicily and Italy. I have just added a better photo satellite to the team, and the boys are now moving it to cover that area. It will take a few hours to get it in place, meantime the older satellite is close enough to see the yacht. Mount Etna, in Sicily is scheduled to erupt soon, I am assuming the Captain had in mind for the group to see that phenomenon. Does anyone think the signal is an accident? Yo, Sticky?"

"If I remember correctly if we hit or squeeze that sender under our arms, we feel some electricity, just to show it is active. The boss would know it and give us a call. But my thinking is we had better get an army together and head for Italy or the Island of Corfu. We need to be closer than we are. What do you say Tuck?"

"I have Josh checking. Evidently you guys did not get a text message from Jerry. I received a broken message, but it did have the word 'h-i-j-a-%-k', I am assuming 'hijacked'. And I am with the Stick, we need an army and we need to be somewhere in the Med. Let's raise the army, alert Stella, and get everyone possible. The boss would move heaven or hell for any of us. I will let you know when Josh puts something together. We will let J Leon and his techies make an educated guess where we should head for, Dallas?"

"Okay I am making an educated guess. Jerry knows about the situation, but not Sherry. We do not have her signal. Let's assume it will be a ransom. It could easily be some wild Islamic Terrorist group needing funding. It must be a fairly elite group to have the information that Jerry is aboard the yacht. If they are sophisticated, I will receive a call on my private line from Jerry demanding a dollar amount. He will delay as long as possible to give us time to get ready for a response. This is that time. I agree with the idea of an Army, but you all know Jerry wants no one in danger for money. His MO has always been, pay them, get everyone clear then blow them and the money away, I want that clear. Buddy?"

"We all understand that, Dallas. Jerry has said it often enough. I hope he can separate himself from the group, I know that will be his first priority. I know Jerry is proud of the new plane, but do you reckon we need a second plane, maybe call Elsie Mae or her cousin Chase and rent a bird? Let's have at least five experts and that many sniper pieces. J?"

"During Mary Ann's kidnapping, I talked with her son, I cannot remember his name, but I did hear him say he had sniper training and if we ever needed him again to call. Pause, *talking in the background*... I just took a call from Josh. He has put the text message together. I will forward it to everyone, but the hijacking is affirmed and he is being forced to comply because every crew member, except a guy named Joe, has terrorists at their homes. If Jerry does not cooperate, the Captain's family and that of the crew will be killed. There is a little more to it, but enough to know we need to get trucking. Sticky?"

"Dusty is Mary Ann's son. I remember it because I have a cousin known by that name. Buddy was telling me about him after that last *Event*. I am inclined to the Islamic Terrorist angle. They have been using the funds raised from ransom in Somali to finance their cause. I speak a little Arabic, and I know Luke and Matt do also, so count me in of course. Tuck?"

"I also agree with the terrorist angle. I also know we will need a real army if there are terrorists with each member of the crew. We need those addresses and someone to neutralize each of those terrorists there. Doesn't Sherry have a friend that is in the embassy in Athens? We need to find out his name and contact him to be working on landings at military fields near where we are going. I don't want the CIA in this myself. I trust us more, but a couple of us have friends there. We might need to try some inroads for permission also. Back to you, Dallas?"

"I will immediately contact the CIA brass who scheduled training at our shops in Pittsburgh, off the record, to see how you can get your arsenal and tricks of the trade into Greece without customs problems. Does anyone else have anything to add now?"

"Okay," Buddy spoke, "I will call Stella and see if she is in contact with Elsie. I think we will need the extra bird. Looking mentally at the map, the hangar in Gastonia is as good a place to meet as any for us in North Carolina. I will be there in two hours. Is that okay with you guys?

"I will be there." J Leon.

"Roger that," Sticky.

"I may be a little late, but hold my seat," added Tuck.

Dallas ended the call, "Okay guys, I love Jerry like a brother, and even left handed I am good with a rifle, I did drop a buck at 600 yards last year. I am available. I will do some investigating and locate Sherry's friend in Athens, if he is still there. Love you guys, and if I don't go, bring my friend and his wife back."

The call was disconnected. Immediately Buddy called his supply guy about all the supplies he wanted available as soon as possible. The other members did the same.

Soon everyone was headed for Stella's loft at the airport. Stella had been notified and was doing her own research. Elsie and her cousin Chase would pilot the second aircraft. Fortunately a local mill owner had a Gulfstream 650 plane stationed in Charlotte, and could have it here on a two hour notice.

In the Charlotte office, Josh was working on a second message. The only thing about this message that he could make sense out of was 'next port Toronto'. He was watching the GPS report and it was about time for the yacht to turn into the heel area of Italy, if the yacht was going to Toronto.

While everyone was getting packed for an overseas trip another signal arrived. Sherry's distress signal had been activated. Yes there was trouble, now there was no doubt. The MVA, though disbanded, now had the most important '*Event*' of its illustrious history, an extraction of the founder. The man whose vision had righted wrongs that normal law enforcement efforts could not do. Yes, now in a foreign country they would have to be as careful as walking around eggs to keep an international incident from being on the six o'clock news.

Josh, Luke and Matt, using the International Seaman's Log had located every crew member's home address. One guy, even though not using his real name on the yacht, surprisingly had a family in Mount Bell,

North Carolina. When they learned this, Buddy, Tuck and Sticky had decided to neutralize that one.

Amazingly enough the address was on Myrtle Street, just three blocks from Sherry and Jerry's North Carolina home. At seven o'clock in the morning Sticky in a Gas Company uniform knocked on the door of Ali ibn Badir Samir. There was a long period of time, but there was an answer, "Yes, can I be of help to you?" An old man answered the door with a dog at his side.

"Yes sir, we need to evacuate this home immediately. There is a serious gas leak in the line beneath the house and it could explode at any minute. Seconds are important," Sticky was forcing himself past the man, catching sight of the man in a mirror, standing behind the door. As he expected, the man was holding what appeared to be an Uzi. Sticky back-handed a fly hit to the man as Tuck and Buddy came in with weapons at the ready. They quickly asked if there were other terrorists and there were not. Asam, the old man, explained there had only been two strange men. The other had left and said he would return at eight o'clock. Sticky explained why they were there and relief came over the face of the old man and younger lady also.

The other terrorist was no problem. When he entered he was taken without incident and both were handcuffed. Within the hour both were turned over to the local FBI agent at the office in Charlotte. They would be held by Homeland Security for as long as necessary. There was an understanding that nothing would be announced or leaked to the media because of the danger to many others.

That took care of one crew member's family now six to go, two members of the crew were brothers and lived together. They had no immediate family listed with the Sailor's Union.

They knew they needed to cover the other four plus the Captain's family. They agreed they did not want to involve the CIA nor local authorities until they were in the Mediterranean area. J Leon was assembling the 'Army' they all wanted and hoped they did not need.

Mark David was available and an hour out. Dusty was cleared and also an hour or two out. All the regulars would go. Sticky had recommended a man who worked for him and had been the foreman on his Grand Jury when he was accused of embezzling from the state of North Carolina. He and Sticky had been on the firing range together, and Ben was a natural with the rifle.

They would take their own medical crew this time. Megan and Jennifer would both be going. Both were top notch nurses. Hopefully in an emergency either Doctor Jerry or Sherry would be available.

It appeared the first trip across the Atlantic they would need only one aircraft. Elsie would be held back with the additional aircraft on standby for an emergency run. It had only been a few hours, but the team again was beginning to work like an oiled machine.

Stella and Vickie were ready and waiting for the gang to arrive. Elsie Mae, her cousin and previous pilot for Wiley Industries, had some vacation time coming and also Chase, who worked with her now, had some time. Both were headed for North Carolina on the next United Airlines' flight. They were presently in Utah.

Mark David was the first to arrive, followed soon by Sticky with his friend Ben Aaron. Then the phone rang, it was Dallas in Pittsburgh. He left a message with Sticky that he would be sending an e-mail with information needed to land at military fields as a Diplomatic flight and would be ushered to a remote part of an airfield. The friend of Sherry's was Tommy Cope, of the Embassy in Greece. His recognition of the Harris name was real and he seemed very glad just to hear it. Their families had been friends in the local church. His mama Georgia Belle and Sherry's mama Susie had been good friends.

After the phone call the four of them were talking and reminiscing when the phone rang again. This time it was Josh. Sticky took the call again, "Just to keep you guys up to date. I am on my way, Megan is driving and I am still following the yacht on my tablet. They are not headed for Toronto; that must be a red herring. I am awaiting a predicted destination. We should be there at the airport in about ten minutes. Take care. See you in ten."

The buzz picked up in Stella's loft apartment.

Chapter 27

The cargo hold was going to be full. It was good they would not max out with passengers. The main players were busy in the hangar with the hangar bay doors closed, sorting out the equipment. In the minds of the original 'Modern Vigilante Association' this was going to be the toughest of all their assignments and the man, Jerry, was this time the object to be extracted. Right now, they instinctively knew bloodshed most probably could not be avoided. For years in hundreds of dangerous '*Event*s' only three deaths had occurred — all unavoidable.

This time it was going to be even more complicated. They would be on foreign soil, violating many agreements and laws, but for their man Jerry nothing, no threat nor danger, could stop this group. This was The Man, the one who believed in them when they were wild crazy kids. This was Rags, S'gar, their boss Jerry Wiley, and they would bring him back or die trying.

They were all present and accounted for. Josh said his system's best software predicted three ports, one of which was Corfu, one of the cruise destinations. They were ready to fly so Stella checked, and there was an international airport on Corfu, Corfu International, that was under government control. A flight plan was submitted. It was approved in an hour and they were off. The last passenger was Robyn, who had been suggested by Dusty, because of her ability to learn languages and interpret. Greece was her dream destination and she jumped at the chance to go. She was proficient in Greek and it had appeared they were headed in that direction.

The flight was going to be about seven to eight hours and everyone was anxious to get close to where that yacht was. Corfu would put them in the Mediterranean. They would be close, anyway not thousands of miles away.

Tuck, Buddy, Sticky and J Leon sat together. Tuck handed Buddy the mike, "Go ahead, you are the mouth with the most," said Tuck laughing.

"The man with the biggest line since James Dean, just said that," commented Sticky with a synthetic grin.

Buddy took the mike, "Okay folks, you need to know some things that, until now, have been kept under wraps. First, Jerry is in serious trouble. He and his vacation party are being held on a yacht in the Mediterranean. What you may not know is, we know they are in danger because Jerry, like most wealthy folk, is subject to kidnapping. He and his wife Sherry have a transponder surgically implanted. When in danger they can activate it and we have received signals from both Jerry and Sherry. Hers later than his, but both are solid."

Not all the passengers could see Buddy because of the plane's configuration, but they were all listening intently. For a couple of them, it was the first time they would be involved in what is referred to *in house*, as an '*Event*.'

Continuing, "Something else all of you may not know. Years ago Jerry Wiley put together a group of men and women who he considered to be the best in the world. People who could handle anything from school yard bullies to international terrorists. Now we are going to be put to the greatest test ever. Bring him home safe, so that is why you are here. We have many theories, but that is all. We do have a couple of sketchy messages from Jerry, but nothing firm. We have taken the shotgun approach, and tried to cover all angles. Everyone aboard this plane is considered intelligent with the ability to be logical. We have about seven hours left in the air. Discuss the situation. DO NOT hesitate to bounce ideas around. We will know a little more as time moves on. Right now, we are told that the next port for their yacht is Toronto, Italy. That is not to be. The yacht has passed the entry to that port. J's satellite is tracking them and we should soon know a destination. Please be thinking and try to relax and rest. Save your strength because we do not know what will be required of us. Last of all, thank you for volunteering. You were told of the possibilities and you came anyway. God bless you and be with us all."

"You can tell the boy's daddy was a preacher, can't you?" asked Sticky laughingly as he looked over at Buddy.

"Now listen to who is talking," said Tuck. "You did good Buddy, but you did not mention the ace in the hole we have." Buddy acknowledged that and handed the mike to Tuck.

"Your attention again," said Tuck, "Buddy asked me to tell you one more thing. He and I talked this over when Jerry talked about the trip. I found a guy in Mount Bell of Muslim descent and hired him temporarily. Jerry has actually met the man but he does not know of the security hiring. He probably still does not know, because of the drastic change in appearance. We placed him aboard the yacht with the permission of the captain as a member of his crew, from monitoring the boat's communications he seems to have weathered the takeover, so at least Jerry has a friend aboard in the crew. We were surprised, the bad guy's intelligence must be good and they must be wide spread, because we found two terrorists at his house in Mount Bell. They are neutralized. We still must deal with the terrorists at the Captain's home and the rest of the crew. The options are still being discussed, got any ideas? Please share them in the next few hours. Also, if you have never dealt with jet-lag you are about to do that, so relax and rest as much as possible. We will have some mild medications to help fight it, but relaxing is the best medicine. I know Buddy has thanked you already, but I want to also say, Thanks."

Everyone had been briefed on a cover story. If anyone asked about them, they are visiting a friend in need. One who would be embarrassed if it was known so no names were to be used. All the crew had been advised also that the 'airplane mode' was not necessary as the aircraft had no electronics in the frequency range of the cell or satellite phones. Calls could be made and received if they were satellite capable.

J Leon was glued to his laptop, knowing everyone was depending on him for solid information. His crew back in Charlotte was monitoring the Tatiana's communications which was very short and apparently in some type of shorthand or code. All radio communications were being fed into software programs for de-coding. So far, the basic local 'shorthand' had the system baffled.

Thanks to the speed of the Gulfstream they were going to be at some destination in the Mediterranean before the yacht docked. J Leon's phone was on vibrate and he felt it. He answered, excited, "Yes, tell me you have something."

"Yes we do boss. The only possible port of any size with an airport is Kerkira, on the island of Corfu. If you guys sustain your speed and the Tatiana hold hers, you will beat her there by an hour. That is our best guess."

"What about the communications?"

"We only have a figure in all the garbage. They could not code this figure and we guess logically it is going to be the ransom. It is twenty-five million dollars. The other seems to be chit chat, but George the computer, is still digesting everything we have heard."

"Thanks dude, this is great, tell George he could be replaced if he doesn't come up with something soon."

"Will do boss, you know we are doing our best. You and the rest, please be careful. We, back here know we are safe but know that you guys are headed into *harm's way* and we are worried."

"Noted my friend, we will do whatever it takes to recover our Main Man. Now get me more!" hanging up, J Leon told the others what he had. They quickly agreed to text Dallas the assumed ransom figure.

Dallas got back with them. He had located Sherry's friend, whom he had researched to find was Tommy Cope, originally from a small community called Browntown, a part of Mount Bell. After hearing the plight, he had agreed to supply codes needed to land in Greece as a Diplomatic flight. He would also meet with them as soon as he could. He needed to know their schedule and the Greek airport destination. He happened to be free at present. His retirement was next week and he needed something to stir his blood. This might just do that.

Since they had decided to go to Corfu, they informed Dallas and he in turn would contact them again after he talked to Tommy. During the flight old acquaintances were renewed and more was learned about the new players. Most everyone knew Dusty who had performed well during the Mary Ann *Event.* Dusty introduced his baby sister Robyn. "Dusty has talked so much about this group I feel privileged to try to help. Something that amazes me is I love Greece. I have studied it and learned the language, and my first glimpse of any part of Greece is not the Parthenon, but a fabled island. For you who don't know, Corfu is just off the coast of Albania. I believe in prayer. Maybe my learning the Greek language was for this time. If not, I still am here to help if I can. I am sickened by the terrorists' attacks, and cannot believe now it is affecting me and my family. Thanks for allowing me to try to do some part to fix this foul deed." She was answered with all thumbs-up.

Four hours into the flight, they received the information and codes from Tommy. Also, Tommy would take a hop to Corfu and meet them personally. Sherry was a little older than Tommy, but the church group had been very close knit and he was concerned about Sherry and her friends. He had been obligated to tell the CIA station chief, who was an understanding guy but had checked on Jerry Wiley and was impressed. Impressed enough to say give them everything they need. His name is gold within the CIA and FBI.

It is nerve wracking to be in the shoes of the captive and the searchers. You are assuming a lot of things, but know they are just that, assumptions.

The four 'leaders' had wandered among the crew members, asking questions and getting ideas. They knew the rules of the situation Jerry faced. They were, to get as many 'out of danger' as soon as possible as you can. Everyone knew Jerry was a good negotiator and he would have already demanded the release of as many as he could.

Dusty and Robyn could not believe that their mama was again the victim of violence. Her life had been filled with excitement since her youth, but nothing on this scale. This was international and it was definitely life threatening. Buddy assured them that Jerry Wiley would put their mother's safety above his own.

They had already figured that; and this time she had a husband and friends.

On schedule Stella came on the intercom. "We have permission to land at Corfu International Airport. We are a diplomatic mission. The assistant to the ambassador, Tommy Cope, will meet us. We are cleared for our own hangar and will be led there by a runway buggy. We will be landing in fifteen minutes. You can buckle up now, but I will make another announcement in ten minutes. Thanks for flying Wiley Industries, we really do care. As a side note, Buddy, I know it is hard, but try to act diplomatic," she clicked off with a laugh.

According to the boys back in Charlotte, the yacht was definitely headed for the Island of Corfu. Since they had no idea why, they were all guessing: To re-fuel? Has Jerry negotiated release of some of the party? Was this to be their base for demands?

In the meantime the team leaders had realized they could not handle the equalizing of the yacht's crew and captain's terrorists visitors. They had decided to confide in Tommy Cope to get his opinion. Could the CIA and local governments do this? They were hoping for some serious cooperation without interference with their goal of extracting Jerry and any of his group being held.

Consistent with Jerry's beliefs of full and open communications, when possible, they let everyone know their thinking. There was no disagreement voiced. Now it was up to what they learned from Tommy.

"This is your pilot, please fasten your seat belts and secure all loose items. I plan to set this bird down smoothly, but if we encounter a raccoon, 'possom or elephant, I want you ready. Thanks for flying Wiley Industries Airways." Everyone got a smile out of that. Stella seldom varied from normal protocol, but this flight was different, her boss's life was on the line, this trip was different. Her levity helped. The landing was a book perfect landing. After landing Stella was directed to follow the 'airport mule' to a remote part of the airfield. There were several men in uniform and an official looking vehicle near the hangar to which she was directed.

Chapter 28

An official looking gentleman came aboard and announced he would view all passports before allowing anyone to deplane. The man was very friendly and not your usual customs agent. He was in and out in five minutes. Sticky and Tuck left the plane to meet Tommy. Some of the team and crew stepped off to stretch their legs and feel some openness. Tommy went back aboard with the team.

Around the conference table Buddy filled Tommy in on everything they knew. J Leon looking at his laptop broke in and announced that the yacht appeared to be headed to the local transit pier area of Kerkyra, Corfu. Arrival time about an hour, which would be around six PM local.

Buddy spoke, "Tommy, I know how Jerry thinks. Although we could take the yacht this evening with little effort, that would put the crew member's and the captain's family in a dangerous position. Jerry would not approve any action that would endanger his family, group or anyone else. Let me request nothing be done until we know the dangers to the families have been neutralized."

"Buddy, it is Buddy, right?" Buddy nodded yes, "I completely agree with you. I do want to schedule some video coverage of the yacht as she comes in. Excuse me a minute." Everyone was silent while Tommy arranged several angles of the yacht.

Tommy was a take charge person; many years of service in the diplomatic corps were apparent. After the photo arrangements he spoke, "Now what I need is all the addresses, and names." He gave an e-mail address and J Leon immediately hit send and Tommy had them on his smart phone.

Tommy then spent only a few seconds and he hit send. That started the ball rolling in France. "We have agreements in France for our international terrorists' teams to work with local gendarmes. They were alerted automatically with Mr. Fletcher's call. This should take less than about four hours for the complete evolution. Our office has been in contact with State and you are approved to attempt the mission before our team gets in the picture. You understand I had nothing to do with this. Mr. Fletcher's call was on our system and it is monitored continually. There is nothing more I would like than for a team from Mount Bell, NC to make the news of saving the day."

"With all due respect Tommy we could care less who gets the credit, we just want an end that leaves our man and his group safe," said Tuck.

"I couldn't agree more sir, but I get a lot of flak for being from 'Podunk, NC', I was being a little selfish. Of course, I want Sherry Harris Wiley to be safe along with her husband."

"Tommy, how much freedom are we going to have here about traveling?" asked Tuck.

"We should have several vans here shortly. They will be at your disposal. I understand many of your group have international driver's license, so all you must do is list the drivers and their license numbers. Unfortunately payment is not authorized, but as I understand it that is not a problem."

"Friend, where Jerry and Sherry Wiley are concerned price is absolutely no object of concern," said Sticky seriously.

Robyn and Sticky were already holding a transceiver on a frequency of the Tatiana which was supplied by J Leon. The transmissions were also set up to be recorded here as well as North Carolina. They were now, in effect, reading the Tatiana's mail.

Robyn had already learned and announced the pier number where the yacht would dock and also that the

Tatiana had requested to discharge several passengers, before heading back to sea. Controlled confusion reigned. Who was getting off? "We need those vans," said Buddy emphatically. J Leon was plotting a course to the pier. Fortunately they were only ten minutes away.

"They will be here in five minutes," Tommy said. "That should give us plenty of time to find a place to observe the docking and for us to record our own video. Please understand, I want to protect any American Citizen, but Sherry is personal, I know her."

While the team was discussing the latest bombshell that the Tatiana was returning to sea, Stella had already called for refueling. Vickie was doing the preflight checks on the craft, engine and body. The plane would be ready when needed.

The vans did arrive in a few minutes allowing them time to be positioned to record the arrival. Once the Tatiana was tied up at the pier, tension rose in the vans. They were stationed a good distance away and from different angles, video recorders were running.

Aboard the Tatiana Jerry was smiling as he spoke to the group, "I am going to stick around for a while. You guys head out and get us a nice hotel, I will be along." Jerry hugged Sherry very tightly and whispered, "Don't worry, all they want is money and we have plenty. Call my friends. I love you sweetheart. Everything will end well. We have too many years left to let money stand in the way. Now go on, your friends need you."

At the same time Jerry was looking around, the language he saw on signs and advertisements was Greek, not Italian, as the skipper had said, he knew right away this was not Toronto, Italy. He thought immediately of his message to the team, saying they were headed for Toronto.

On the pier he could see Sherry. She was a trooper, waving enough cabs for everyone and their luggage. Everyone laughing and carrying on. Silently as he stood with Captain Jamal Rahim he prayed, ***Lord, I know I don't talk to you enough, but right now it is Sherry I am worried about. Please give her strength. As for me? I want to live, please give me wisdom to handle whatever comes my way. I prefer to be in charge, but for now, I don't mind if you are, so I submit to your control.***

He was brought back to the present situation. "I am a man of my word. You alone are left. Now Mister Wiley, I suggest we go to the yacht's bridge and make a telephone call."

"As you command Captain." On the bridge Jerry took the phone and placed the call to the states.

“Yes, may I ask who is calling?” was the answer over the speaker, Jerry recognized Dallas’s voice.

“Hey Dal, this is Jerry, I have gotten myself in sort of a jam, I need twenty-five million dollars. I seem to owe some folk here in the Med. I am going to let you speak with Captain Jamal Rahim, he will give you the details.”

“Mr. Fletcher, my name is unimportant, but your friend and his friend’s lives depend on the delivery of twenty-five million dollars cash within three days. You are familiar with beheading I am sure. If we do not have the money in three days, your friend will lose his head along with his wife and friends.”

“Let me tell you something please, I have never in my life put together that much money in cash, so I am not sure it can even be done. I do not want to lose a friend, but I am not sure I can deliver in three days. I don‘t even know how to get it out of this country in cash. Always for moving money we use internet transfers. Can I call this number after I find out something? PLEASE?” Dallas sounding frightened and at a loss to act.

“You raise the money, then call this number. We will instruct you how to get the money out of the country and to us. Please be aware that Mr. Jerry Wiley’s life depends on that understanding.”

"Sssure I understand and I will start working on raising that amount of cash immediately." The connection was broken. Dallas had already started the ball rolling for the cash before the call. He noted the number he was to call, and then hit speed dial on the team's number. The answer was immediate.

"Yeah Dallas," Tuck had been standing by in one of the vans, "What is the story?"

"Things are exactly as you guys thought. Jerry is being held hostage for twenty-five million dollars. I am to raise the money and deliver it in three days. If they are as smart as I think, they know that time frame is impossible, I will call them back in two days and tell them it will be Tuesday before the money will be ready, since we are facing a weekend."

"We don't want to endanger Jerry," Tuck knew he did not have to say that but it just came out.

"No problem Tuck. If they refuse I will send a package of newspaper with some hundreds on top and bottom, but I am sure they know three days is impossible, and if I agreed they would expect a trick."

"We trust you Dallas. Jerry said you were the best at negotiations. This, my friend, is the most delicate deal you have ever negotiated."

"Don't I know it Tuck? You know I will do nothing to endanger the man who trusts me with everything he has. I will be in touch. You know any communications will be on this phone, unless we want to leak something. I would think they are monitoring our normal calls."

"I agree, so if I get a call on the other phone, it will be an intentional leak, Gotta go Dallas, it looks like everyone is off the Tatiana except Jerry. We have two vans, one will stay here and the other will follow Sherry and her friends."

"Yes, take care, I have work to do. I knew Jerry would get his wife out of harm's way if at all possible. Get to work, God be with you guys."

The van carrying Tommy, Robyn, Mark David and Buddy were to follow the released passengers. Tuck, J Leon, Dusty and Sticky were in the other van. They sat helplessly making a video of the Tatiana as she prepared to leave taking Jerry back to sea. J Leon was following the yacht on his laptop screen. It was too soon to determine where it was headed.

J Leon felt his phone vibrate. After listening for a few seconds he breathed a sigh of relief. His boys had been able to get in the back door electronically using their own software. They could now monitor the ships radio, cell phones and read the e-mails. It appeared they could read all the bad guy's mail now and start some plans. They were in the process of patching everything thru on different channels. Just as soon as a base was set up on the plane or a hotel, the feeds would start. Also they would have his satellite in positions soon. In turn he informed the guys in the van. Everyone gave a thumb's up.

****

Sherry and the group were headed down town it seemed, but they ended up at the Archadian Hotel. The van parked at a discreet distance to observe if anyone suspicious was watching the party. After about thirty minutes, Robyn, wired with a transmitter and dressed as much like a local as she could, did a casual walkup. Being able to speak Greek she asked a few questions, but mostly observed. The lobby of the hotel was empty.

Robyn then approached the desk to ask the room number of a friend, Sherry Wiley, who had just arrived and at the same time slipping him a 100 euro bill Tommy had given her. She received a note with all room numbers of the party, noting Sherry's room.

The clerk busied himself and Robyn walked past the elevators to a side door. She spoke over the microphone to tell the guys where she was. The van moved to the back of the hotel and everyone walked in and up a set of stairs out of sight of the clerk. On the second floor they took the elevator to Sherry's room.

As they passed the room for Mary Ann and Buck and Robyn indicated she wanted to knock, Buddy nodded his approval. After a few minutes she got no answer and they continued and knocked on Sherry's hotel door. Buddy was standing with Tommy as the door opened.

Sherry answered. She almost fainted as much of her anxiety was removed, "Buddy, Tommy? Tommy Cope, is that you? In the Lord's name, how did you know? How in the world did you get here?" Buddy motioned they needed to be inside the room.

Chapter 29

Once everyone was in the room and after fully recognizing Tommy as 'a boy' from home, Sherry had latched on to Tommy hugging him and tears began to flow uncontrolled. She squeezed as if trying to roll time back, back to a time in Sunday school, back to a time when a big problem was a bad name or a skinned knee. Back to a time in Mount Bell as kids.

As Buddy looked around the room it was apparent the entire group had been crying. Then Mary Ann saw Robyn and her jaw almost hit the floor with the look of HOW? Then they rushed to each other and embraced, and the tears flowed from both. It took about fifteen minutes to calm everyone down and get the stories.

Sherry explained, "I had just finished trying to explain to everyone here what was happening. I was going to call you guys, Jerry's MVA, the *miracle workers*, to see if you could help. Now what is the plan?" asked Sherry.

Buddy answered, "Right now, all we have is information, not enough for a plan. Elsie and Chase are standing by with an extra aircraft in Gastonia, in case we need anything else. Jerry is being held for twenty-five million dollars ransom. As far as we know now, the terrorists only want money. We plan to be around to make sure that is all it is. Tommy here, has been the cement that allowed us to build what we have so far. His knowledge and influence has allowed us to land here with our supplies. As for now and for everyone's safety, you guys shouldn't know any more than that."

"Seriously Buddy, what are Jerry's chances that the ransom will set him free?" Sherry had to know.

"Sherry, Jerry has always wanted all the players to know how the deck is stacked, so we consider everyone here as a player. This is *Very* serious. Our best guess is we have a sixty to seventy percent chance of getting Jerry back uninjured. We are confident we can get him back alive, that confidence level is over eighty percent."

"Thanks for being open. Something you guys need to factor into your equation are our prayers; I know that Jerry's prayers are there also."

Tommy talked to the group about Greek law and the problems everyone could face if this turned nasty. There were a lot of questions. Buddy and Tommy answered as well as they could.

Buddy got everyone's attention, "Now folks, we *DO NOT* foresee any problems you guys would have from the terrorists here at the hotel. However, for peace of mind, we are arming Don, Ed and Buck. We have enough information that tells us each of you are proficient in fire arms. These pea-shooters are only small nine millimeters, but that should be enough."

Quickly Mark David issued the weapons along with quick instructions for caring with the holsters furnished. He also had a fake license that would pass casual scrutiny.

There were a lot more questions, but the crew needed to get back to where the intelligence was being gathered. "We are going to get out of here as quickly and quietly as possible. Sherry still has a secure phone and a couple of numbers. There is an outside possibility that we may ask for volunteers. Be thinking about it." With that they said goodbye telling the group that they would keep them up to date. But this is a touchy situation. We do not know if they have more assets here in Corfu watching this hotel.

They made their exit to the van without any detection from the hotel staff and headed back to the airfield. On the way back Buddy called the hotel to see how many rooms were available for the night on the same floor as Sherry and the tour group. There were six rooms left and he reserved them for the night with an option to cancel within the hour.

Back at the hangar, J Leon and Josh were intently studying the Tatiana's course. It seemed to be in no hurry to leave the immediate area. Taking that fact under consideration, there was unanimous agreement to spend the night at the hotel. Some of the crew were already dozing.

Stella and Vickie had already scoped-out the hangar area. It was fitted with a very nice shower and toiletry area. By the time the vans returned, they had already showered, finished the fueling and decided if everyone else went to a hotel they would stay with the plane. The plane had two areas that make queen size beds.

The vans were loaded and they headed back to the hotel. They had agreed to record all message and phone traffic then review it in the morning. There were enough of the group to stand an hour watch on the phones, so Tuck made a quick schedule. Tommy wanted to stick with them and also wanted to stand one of the phone/radio watches. Everyone felt good about security. At Tommy's request the airport was glad to provide extra security for the 'Embassy' plane. When everyone was settled at the hotel, Buddy, J Leon and company were still wound up, it was near midnight heading into Saturday.

A quick contact with Sherry via the hotel phones put them back in Sherry's room. The girls were with her and the guys were together trying to work out their own plans should all fall through.

Everyone knew at a time like this, the unknowns were too big to allay the fears. But they all understood the need for human support of the physical nature. They just talked. Near 1 o'clock AM they said their good nights and headed for bed. There was no need to check messages, the person on watch would alert them of an emergency situation. There was not much they could do to extract Jerry until they heard from the authorities in France that all crew members' families were safe.

****

Back aboard the Tatiana and after the phone call Jerry headed back to his quarters. On the way the cook waved him down with a steak sandwich and a thermos of coffee. Both smiled weakly knowing they were in the same boat. "Thanks Cookie, I may need something stronger if my nerves don't hold out." In his room he sat on the bed, *I have never been this much in the dark. Did the guys get a message, are the senders getting out?* Sitting on the bed he looked in the mirror and realized he was depressed. *Look old son, you don't have time for depression, of course they got the message. If not they have by now. I think I see Stella smiling and she and Vickie are checking the plane with the anticipation of flying across the Atlantic.* Then he smiled and poured himself a cup of the cook's good coffee.

Now what are the odds that this is a straight swap, my life for money, and who is my friend aboard ship? He needed a weapon. This old guy did not plan to leave this world alone. He searched his mind for anything he had left undone. He always liked all loose ends tied neatly.

After sitting in the dark thinking for hours, he thought, *Lord, I need some help. I know you have heard from Sherry already. I am in a heap of trouble, help the boys to know what to do. Now if it is my time, please accept Jerry Wiley with all his spots and wrinkles. All my life I have tried to do the right thing, but then you know that. Just keep an eye out for me, and if I must come to you, make it easy on my girl. She is the best, but then you know that too. Night Lord, You have been much better to me than I deserve.*

Normally Jerry could compartmentalize and go off to sleep, but this night was unusual. Then he thought, I have a friend aboard, I wonder how much of a friend? Then I might ask, why do I have a friend? I do not know anyone who would have been associated with the Tatiana. Jerry drifted off into a fitful sleep.

Chapter 30

Saturday morning everyone was in the hotel restaurant except Josh and J Leon. They had both chosen to go down for coffee about the same time. Megan was still sleeping, the two picked up a couple donuts and coffee and headed for the room that J Leon was sharing with Matt and Luke. The monitors and electronic equipment was there. The two roommates rolled over to see what was going on and went back to sleep.

They dumped the last night's e-mails and text messages. While they were printing, they played the three phone calls. They were in a foreign language, both agreed it appeared to be Arabic. Immediately Josh called up his translator software and they listened to a mechanical English conversation. Nothing new in the first, a report of the demand being made. The Captain here believes Jerry is cooperating. *The infidel will do anything to protect his life and that of his woman.* He laughed at how he had scared the money man. That conversation proved Dallas was right, they know he cannot put the money together in three days.

The second call seemed to be from someone higher up the ladder because the Captain seemed to display more respect in his words. Josh and J Leon both became tense when the caller said, 'Remember we want a good video of the faithful beheading the infidel.' The fools think money can redeem their souls. The Captain's answer had been, "The video technicians have been alerted and they will be on Corfu within three days. We have rented an isolated house that is in sight of the beach. I think your choice of the beheading of infidels on the shores of the Mediterranean is an insight from Allah."

Both Josh and J Leon looked at each other, knowing this is not good. The third conversation was only about the yacht cruising in the local waters for a few days. However there was a little gem. *The terrorists had planned to furnish the aircraft to transport the money, but it has been decided to let the money man use the company plane or lease one.*

Stating at present we do not want any tracks in the land of Infidels.

There were no text messages. The printed e-mails did not produce anything and the ships radio was only about course changes when alerting the area shipping lanes.

After everyone had finished breakfast they held a quick briefing. It was decided they would rent the rooms for a few more days and set up one room as an operations center. They would suggest that Sherry continue to reserve their rooms separately.

The crew sat around very solemn following the knowledge that the terrorists had decided to take Jerry's life after the money had changed hands. "Okay now we are sure there is going to be loss of lives. We must put together a plan, remembering what General Patton once said, *let the loss be theirs not any of ours.* I think we can handle this, but my question is do we tell Sherry?" asked Tuck.

There were a lot of pros and cons and lastly Sticky spoke up, "We are talking about a woman who endured being kidnapped and was nearly killed herself. Remember we got tied up in traffic and she saved herself. She deserves to know. Jerry always wanted the players to know the score. I say we tell her and then let her, or help her, decide when to tell the rest of the party." Without speaking Buddy gave the thumbs-up. He was followed by J Leon.

"I feel the same," said Tuck. "I just wanted to know how you felt."

"Actually we girls are pretty tough when we have to be. I agree Sherry should know," spoke up Jennifer. Then it was Megan's and Reece's time to produce the 'thumbs-up.'

"Thanks ladies. It's always good to hear from the prettier side," smiled Tuck. "Buddy go ahead and invite Sherry over."

In a few minutes Sherry knocked and was let into the room. "I can see this is not good news. You think they plan to kill Jerry, don't you?" She said with tears welling up.

Buddy walked over to her and put his arm around her. "Sherry, you have that partly right. What we know is, they plan to take Jerry's life after the ransom is paid, *but* what I am telling you is, that ain't gonna happen."

"Sherry, we debated whether to inform you or not but Jerry's rules won out. He would want you to know the game, cards and chances. I also want to remind you of what you know already, Jerry is still on that yacht, and he is sure his team is going to be there for him, just as he has been there for each of them." Sherry did not miss those misty, 'never misty', eyes of Tuck's, when he finished. The room went quiet except for the sounds of a keyboard.

"Sherry, we learned what we have told you from their phone calls. We are reading their mail and we are positive they are going to make the exchange here on Corfu. We hope to know where, soon. Until then we will be making some educated guesses and forming a solution scenario. Josh is already searching the net for rentals near an isolated beach." Buddy spoke breaking the silence.

Sherry looked first at Buddy then around the room before speaking, "I will tell the others in a few minutes. Before I leave, let me tell you guys and gals something. I believe in prayer. I prayed most of the night. I now have faith and confidence that again you guys will win. You will bring Jerry back to us. I never knew I could love and respect a man the way I do Jerry Wiley. You do what you must. Methinks God is on our side, and that is not spoken flippantly."

Again the room was quiet. Sherry nodded to them. As she reached for the door to leave, she turned to say, "Thanks everyone, I know it was a tough decision to tell me the hard truth." Then quietly she left.

Megan said, "What a lady." Breaking the silence, the room was filled with 'amens'.

"Okay, back to work," said Tuck. "Robyn, it would probably be good if you wandered around the area. Take Dusty and Reece with you. Wander around the Hotel area then range out a block. Paying close attention to shaded vans and construction trucks that might hide someone with electronic equipment."

Tuck explained the majority opinion. It was possible, but unlikely, that the party would have been allowed to leave the yacht without some surveillance. We are hoping they are confident enough to leave them alone, but it is better to be prudent.

After some discussion, it was conceded that Sherry and the tour group should tour a little. That would occupy their minds some. Sticky suggested he dress in local apparel and be a guide, taking them to a local attraction, the Kaiser's Palace. He visited Sherry's room where he found everyone. Sherry rented a van thru the hotel and they scheduled an outing. They hung the 'Do Not Disturb' signs on each door.

As was his practice, J Leon had pasted cameras facing both directions in the hallway outside the rooms to monitor any suspicious actions. Getting the tour group out and on the road could serve two purposes: to see if anyone was interested in the rooms and also Sticky could keep an eye out for someone who may be tailing the group to keep track of their movement.

Within an hour the tour group was on their way trying to enjoy this island with which Jerry had been so impressed.

Back at the command post many ideas were being put forward. Most had to do with snipers placed near the transfer point. Tommy was there to give them past history of how several ransoms had been paid, even though our government had denied that was done. Tommy said in other cases it had been a simple walk up and switch with armed men on both sides to guarantee compliance. But as he stated, this time you guys know they plan to kill the hostage, so there will be no visible armed men on the good guy's side or each of the armed men will be targeted from a distance. They were still in the dark as to how the money transfer was going to be completed in this case.

"I have counted our sniper assets, ten including Reece, but that leaves no one at the command post. We will need our medical folk within minutes of the site. We will need local observers of the roads, paths or lanes heading to the transfer area to prevent *'that surprise'* which we do not need," said Buddy, "We need one or two of us, *the unholy four* here, monitoring and directing." Buddy used a term that Jerry had used many times to describe the tattered bunch he had met at Mount Bell as kids: Buddy, Tuck, Sticky and J Leon. They were the *'unholy four'*.

J Leon took the floor, "I know we will need at least five more secure radios with hidden mikes for the road watchers. We need to get a list together for Elsie to bring when she brings the money. It needs to be labeled and ready to distribute, *unless*, y'all think she needs to make two trips. She does have time but that window is closing."

"Good points J Leon, we do need to work on that. It sure would be good if the bad guys would tell us where the transfer is going to take place. It looks like right now we have about a day slack to decide." Spoke Tuck.

On the tour the group could not help but be impressed with the Palace. Its history was intriguing, and it was easy to see how people in Germany and even Russia would prefer the mild beautiful weather of the Greek Islands. The sculptures were all by famous artists along with the paintings. They also toured the Kaiser's Throne.

This was intentional on Sticky's part. It was a tough climb. Everyone was winded when they reached the top. No one disagreed that the Kaiser had great instincts for a place to contemplate. There was a stunning view of the coastline. The flowers and shrubs were out of this world beautiful. They had passed several huge deer as they climbed. Even from the top most view point Ed had pointed out a twelve point buck casually grazing. The views were three hundred sixty degrees of stunning flora and fauna. They all rested here for over an hour, enjoying the water Sticky had packed in his back pack.

It was time for dinner by the time they made it back to the hotel. Sticky had seen no sign of a tail following them. It seemed they were being left alone — at least on the road.

Back at the hotel there was no suspicious action in the hallway. The staff cleaning crew had read the do not disturb and smiled as they walked off. No suspicious persons appeared in the hallway during the group's absence.

Saturday passed with no communications of importance. All sources were monitored around the clock. It was four o'clock Sunday morning, Matt was on duty, and listening intently to a phone conversation. The phony Captain had received a call from someone who was under him judging by his attitude, "Why do you ask again? I made it clear. You have a GPS. Put the following coordinates in the box and follow the instructions, 39 degrees 33 minutes and 58 seconds N and then 19 degrees 50 minutes and 3 seconds E. This will lead you to the rented house. Stay inside and await further instructions. Surely you can follow these simple rules, Allah be praised." He had hung up abruptly. The golden number was recorded: 39° 33’ 58”N 19° 50’ 3” E. Smiling as he woke up the crew, he ordered a pot of coffee.

It wasn’t long until the room was bustling. The coffee had arrived and signed for. J Leon was positioning his satellite over those coordinates and displaying them on the four foot screen for everyone to see. It was night and he switched on the night vision. It was clear enough to see the area. There was one pier approx. 100 feet projecting into the Ionian Sea, the site was on the opposite side of the island, only twelve to fifteen miles from where they sat.

Using a pointer as he spoke, J Leon said, “This is obviously the house they have rented. I will guess, they expect the money to be delivered by sea so they can observe it coming in. It seems to be a long way around from the airport. Probably not but thirty five miles, but still a long way by boat.”

Buddy spoke, “They could drive across the Island a few miles from the site and start from there, and it would take no time.”

“True dat,” said Sticky, “And that is most likely if they plan the exchange money to come by sea.”

“Okay, first let’s figure the pier area. Where is the most likely place for our snipers to be stationed?”

The discussion went on until they broke for breakfast. They were pumped up. This was solid information. They could check out the roads and take a look.

Chapter 31

With the new information all minds were hopping. They all knew not to discuss this in the open restaurant, so most of the team rushed thru their breakfast to get back to the business at hand. This was one piece of the puzzle they had needed desperately. Most of them knew they did not have a lot of leeway to study the area and post the team before it would become dangerous to the point of blowing the mission.

Sherry again had scheduled a tour thru the hotel for her group. Robyn, Jennifer, Megan and Mark David would join the group to add eyes, looking for any sign of a leak or observers in the area. The tour left mid-morning with a stop at a local Greek Orthodox Church that had been gladly arranged by the hotel. The Manager was proud to say the small church was his home church since birth.

They were pleasantly surprised as the Priest greeted them and pointed them to an area that was set aside for small groups and their interpreter. Robyn would be their translator. Following church they would do a sightseeing tour of the entire island, strictly avoiding the area designated as the final scene of this terrible drama. They would all be able to speak freely in the van since they opted to allow Ed to drive because he had an international driver's license. Just to be on the safe side, J Leon had already scanned the van's interior for transmitter bugs.

Back at the Command Post J Leon using the four foot screen had blown up the area of interest and everyone was looking for the best angles to station shooters with the least danger to Jerry. Deciding the number of actors was the big problem. The question kept arising, how many bad guys will be around?

There was a consensus that the bad guys would also post shooters. The good guys needed to be there first, even if they had to remain in position thirty to forty hours. J said he would use split cameras and screens. One camera on Jerry at all times and the other covering the area and occasionally scanning.

"J Leon's cameras cannot see under the trees. Note the sand roads about a quarter mile on either side of the house. They appear to be some developer's ideas for later construction. We need recon on the ground of those woods as soon as possible. Our communications have not told us if there is life there. J's heat sensors show nothing in the house. We need to monitor the screen to see if there is ever movement around the house. But we need a team today to do the boots on the ground deal. We can drop two teams off and let the van return upon notification. That will also let us check out our communications. Okay, who goes?"

The teams were being picked when they all heard what was obviously Arabic being spoken, Ben stood up. "I was just fooling with you guys. What you just heard was me asking to go. I have been learning Arabic for the last few years. I have a good friend who lived in Saudi Arabia for many years who has been teaching me. I would like to go on the recon. My language knowledge may come in handy." The team was taken aback at this quiet dude and his ability.

"You got it Ben, you are with Buddy." Buddy and Ben high fived each other. The van stopped by the plane to pick up some gear and 'silenced' weapons on the way.

This was to be a big test and everyone's eyes were glued to the screen. The screen would show body heat thru the tree cover and they could follow the team on its recon. There was also radio contact with the members of the reconnaissance teams. This was common in the MVA when they were active. It was followed live and recorded. The team members ran into no hard barriers and the woods were clean. Each possible viewing site was clicked on the GPS system. Later they would all be displayed on one screen. No one ran into anything they would deem an obstacle. With night vision travel at night in this forest would be a cake walk. There were many pictures of the house. They all agreed this time it was not occupied. They had what they came for and called for extraction.

It was late Sunday evening, after dinner. The coverage looked good. Buddy made an announcement. "My guys say they have perfected the ideal hiddee-hole they call The Rock. It is for an observer or if need be, a sniper. In a pinch it will house two shooters. J Leon is going to help me with a video. Roll it J."

On the screen they saw a man in camouflage in the woods. From his pack he took out a small circular packed device and pulled a tab, immediately there was a three foot by seven foot tunnel. The actor looked at the screen and said, "That is simply an enlarged camper's laundry bag. The next thing is what makes this different." Next was a gray green camo sheet he spread over the tunnel. Then using several spray cans, he began to spray, explaining each one. "This sheet is camo on one side and granite colored on the other to look like a rock, therefore our name, The Rock. Now notice this can is labeled 'hump'. As I spray it the material will contract and expand to cause the material to rise—watch." He did this in several places. "Next is a can labeled Flat, using the cans you can move this cover to form a rock or a rise in the ground. As you can see it also becomes sturdy," and he thumped the surface. "Now you have a house with no door. You can, of course, lift it, but for long term it is good to pin it to the ground," and he inserted thin ground stakes. "Now using your knife cut three sides big enough to crawl in. Then to form a hinge for the door, use the can labeled 'Relax' and spray down the uncut hinge side and the door will be hinged to open. This baby is very hard to distinguish from fifty feet. There is room inside for power bars and water for two or three days. Room enough to change your diapers when needed and a self-sealing bag to store them in. The original laundry bag coil can be removed once the sheet is hard. This gives more room for two occupants. Using your discretion and ingenuity, you can cut slits, flaps and even a shooting flap. If you were ever a sniper, you can see this is much better than digging a hole and spreading a blanket over it. What do you think, Buddy? Do we get paid this week?" The video faded to black.

Dustin who had been trained by the FBI like Sticky, Buddy, J Leon and Tuck said, "Buddy, that is cool, did your guys do this for your company?"

"No Dusty, this is a contract with the CIA and the Pentagon. My guys came up with the idea and it was snapped up quickly by the government."

The lab boys had put this video together fast for Buddy. They had twenty five in stock. "I am going to have them ship twelve of them along with what Tuck and J Leon are donating. The weight of this hiding hole, cans and all, is less than two pounds."

Tuck, pointing to the refreshed screen of the beach and house area said, "Now that we have seen this, where can we use those best? I asked J Leon to print these layouts of the area of interest." As he passed them out he continued, "I want everyone to pick ten spots where you think we need coverage and mark them. Also mark an 'o' anyplace you believe we need observation with the possibility of fire power, but mostly for observation so we don't get blindsided by '*that surprise*'. We will put them together to see how close we are in our thinking"

Sticky spoke up, "Very important, Dallas is calling the bad guys tomorrow to tell them it will be Thursday or Friday before he can have the money ready. He tells me they will say 'have it here Thursday or Jerry is dead,' so he will have a delivery this Thursday probably in the AM."

Reece asked, "He isn't actually bringing the money is he?"

"This is not to leave this room, not even to our friends down the hall, because if by chance the terrorists learned this, we wouldn't have a snowball's chance to save Jerry. There will be up to five million in cash but the rest mostly green paper topped with one hundred dollar bills. Dallas has been told it will take five locked aluminum suitcases at one hundred-ten pounds each for twenty-five million."

****

Back aboard the Tatiana, Jerry was thinking. He had just received another note from his unknown friend. It read, *they know you have a phone. Your cabin has been searched looking for it. Be careful. They are monitoring for a transmission. I think they have some device to blank out all signals unless they want to transmit or receive.* In spite of himself, Jerry smiled. Even in captivity you wanted to win something. He knew someone had been in his stateroom. He always left a signal, usually a hair in a strategic place when he left his room so he would know if his area was violated. At least three times they had entered and had not found the phone in the vent. It was good to know about the killer signals. He must figure a way to know when they were able to transmit.

Today is Sunday and I know Sherry found a church to pray in, thought Jerry. He was sure of that. What are Dallas and the boys doing? I know they are working. Are they here yet? Are they monitoring the ships signals? Surely J Leon and Josh can hack into this rig.

Jerry knew they had not sailed far out of the area where they dropped off the others. He was learning the coastline pretty well. He had concluded they had actually made it to Corfu and that Sherry was ashore with the others in Corfu. He thought, *this isn't exactly how I wanted to show her Corfu, that's for sure.*

Funny, being held here on this fancy yacht is pretty much like one of those country club prisons rich dudes are sent to. Good food, great scenery, but no walking around. I hate to put Dallas in the middle of this, I imagine Dallas will call sometime tomorrow to try the delay tactic. The delay had been set up for years as a Standard Operational Procedure (SOP) of the MVA to use in any negotiable situation. The delay would give the MVA more room to act and plan. He was sure this would be the same. Late Sunday night Jerry decided to try a fast text. To his disappointment the charger had taken this time to give up the ghost, and the battery was dead. Maybe he could work out something. Churchill's words rang in his ears, *never give up!*

Chapter 32

Monday morning on the Tatiana, the Captain's cell phone rang. "Yes?"

"Captain, it is impossible to have that much cash ready before Thursday or Friday. I've got to have a few more days, no matter what story I use, the banks insist I am talking about over five hundred pounds of one hundred dollar bills. How can I carry that much?" pause for effect, "B-but then you must know that, right?"

"Mr. Fletcher, of course, I know how much money I am demanding. It will be only five suitcases, very simple. I know you are an old man, but surely you can handle one simple hundred pound suitcase, you do not have to carry all of them at once. As to the time, I am an understanding man, you have until Thursday morning to have the cash at an airport here in the Mediterranean. If it is not here, I will send Mr. Wiley's head to you, is that clear?"

"T-thank you, thank you," Dallas tried to sound as contrite as he could, "Where am I flying to? We will need a flight plan and entrance visas."

"You raise the money sir, and I will give you the instructions when you are ready to depart. Call only then." The connection was broken. Dallas gritting his teeth, thought, *if I can Captain, I will send you to hell for putting Jerry thru this.* Dallas immediately called Tuck.

"Yeah Dallas, of course we heard, but how do you feel about the whole situation, you did a great job appearing to be a frightened old man?"

"To tell the truth Tuck, I am scared, scared I might do something to get my friend killed. I have been thinking, and consulting with a 'friend familiar with this type of exchange.' I want to run this by you guys. Is everyone listening?"

"Yeah, we are all ears, shoot."

"He suggests I put a fake bomb in every suit case with a digital clock easily read set at two seconds. I should be holding an electronic clicker easily seen, maybe even red. Letting them know up front if I release pressure no one gets the money. He suggests two million or more in the first suitcase. He said they will probably scan the suitcases and either way I should let them know that if things go wrong, we all go up to meet Allah or God. Allow them to open the one case to see the clock and check the money. I want you guys to brain storm on that for holes, fixes or drop the idea. Since I know they do not plan to release Jerry no matter what, I am sure not bringing twenty-five million."

"There is some logic to that Dallas. As it is, the deck is stacked in their favor. As soon as you show up with the money, they could do you and Jerry in, and then leave with the money. It does need to appear that you are trying to save both your necks, and it is for danged sure you are."

The conversation was closed shortly and the group began to discuss the possibilities. As they talked J Leon and Josh were monitoring a phone call by the captain. The Captain was saying the money would leave the airport and go across the Island just a few miles to Gastouri. There he would put it aboard the yacht and order Dallas to remain on the pier. Then they would move out into the sea to verify the amount, and then put Jerry in the skiff to row back to shore. Josh was looking at a map. The Captain was evidently talking to a superior. The superior had said this infidel is not an ignorant person. He is not going to let you leave the pier with both the hostage and the money. The Captain said his impression was that the infidel was a scared old man, and his order would be followed. If not, he could be killed or they could take the Tatiana with all aboard to the beheading area and do it there. Either way they would get the finances they needed. The superior had said he trusted Jamal Rahim and Allah be praised.

"Gastouri, does that sound familiar. Maybe Karma or fate. Maybe even a sign from God," said Buddy, "But we need to get Jerry before the beach area if we can, what say ye?"

Everyone agreed the pier near Gastouri would be ideal and less complicated, but the area was light commercial fishing, so more chances of failure and civilians being hurt. But still they had to try. J Leon had found the only pier that would accommodate the yacht's draft. A blow up allowed them to do some figuring for snipers. They could only find four possible spots that would hide a sniper.

"What about renting a fishing boat to be on the opposite side of the pier. We could rent one under the guise of filming a commercial, requiring no crew. The boat only being a prop," suggested Sticky.

"Sticky is on to something here. We will need some tight planning. If the pier near Gastouri does not work, we need to get to the rented house much sooner than the Tatiana, to be set up for plan B. That would also mean the guys on the yacht would probably not make it to the plan B area until too late," input Buddy.

While they discussed this, Matt, Luke and Dusty took a van and GPS, plus a map, to check how long it would take to get from pier A to pier B, with time to set up. As they left they passed Sherry and the tour group heading out on a tour. There was a friendly wave, but no contact.

Along with the plans at the piers, Monday was the dead line to order the extra required equipment. The schedule was too tight for Elsie to fly over and back. FAA would not approve her a flight plan because of the required rest between flights. J Leon's crew was flying the supplies. J Leon's plane would not fly nonstop, it would stop in the Azores for refueling. But it would be there by Tuesday Noon for a turnaround Tuesday Evening.

Nerves were getting on edge, J-Day (Jerry's Day) was fast approaching.

In two hours the crew was back from doing the reconnaissance on the pier area. They were sold on the idea of ending it all at the pier. The set up was near perfect for snipers, the added flexibility—a forty or fifty foot trawler there at the pier would seal the deal.

They also wisely calculated the longest time to drop plan A at the pier area and set up again with Plan B at the destination pier. There was time with some room to spare.

It was quickly decided they could use the help of some of Sherry's entourage. Everyone had crowded into the 'Command Post'. Everyone in the tour group volunteered to the man. This was the largest room and everyone made themselves comfortable on beds, the floor and chairs.

J Leon was not happy, but everyone agreed that he would be at the command post and direct the '*Event*'. Tommy, Sherry and the rest of the group, not out in the field, would be watching the evolution unfold. By this time J Leon would have several monitors to match the head mounted cameras on key members, all coming on the supply run from the states.

They first started on Plan A. Priority was Megan and Jennifer in the Medical van that is also the mobile command post, where Josh would be for immediate tech assistance if needed.

Buddy spoke, "Folks, the day for the extraction of Jerry has been designated 'J-Day'. Sadly we happen to know there is no way, other than a miracle, to avoid bloodshed. The bad guys have already decided that for us. I am taking you into confidence here. Our best friend, Jerry Wiley, sits on a yacht with his life at stake. We have heard from the terrorists themselves. They do not plan to honor the ransom, but they plan to take Jerry's life as a statement to the world." Pausing for a drink of water, Buddy continued, "Some of you know the story how Jerry befriended four little boys once. He saved one's life by doing surgery with a pocket knife and a quart of whiskey donated by a drunk as a germ killer. He followed *our* lives and educated us. We became some of the original members that formed a righteous group he called the MVA, the Modern Vigilante Association. We, the MVA, performed hundreds of operations for good. Jerry was always righteous. This is the first time he has personally needed us, and we *will* come thru for him." Buddy nodded at J Leon.

"The Terrorists are Islamic. All of you remember nine-eleven. You have also seen the videos on the news of the atrocities committed by this group. They have demanded twenty five million dollars in cash, do you have any idea how much that weighs?" All heads indicated no. "A million dollars in one hundred dollar bills weighs twenty-two pounds. Twenty five times that is five hundred and fifty pounds, the terrorists have now involved Jerry's closest friend, Dallas Fletcher, through threats to deliver the ransom. It is our job to stop them without injury to Jerry or Dallas."

There were gasps and some tears among the small audience. It was Sticky's time, "It sounds bad and it is, but this is not our first rodeo. As far as we can determine, they do not expect our involvement and that is why secrecy is so important here. They can have eyes and ears anywhere; therefore, we must be vigilant. Trust us, we can do this, no, let me change that, we *will* do this. We are going to ask the help of Ed, Don and Buck. But we want you all to know, anything can happen. We, as the MVA reunited, want you to discuss this among yourselves before committing. Nothing will be held against anyone who has reservations. We have some time, so take yours and discuss it."

Before Sticky could move back from his speech, Ed spoke, "Guys we have already decided. We all talked about this after someone said you might want volunteers, we are in. So what do you need of us?"

Tuck stood, "First we have two options to extract Jerry. The first and the one we all prefer is when the ransom and Dallas are being transferred to the Tatiana. It is the most likely and we expect it to happen there. You might get a smile out of this. The transfer is to be close to a fishing village of Gastouri. Sounds a lot like Gastonia."

J Leon put the pier up on the four foot screen, "Folks this is the pier. We plan to rent a trawler and tie it up at the pier where the Tatiana is scheduled to tie up. Elsie, flying in from the US, is to land Dallas and the ransom and probably transfer them to a van or truck and be transported to the pier. Looking at the pier, here is what we want. We want Buck, Stephen, Buddy and Robyn aboard the trawler. I am still discussing with Sticky whether he will be on the boat or with me in control. Robyn speaks fluent Greek just in case anyone is required to answer incidental questions or to pass the time of day while waiting. Everyone will be armed with short guns that are silenced. That is the close up part of the team. This vacant building will be occupied by Ben," Ben stood and nodded. "Dusty will be in the vacant building to the right," indicating Dusty and pointing to the building. "Our man Tuck here, will be in a van straight out from the pier. He will also act as the driver of the van in case we have to go to plan B.

"That is the basic plan A. It will be tweaked as we get further information from the bad guys.

Chapter 33

Everyone talked among themselves as the stage is reset. The screen now shows the area of Plan B. J Leon continues, "Okay, let me have your attention. We are hoping and praying that Plan A solves the problem, because Plan B is more involved and more complicated, but it will work. First of all, if there is any glitch that would endanger Jerry or Dallas at that point, we silently drop plan A and go to B. So if we must relocate and set up for plan B, we have checked and rechecked, *we do have time.* Our medical and mobile command center will have to move to a predesignated position. I will jump ahead here. The medical folk and I will start into the action area as soon as the contact begins. We want the medics on sight immediately after the firing ceases to handle injuries, if there are any. We should see none if the plan goes by the book. Now, back to the plan. Ben, Mark David, Tuck, Dusty and Buddy will beat feet just as soon as possible and head to the Plan B location. Robyn will join me, in case I encounter a need for a Greek person with the locals.

"As of now, we plan to station Don, Reece, Luke, Matt and Ed on site twenty four to thirty six hours ahead of J-Day. This is a tough assignment, they will have a new innovation—a sort of camouflage tent. Don't laugh at this ladies, but they will wear diapers since there will be no toilet around for them to use. That is common for this type of mission. There will be helmets and body armor, power bars and water enough for two days. They will be in constant radio contact which will be invaluable to us as we move forward. They will have the latest in weapons, silenced, and scoped. They will have night goggles as they wait, and helmet cameras. That is the long term guys. Buddy and Mark David will move in and out. We want them there incase fire power is needed when the Tatiana drops off Jerry and the crew. If there is any chance we do not want to miss it."

"The other positions will be here. Dusty and Ben will share a site. You guys will have a two hundred yard shot. In the wooded area about 25 yards below them will be Tuck with Stephen. Those are in the wooded area. Tuck with, Stephen will have about a hundred fifty yard shot. Then down at the water's edge will be Buddy in the rocks. Buddy, you and Mark will have about a hundred yard shot. These last positions will be set up tonight and secured.

"We believe the Tatiana will pull up here at the pier and tie up. From the phone conversations we have heard, it appears the execution is supposed to be at the water's edge. We think the ransom money will be checked here. Dallas has a few ideas he will incorporate into the plan. At present we think by Thursday afternoon we will be dining with the greatest guy we have ever known and joking about his time away from his wife. Folks that's a lot of words, but we have put a lot of thinking and planning into this and it is far from smooth. We do have a couple of days to tweak this also."

"That's the most J Leon has spoken in years," joked Buddy, "But he is the best and we are all anxious to put an end to this invasion into all of your lives." Then he held up his hand as Sticky started to speak, "One more thing that needs to be said. I noticed some eyebrows raised when Reece was numbered among the long termers on site. She is cute as a button, but as one kid she met once said, 'that's Wonder Woman!' How many of you have heard of Doctor Ruth?" heads nodded and hands also indicated affirmative, "Doctor Ruth lost her family in the Holocaust, she grew to be a four foot seven inch dynamo. She joined the paramilitary group Haganah and trained to be a sniper, and in her own words she said, 'I had a knack of putting bullets where they were supposed to go.' Well folks we have our own Doctor Ruth with a rifle. That is just so you will know Reece isn't just decoration, but the real thing." As he spoke, Reece reddened, embarrassed at the attention. Buddy nodded to Sticky.

"I said when I first heard of this situation that we needed a small army. I think we have it. I would like to welcome Robyn, Don, Ed and Buck in as honorary MVA members," said Sticky, "and welcome Dusty back. We were fortunate to have him aboard when the MVA went down to Florida to bring his mama back." Mary Ann was looking at her son and smiling.

"Okay that's about it for now. We are expecting my crew to bring our supplies in tomorrow. We are happy to have Tommy with us. He tells us he wants to remain here until the situation is resolved, and we do welcome his smile, input and wit as we wait. He and Sherry and some of the guys from Mount Bell have been talking of the past and the many happenings there and over in

Browntown where Tommy's family lived. We have talked to Sherry and think another tour of the Island would be good for the tourists using the rest of the day. Again, avoiding the areas of interest."

Tommy stood and was given the floor. "If it wasn't for Mr. Wiley's situation, this would be one of the highlights of my time in Greece. I am amazed at the ability and professionalism of this group. I cannot wait to meet an amazing man named Jerry Wiley, who was lucky enough to land Sherry Harris. If there is anything I can do, I am here as an observer and also to aid where I can. And yes, J, it has been pleasant to rehash the times in Mount Bell."

With a lot of chatter the meeting broke up and it was business as usual in the command center. There had been very little communications to monitor, mostly course changes of the Tatiana.

Constant viewing of the rental house showed no movement other than wild life. The rental company had been located and records checked. The rental was paid for the week from Tuesday to Monday. The crew departed to allow everyone concerned to physically view the area and let the snipers pick their spots. They all wished the camouflage material was already here. On site, some minor changes were made and it all looked good.

They talked in the van on the return trip to the hotel. The only problem they could discover was the time frame for the late comers to prepare their sites to be ready in case they must go to Plan B. Consensus said to do it in the early morning hours of J-day. It would be touchy because they were sure there would be occupants in the house, but they would have the benefit of the guys already set up to assist in monitoring the movements at the house.

Monday ended and tensions were growing as they wonder how Jerry was holding up as the yacht cruised the Ionian Sea and at times even up into the Adriatic Sea.

****

Thinking of the loss of the phone charger, Jerry mentally reinforced himself by repeating Sherry's oft quoted phrase, *all things work together to them that love the Lord.* He had no more communications with his mysterious *friend* here on the yacht. As he sat on his small balcony alone, his thoughts were running the gambit of his life. He was doing what he had been trained to do—compartmentalize. He had always admired the Serenity Prayer. Even when he was agnostic, the words fit his philosophy. He was in his seventies and many of his peers and friends had not enjoyed this many years. If this was his end, he would accept that, but if he could go out with a fight he would.

He smiled as he remembered what Sherry had said of a lady she admired. The lady upon learning she had terminal cancer told her friends. One friend gasped, "Not you! For heaven's sake not you!"

Sherry said the lady sweetly turned to her friend and asked, "Why not me?"

So here I sit on a beautiful yacht, near an island of my dreams and I may never see that beautiful lady of mine again. His eyes went heavenly, taking in the vast Mediterranean sky filled with stars, they blurred as the tears welled up. *God, thanks to my Sherry, I am ready. I am at peace. However, if you can see it in your will, I want to walk on that island with the girl you gave me. I want to share my feelings one more time.* After sitting there, clearing his eyes he looked back up, *but if that is not allowed. I thank you for what I have had.* Unbidden the tears came again, this time he did not attempt to quell the flood.

Chapter 34

The plane was on time—Tuesday mid-morning. It taxied to the hangar where most of the crew was waiting. Josh had taken the duty at the command center and J Leon was there to greet his boys. The hangar doors were closed and a scan was made of the hangar. Everything was there. One of the incoming guys worked for Buddy and gave a quick demo of setting up The Rock. Each person who was to use them got to try their luck on some parts. The actual doing was much simpler than they all had thought. They were also amazed at its strength. One could not sit on it, but you could lean on it a little. The demonstrator said it would withstand sixty pounds of direct pressure. It was colored to give the impression of a rough dirty granite. A small kid could climb on it.

Each user took a few minutes climbing in and out and practiced cutting peep holes; just getting the feel. They were satisfied with the results. A netting of the color of the structure had been added since the video demo. It covered a slit six inches wide and about thirty inches high. The occupant(s) simply cut what he needed for a good shot. This would allow the user to see and fire from a prone or sitting position.

The guys also brought J Leon a new device they had developed. If a distraction was needed, this would do it. Remote controlled, it worked on the principle of the auto air bag, immediate inflation and it stayed inflated. It could be weighted and used underwater. The colors were wild. It definitely would draw attention.

The plane crew was logged in to rest at the airport pilot's lounge. They would have no contact with the others before they flew back to the states. They had room for four passengers, but no takers. Everyone here wanted to see this through.

Around four PM, Josh reported a call from some men headed for the rental house. The Captain had asked how many, the answer four. Two cameramen and two power supply guys. It wasn't long until the screen that had been static showed a van pulling in. Four men carried supplies into the house. The screen was monitored by several. The actions were normal. The men came back outside in a few minutes and walked down to the pier. A couple waded in the water. They playfully kicked water on each other. The dress was mixed, Arabic and western.

That evening the meal back at the hotel was steak and potatoes especially for the five who were going to live off water and power bars for about forty hours. Their plans were to head out to their stake out positions when the action at the house died down or at eleven PM whichever came first.

The briefings had been intensive as to what actions to take and when. Constantly emphasized was the safety of Jerry and Dallas. Every sniper knew where to aim to avoid body armor. They still did not know how many bad guys would be there. As of tonight the team knew only of the two on the yacht, and the four member camera team. No one was buying that as the total for such a large ransom. Each person was assigned a sector to fire in if it came to that. The odds were very low that Dallas could bluff his way in and out of this situation. Dallas had always been admired by the MVA guys because Jerry himself held him in such high esteem. But Dallas was no one's fool. He knew he was stepping into the lion's den. Everyone could sure breathe better if he could pull off a miracle without bloodshed. That sort of fantasy could be hoped for, but the decision had already been made. Jerry had to die, according to some voice on the phone, but they had a different idea.

Just a few doors down in the hotel, Sherry was out on the small balcony. She was remembering a song from her youth about a young lonely soldier singing to his love in Germany. One line was, "By the same stars above you I swear that I love you." Then she prayed as was her practice. *Lord, I know I have bothered you more than many of your children, and here I am again. Please let Jerry know his 'boys' are going to get him back to me safely, with your help of course. I feel so selfish asking this, since I have been blessed beyond my wildest dreams. Our lives have been special since you brought us together. If you can, allow us to enjoy a few more years. I never knew I could love a man so much. Your sky is beautiful tonight. I am picturing Jerry, somewhere out there on this beautiful water, talking to you also. Please, tell him I am fine. He has wanted to share this beautiful Island with me since we fell in love. I am asking you to allow him to do that. Let him live to fill that dream. I love you Lord. Good night.*

Back in the command center it was getting late. J Leon had added two more four foot screens that were sectioned off for head cameras. The original four foot screen was split showing the Tatiana at sea and the rental unit. Both were showing infra-red and indicating body heat. He had masked the heat of the engine on the Tatiana as well as possible. The house indicated that the film crew was in one room. The assumption at the command center was that they were expecting more guests (soldiers) for the big *Event.*

At the command center they were starting to intercept some text and e-mail. They had sadly learned that the yacht's crew was to be killed also and they planned to keep and rename the Tatiana. It was not looking good. That was eight more bodies.

Would they line these up by the sea as they had the Coptic Christians in Libya? Is this becoming a pattern? With this news, *The Unholy Four* of the MVA were beginning to expect at least ten soldiers to show up before the *Event* took place.

****

Back in Pittsburgh, Dallas called Elsie who was staying at Stella's loft apartment at the airport in Gastonia.

"Stella, this is Dallas, how are you guys doing down there?"

"Hi Mr. Fletcher, we are going stir crazy wondering what the story is."

"Are you ready to fly to the Mediterranean?"

"Has a cat got a climbing gear? Of course we're ready. What is the schedule?"

"Get the plane and fly to Pittsburgh, Taxi to your old home. We will head for the Med sometime tomorrow evening, we must be in Corfu, a Greek Island, by the next morning."

"Are you kidding? The times I flew Jerry around the country he always talked about stopping there but we never did. Anyway, Chase and I will see you tomorrow. We want the whole story of what is happening, Mr. Fletcher."

"You will have it, see you tomorrow."

****

On Corfu, the van stopped by the hangar. Each sniper had a check off list and they made up their packs. Everyone had a partner to act as a double check, because this was it for them. They would see no one else, no supplies, no physical contact until the end of the *Event*. Each one knew how serious this was. With the last check being with J Leon to make sure their microphones and helmet cams were working, so he could label the displays. Tommy was there with Sticky to say good luck and wish them well. This was real. They ran into no problems and there was no traffic on the road trip. The drop off point was the end of the road journey, the rest was on foot.

The MVA members were in the woods by midnight and headed for their assigned spots. The night vision goggles made the quarter mile trek a piece of cake for them. There was no talk and they observed radio silence. After hearing that a massacre was planned, they were on a high. *How dare they plan to kill Jerry and an entire crew?*

Back at the command center J Leon and several others were watching the screens. As the last 'click' came thru he spoke to the troops on site, "Do not respond. The house is as it was when you left. It seems the bad guys are sleeping well. We are receiving all cameras four by four, we all wish you luck and wish we were there. Take care and goodnight. Please click in order so I will know you are hearing me. All screens and clicks responded in perfect order.

"Well, it starts. We are on our way Jerry." Tuck said to no one in particular. The guys on site would sleep in the roomy Rock. One of them would be awake at all times. The relief would be awakened with clicks of the mike into their earbuds. It looked like everyone in the hotel was awake and watched for an hour. They set up a watch and tried to get some sleep.

Chapter 35

Wednesday morning another van arrived at the rental house with six men aboard. Stephen was on watch at the screen and reported to the guys on sight. Zooming in, Stephen could see large bags were moved inside the house, large enough for rifles. He alerted the guys in the room. Soon there was a crowd around the screen.

On site other activity movement was reported. Audio was authorized after a scan was made and there were no intercept devices active. That was good. It indicated no one suspected any interference in their dastardly deeds.

Reece was the closest to the water and she reported two men had walked to the end of the pier. They had looked closely around the pier. One lay on the pier looking beneath it. They appeared to be looking for anything suspicious. As they headed back to the house one of the men waved his arm extended back and forth then pointed at a can he held in his hand. He set the can on a small pile of sand, and then walked on back to the house.

Luke reported that he and Don were watching a man on the roof of the house about the same time. He said Don called the small fenced area a Widow's Walk. It was a small deck a carryover from the old days when a Ship's Captain built his house near the sea and the captain's wife would go up to look out to sea for the returning ship. However this was no widow because he had a rifle with a scope and he was sighting at the pier, Don had said, "He is not a widow, but he thinks he is going to make a widow."

At that time he assumed the prone positon and rested the rifle on the lower rung. "He is going to zero in the rifle," Luke said. Then he reported that the man had fired a round.

"He is adjusting the sights," Don said. "He is aiming to fire again. He got the can, the sights are set. Wait, he is moving the rifle as he looks thru the scope. He is scanning the area, and he appears to be looking directly at Reece's Rock. Wait, there is a gull near the water's edge. Whoa, the gull flew and he took it in flight. Hey guys, this fellow is good, he's not one of the cameramen."

"I heard the firing reports and also heard the hit. The bird is fifty feet in front of me. I could not see him once he was prone. I barely could see the barrel. Let me know if anyone heads this way to check the bird," Reece very calmly said.

The shooter did leave the widow's walk and walked down to check the can, he ignored the dead bird. He then walked out on the pier and looked back to the area from which he had fired. He walked the beach a bit, constantly looking back toward the house. He seemed to be satisfied and returned to the house.

"Standby everyone, we have men leaving the house with equipment," Ed whispered. Reece and Matt gave a 'roger that'.

"I think it is camera stuff, yeah, that's what it is. If they are going to do a run thru, it may tell us where they plan the activity. I like that." Whispered Reece.

They did exactly what Reece had hoped. They set up about twenty-five feet from the pier toward Reece. It was four men and they did all appear to be related to the video they planned to make. The professional tripod was set up and two men walked over to the pier head area. While looking through the lenses the cameraman gave the thumbs up. One of the guys acted like he cut a throat and with a motion threw the imaginary head toward the water. They played that game for about fifteen minutes then wrapped it up and headed back to the house. The MVA team back at the hotel saw the whole evolution. Standing and looking at the screen Tuck said, "This movie is going to turn out much differently. We infidels will win this one." Around the room there were silent thumbs-up.

****

Back in the states the rental for the plane was paid. Dallas had called to alert Elsie and Chase to get the plane and have it ready to fly. File a flight plan to Pittsburgh and head on up that way Wednesday afternoon. They were to top the fuel off in Pittsburgh for an international flight. The destination was in the Mediterranean, but as yet he did not know the exact destination.

After talking to Elsie and verifying with the boys in the Med, he placed his call to the terrorist Captain. The phone was answered on the second ring, "Yes Mr. Fletcher?"

"Captain, I would like to speak to Mr. Wiley."

"Do you have the money in cash, Mr. Fletcher?"

"Of course, I have the money. You know I am scared to death, Captain, but being scared doesn't make me stupid. I need to know my friend is alive and well and if he is sure he wants me to do this. He is my boss and sooner or later I will have to answer to someone for this money."

Jerry was called into the cabin when the phone first rang, so he was present. "There is no need for fear sir, this is simply a business transaction, and here is Mister Wiley."

"Hello Dallas, did you have any trouble from Mr. Thomas about the money?"

"First, are you okay? I mean really, you are okay? Do they have a gun at your head?"

"Dallas, yes, I am perfectly okay. As the Captain says it is just a business transaction. One I am not crazy about, but I am convinced all they want is the money and I will be back with Sherry." At that the Captain took the phone.

"Satisfied, Mister Fletcher?"

"You know very well I am not happy nor satisfied. Until this is over I cannot help but be scared. Now, please, W-where am I flying to Captain?"

"You are flying to Corfu International Airport located on the Greek Island of Corfu. You are to taxi to the transit hangar for businesses as Wiley Industries. You will be met at ten AM local time, by a gentleman named simply Emil. Please, for the sake of your friend, keep this simply a business transaction and all will be well." The connection was broken.

Jerry returned to his cabin, he did not know what or how, but the MVA was at work again. When Dallas said in his conversation 'you are okay instead of *are you okay*?' *You are okay* meant there was a solid plan. The word *gun* used meant it could be violent. And when he used the word '*perfectly*' in his conversation Dallas knew it meant he understood.

****

Dallas called Elsie to say they needed to fly out of Pittsburgh by nine PM flying to Corfu International located on the Greek Island of Corfu. When he called the girls were headed for the plane.

He speed dialed Tuck and the answer was, "Sounds good, I am glad he now knows we are going to do something. We did monitor the call and fortunately we could hear it well. Thanks Dallas."

"Yes Tuck, I too am sure he knows we are pulling out all stops. I won't see you in the morning. So we are all praying it comes off without a hitch."

Tuck went over Plan A and Plan B again. Letting Dallas know the number of men present and that some of the good guys were already hunkered down and on site. The conversations broke off. Tuck promising to contact him once they were airborne and keep him up to date. He also suggested Dallas rest on the flight.

****

It wasn't long until the phone opened again on the yacht. "Yes?"

"Have the infidels raised the money?"

"Yes, it will arrive in the morning at 10AM. What do you want me to do with the messenger?"

"If he insists to accompany the money to the end of the transaction, then he will meet the fate of his friend. If he will trust you to return his friend, then he can live. It is as simple as that."

"Allah be praised, it will be as you say." The conversation ended.

Tuck knew it would make no difference to Dallas so after talking it over they decided to wait until the flight was under way. At about that time the phone became active again, this time initiated from the yacht. It was ringing, the number was automatically recorded on J Leon's system, "Yes?"

"This is Jamal Rahim, we will bring the boat to the pier at about eight AM. I want everyone awake. The cause is about to be forwarded in one great leap. I will leave the rich infidel and the crew in your care. I see no problem but I want them all in the proper suits and bound. The boat's Captain will be with me and I will keep Jomen aboard with me to handle lines. You know what I expect when the boat ties up. The leaders expect a solid professional video of the beheadings. They want the final pictures to be with the infidels 'thinking on their chests'."

"Allah be Praised, it will be as he desires." The phone call was ended.

The room was buzzing. "I guess we can scrap Plan A," said Buddy. "But I still think it may be good to have the men and Robyn aboard the rented trawler, just to have someone close."

"I agree Buddy, what about the rest of you, any ideas?"

The information was passed to the crew members on site and they were asked to be thinking of any problems. Back in the command center Sticky spoke, "In my opinion Dallas is going to serve no purpose after delivering the ransom. Let's ask him to act relieved, if the Captain suggests he wait at the airport for Jerry. If he is clear, it will be one less for us to be concerned about. Also, I think Jerry would want us to keep Dallas out of harm's way."

"Good thinking Sticky. We know that we have the crew and Captain to worry about now. We did not know that for sure before," threw in J Leon.

"Dallas ain't gonna like it, but let's not give him a choice. If it comes down to it tell him we will kidnap him and send someone else in as Dallas Fletcher." added Buddy.

"What about the bombs?" asked Dusty and Ben at the same time." Laughing Dusty continued, "Did he decide to go with the bomb?"

"Last I heard, yes. I will ask him once he gets in the air and settled," said J Leon, then added, "There was a question a while ago during the phone conversation about the statement, 'thinking on their chest'. That is the disgusting practice of placing the severed head on the chest of the corpse. Just to make that clear."

They were concerned about the pier and the crew that was going to remain there until the Tatiana departed. The final decision was that Stephen would double with Tuck while Robyn would join the command van with J Leon and the Medics. Buck was very familiar with tree stands and was used to looking for movement in the woods. He would be armed with a silenced rifle and scope and take the watch on the input road. Movement from plan A would take place after the Tatiana was out of sight. By now they all knew this was going to end in blood shed, but they planned a completely different ending than the mass beheading reminiscent of the Coptic Christians in Libya.

Chapter 36

Elsie had filed the flight plan and they were in the air headed for Corfu when Dallas's satellite phone rang, caller ID was Tuck. "Yes Tuck?"

"Hey Dallas, I assume all is on track and you are in the air in the skillful hands of Elsie the plane driver."

"Yes Tuck, have you learned anything new?"

"We have learned enough that we must change plans. The terrorists plan to discharge Jerry and the crew at the location of the rental house. Then the fake Captain and the Captain Solomon along with one crew man will meet you at the pier near Gastouri. Dallas, they plan to execute everyone aboard the Tatiana, including you.

Now my question is, did you install the fake bomb or bombs?"

"Yes, but only one and it is in the number one suitcase."

"Dal, it is the consensus of everyone here, after listening to these suicidal fools, that the threat would be an exercise in futility, especially since Jerry will not be aboard the Tatiana while she is tied up for your meeting."

"I completely agree Tuck. What are your plans and what do you suggest on my end?"

"Dallas we know beyond a shadow of a doubt you would die for Jerry, but that is not the goal. We want you to find a way to agree for them to take the money and deliver Jerry to the airplane safe and sound. One thing that we are hoping is for the Captain to be so engrossed with his ability to cow you down, he will not look at the other cases. We have some other ideas of keeping the Captain from going thru the other suitcases. We have a young lady, proficient in Greek who will be in the trawler at the pier. Several of the ideas sound good. We hate flying by the seat of our pants, but this seems to be a time we have to. The ideas sound good, but first of all we want you out of there if it is at all possible."

"Yeah Tuck, I know. If I stick around to the end, I will be an abstraction to saving Jerry. I do not want that. I wanted to see the end, but I am logical and a businessman. You are choosing the correct direction. I will give in to the will of the MVA. I trust you guys. During the rest of the flight I will be working on my end."

"Everyone thought you would understand, but even understanding, of course, we know you want to be there. By the way you will be covered by our people from across the pier. Now if you get off the pier in one piece have the driver drop you off at the airport. Call a taxi and then you and the girls join the Command Control Center at the hotel and y'all can see the whole *Event* on the screen."

"Got it Tuck. Now get back to taking care of Jerry. I will do my best to do my part." The connection was broken.

****

It was a long night. No other calls or communications from the yacht. It was now Thursday morning. It was J-day. Tension was tight. Before daylight the rest of the crew took up their positions. They had all debated about the distraction. Buddy was going to deploy the little container. Mark David would be with Buddy for close cover if needed. Mark was an all-round operative. Buddy chose to swim to the pier to deploy the distraction near the shore. It had the appearance of drift wood.

"Alert everyone," said J Leon into the mike, "Listen only. Do not transmit. Extreme quiet. The screen shows three warm bodies moving out. One swinging right and the other left. We have one on the widow's walk scanning with night vision. It appears both left and right will come close to you guys. Have your silenced hand guns ready." J Leon was tense. He could see his guys in blue on the heat screen. To the bad guys he had assigned red. For thirty minutes they scoured the area and moved around. One approached the pier with a light.

It was unfortunate Buddy was under the pier and did not have his ear buds. He started to swing out and head back to The Rock, when he heard shifting feet. He froze. He was fortunate the terrorist did not turn on his flash light until he was a few feet on the pier. Buddy berated himself. Here he was without weapon or radio. He knew Mark David had the bad guy in his cross hairs, but this could blow the mission. The terrorist searched the water and the area around, the light was extinguished as the man reached Buddy's positon. Buddy breathed a *thank you Lord.* After giving the terrorist plenty of time Buddy swam back to his position and stayed under water as long as possible. In the Med that didn't help much. The water was so clear. He was soon back in the safety of The Rock. Mark David handed him a towel. Buddy was surprised at the room inside The Rock after Mark had removed the original coil. The coil was not needed once the cover was solid. They sat cross legged and silent. Finally he heard J Leon give the all clear. All the bad guys were back in the house. Buddy crawled out, dried off and dressed. Now they could only wait for the arrival of the Tatiana.

At 0800, the Tatiana arrived. Every shooter was on highest alert. If they could end it here, it would be a miracle, a God sent. It was Buddy's call. If it appeared the bad guys could be dealt a solid blow with no danger to the crew or Jerry, Buddy was to give the order to fire. But as the debarking took place, it was apparent to Buddy, that if they tried it now, they would lose Captain Solomon for sure and very possibly Susa, the crew member. They were never in the clear at one time.

"Stand down, I hated to say that, I wanted to end this. We will take care of these guys when the Tatiana returns," said Buddy with true regret.

Every one heard J Leon, "That was the correct call Buddy, we were staring at the screens and didn't see the shots either. Just as soon as you are clear, head back to the pickup zone. We will pick you up in ten minutes, and you can assume your positions at the pier."

****

In the sky, Elsie announced they were landing in ten minutes. Dallas had decided to remove the fake bomb. And had jammed every lock on the other bags. Unless the Captain had something to cut aluminum and steel webbing he could not get in the bags.

They landed an hour early. Elsie and Chase went for coffee. Dallas was too nervous to leave. He was wondering if he could pull this off. Dallas was orderly, a planner. He could, but did not enjoy 'winging it' as Jerry would say. To say the least Dallas was out of his comfort zone, mainly because he was not in control.

Elsie returned handing him his coffee. "Is there anything Chase and I can do?"

"No. Be aware this is all a mission of life and death. A lot depends on fate and prayer. I am not sure how receptive these terrorists are to prayer."

"Dallas, I have met your wife, Marian. I also got to love and appreciate Jerry's wife, Sherry. I know you are worried, but if I was a betting person, I would bet those two ladies have talked the Lord's ear nearly off. I would also bet He likes them. I think I would trust their prayers over some crap head that wants to kill my old boss. I say take the situation by the ears and you and the others will win."

Dallas smiling, "Thanks Elsie, I believe that talk is what I needed." In a few minutes a van drove up and a man came to the plane.

"I am Emil, a local contractor, I am hired to pick up Mr. Fletcher and five bags. Am I at the right plane?"

The big countdown had started.

Chapter 37

There was no conversation. The trip was a short fifteen minutes. As they rounded the last turn, there was the pier. A trawler on the left and the big yacht, Tatiana on the right. The van drove out onto the pier. Dallas did not have to act, he was not armed and did not have the full amount of money demanded, and he was shaking.

A dark skinned man who appeared to have put in many hours at sea, stepped off the yacht and opened the van door. "Mr. Fletcher, it is nice to see you. Please step aboard. My man Joe will bring the luggage."

"Captain, I was expecting to see Jerry. I would like to see him before I leave the van."

"Mr. Fletcher, please step this way. We will take you to the island where Mr. Wiley is located."

"That is not what I expected, nor agreed to. I brought the money and was to exchange it for my friend, Jerry." The Captain could see there was stirring on the trawler and the last thing he wanted was to stir a hornet's nest.

"I tell you what Mr. Fletcher, you let me have the bags and I will have Jerry at your plane in two hours. Before we go any further with negotiations, let's look inside the cases."

Dallas started to open the case, but appeared to change his mind, "Let's say you take one suitcase and get the rest when Jerry is brought back here or to the plane." Dallas had then opened the case, the Captain looked in and reached deep for a random 10K bundle of one hundred dollar bills and fanned them."

"Ahoy there mates," came a Greek woman's voice, "Hey is the taxi available?" Robyn rounded the van saying, "Me 'n my mates need a ride into town."

Dallas quickly slammed the case shut and the Captain stuck the bills in his pocket, "This is no taxi and no fishing boat slut will be riding in it." Robyn jumped quick and slapped the Captain, when Joe grabbed Robyn.

Robyn yelling, "Nobody talks to me like that rich big boat snot!" Still kicking and scratching at Joe with all her might. At that time three mean looking sailors appeared, armed. Buddy at the front with a sawed off shot gun he had found unloaded on the trawler. Buck and Stephen at the back with pistols. Joe released Robyn. "It's okay mates," turning to the Captain, "The Captain was about to give us some of the money he just stuck in his pocket, so we could go to town later. Right Captain?"

The only sniper left assigned after Plan A fell apart was Mark David. He could hardly aim for laughing. He just had to respect the guts of that gal.

The Captain, hoping to calm the waters, pulled four bills off the stack and handed them to Robyn. She jumped and hugged him before he could think, "For a rich boat guy you ain't half bad." Turning to Buddy she said, "Let's get back on the fisher and talk about how we divide this." They all backed away and around over to the trawler.

Dallas acting as if he was scared within an inch of his life faked a stutter, "T-take the suitcases, Captain. I'm a businessman, not a rough neck. You promise to have Jerry at my plane in two hours. Right? They shook hands. In my country that is as good as any contract. If you break the contract, I will report to the authorities."

"Certainly, Mr. Fletcher. I do appreciate your trust. The slugs from the trawler even gave me a scare. I want to get out of here. I said two hours. Please allow me at least a little leeway just in case I have boat trouble or something."

Dallas nodded and Emil backed the van off the pier. "I see a problem you have with trouble that comes around you. That was a scare so I am glad my van is not damaged." The driver spoke in broken English as he accelerated toward town.

Aboard the boat Captain Solomon eased the Tatiana away from the pier and set the course for the rental property. In a few minutes he heard cursing from Jamal Rahim, He was yelling something about the *Boat Witch* picking his pocket. Solomon just smiled.

Over on the trawler, everyone had hugged Robyn and congratulated her on her acting. The crew back at the operations centers had watched. J Leon had said they needed a distraction that would prevent a close inspection of the suitcases and checking the money. Robyn had done a superb job. Dallas was out of danger and Plan B was on a count down.

The crew on the trawler remained on the boat until the Tatiana was out of sight. As they sat there at the mess table, Robyn smiled big and took the stack of one hundred dollar bills out of her loose fisherman's clothes. She had picked the Captain's pocket when she hugged him. They all got a big laugh, one that was needed. The tale got around fast. Sherry and the crowd were given a short respite that did relieve a little stress.

The trawler crew all went to their assigned spots. Mark David was doubling with Buddy. Don and Luke's positions were highest and Luke was giving the report that the incoming members should have no problems if they used extreme caution. All attention was down by the water. The crew and Jerry had been dressed in orange jump suits, reminiscent of the beheading of the Coptics of Libya, and had been bound with the standard tie-wraps. They were sitting loosely in a circle. All the bad guys were armed, even the camera crew. Everyone was in position and everyone's nerves were stretched tight.

"Uh oh," it was Don, "We have our sniper getting in position on the widow's walk."

"Luke, that guy is your responsibility. Take him out with one silent shot. Try to get him when his finger is out of the finger guard if possible. We don't want his last act on earth to be a warning shot before he meets his virgins," J Leon said without mirth.

"Roger that my friend. Roger that."

"Okay, attention on deck. The Tatiana will dock in about five minutes. Everyone breathe deep." The crowd in the Operations Center could see on the screen as the Tatiana neared the pier. Instead of breathing as directed, they were holding their breath.

Joe jumped off and secured the lines. Aboard the Tatiana Captain Jamal Rahim ordered Captain Solomon to cut the engines. "Why should I do that Captain? Please send my crew back aboard and we will depart. That was your assertions when we were taken captive. We have complied."

"Ah, but Allah has other ideas," Jamal reached over and cut the engines. "Now off *my yacht*, Jewish pig."

"So, we are to be sacrificed for your bloody cause. I will not leave my ship."

One pistol hit to the head and Captain Solomon was out like a light. "Jomen," he called, "Loose Susa Muhammad and bring him here. Captain Solomon needs help getting ashore."

"The Tatiana's true Captain appears to have refused to leave the yacht and the terrorist leader hit him and he is down," reported Reece quietly.

Susa and Joe dragged Captain Solomon ashore. He was slowly regaining his senses as he was fitted with the orange jump suit and forced to kneel beside Jerry at the end of the line. The cameras were rolling. "Susa

Muhammad that is a true name of Islam. I will ask you once, can you slit the throat of an infidel?"

Susa bowed slightly and spoke, "As Allah decrees my Captain."

"You have your choice as a warrior, the Jew Captain or the rich infidel?"

"The Captain has been good to me so I choose the wealthy infidel. I have been his slave."

"A wise choice Susa Muhammad, a task worthy of your name. Quickly remove the clothes of the condemned and be a true jihadist." Susa stepped out of the orange jump suit and was handed a black hooded cape and a razor sharp knife with a serrated blade." He took his position at Jerry with a scoff. He slowly ran the knife in front of Jerry with both hands. Jerry felt anger and fear first, then he felt some relief, because as the knife had passed before his eyes, there was also a white card discreetly held from everyone else's view, and on the card was the Coptic sign. Instantly he remembered a man's words from a few weeks back, *and if you ever see this sign held by a man nod your head slightly*, he did.

All action was to the front. The Captain was giving a speech to everyone but facing the camera. Ever so quietly Jerry heard, "Struggle slightly, so I will have reason to grasp you and at the same time, I will cut your hands free, but please let them remain together. We will try to take out as many of these fools with us as we can." It was Susa, his unknown friend from aboard the yacht.

Jerry did what he was told. Susa held his shoulders and slid his knife hand down to cut the nylon hand cuffs.

Tuck said quietly, "The man behind Jerry just cut Jerry's hands loose. Is that our man?"

Sherry said excitedly, "Josh, this is important. Can you zoom in on Jerry and the man behind him and back it up. I saw something!" Josh was busy concentrating. This was so close to the end and he could not make a mistake, but he did not hesitate, as he heard the urgency in Sherry's voice. You could plainly see the Coptic sign in the man's hand and easily see the nod by Jerry.

"That is a good man behind Jerry. Don't hurt him."

The pressure was on Mark David. That was his man. Buddy lay beside him. "Mark, he could be a turn coat. He doesn't know we're here. It's possible he is saving his own rear. If you see one drop of Jerry's blood, take him out."

This was going to be tight. Scoping Jerry's neck, then if necessary switching to the head shot. Mark was thinking, *I can do this, I will hit the knife hand first, then take the head shot.* He held his cross hairs on the knife hand. Staring at the hand his mind kept saying *something is not right.* The black sleeve was too long covering most of the knife, then it hit him, *the knife was backwards, the sharp edge is away from Jerry's neck.* He did breathe easier.

****

Back at the hotel there was a knock on the door. Dianne had opened the door. It was Dallas. Sherry turned and motioned for Dallas and the pilots to come in. She pointed to the huge screen. Dallas, Elsie and Chase stood, joining the crowd to watch the end. Greetings could wait.

On the screen Dallas saw Jerry in an orange jumpsuit, kneeling with an assassin behind him. Tears came to his eyes as visions of videos of beheadings by these crazy Islamist extremists came to mind. Now here on the screen, standing by the beautiful waters of the Mediterranean were men in black, standing behind kneeling men in orange. This was real and real time.

****

Back at the beach and on the screen, the speech was over. Jamal Rahim walked defiantly to his position behind Captain Solomon. "Take the sniper out Luke," J Leon's voice was calm. Everyone be ready in case the bad guy squeezes off a round. No one heard a thing.

"Done," was all Luke said. On Luke's screen the hit was clean and clear.

"Get ready everyone, Buddy planted the distraction at the pier head. When it goes, that is your order to fire. Mark your targets" said J Leon.

Jamal Rahim held his knife high and said, "Let this be a lesson to all infidels, there is no god but Allah."

At that instant the multicolored balloon popped up out of the water. All eyes went to it. That was the last thing ten men saw. If their belief was correct, they now had their virgins, if not……

Mark David had been intent on the knife to see if it was turned to cut Jerry. Thru his scope he saw the man behind Jerry push Jerry to the ground and throw himself over him, obviously to protect him. Mark's mind said *Good Guy,* and he smiled. Quickly, he searched for any threats to Jerry. All he saw was prone bodies.

At the instant Jerry heard the strange loud pop and water splashing. He felt himself being pushed forward and felt Susa as he fell on top on him. Susa said in Jerry's ear, "Someone must be shooting. People are falling but I don't hear anything."

"Are you hit?" asked Jerry quickly.

"No."

"Then just lay here my friend and relax. What you are seeing is salvation. It is shooting from silenced weapons and it is the good guys, my people," his voice had a smile in it. "All is well, my friend, thank God and you for saving my life."

In seconds every team member had taken his/her target. All the bad guys were down. Then Jerry's MVA team was there. The medics came in, but had nothing to treat except a few bad scratches, a few cuts on the throats of some of the crew that happened when the assassins fell and of course, the banged head of Captain Solomon.

"Don't touch a thing except the injured men of the crew," called out Jerry as he stood and Susa cut his leg bonds.

Susa then removed the black hooded robe and disgustingly threw it at the body of the now deceased terrorist Captain. "You are a disgrace to Allah and Muslims, a disgrace to the human race. These men are good men, Christians all." Susa yelled with all the venom he could muster, releasing the stress of the last hour.

Jennifer was treating a bad cut on one of the crew where the terrorist's knife had come close to the carotid artery.

Megan was looking at the cut on Captain Solomon's head. She used a field test to check for a concussion. The nurses completed the check and applied first aid in record time. Jerry hugged everyone and thanked them and into Buddy's helmet camera, he spoke, "Hi Sherry, I know you are watching. Thanks and I love you more than the whole world. I am not sure but probably Dallas is there. I can't wait to hear the tale of how hard this was without my help." Jerry laughed a big relieved laugh. "I will see you in a little while. Meet me on the Tatiana at the pier. I want a big hug and kiss." He paused, "I am still trying to get used to being free again. I just wanted to say, I love you all. But darling, I see Ed with a rifle, I can't believe you allowed that. Someone could have gotten hurt badly. Just joking, you guys are the greatest! I have known that for years."

Everyone went back to their sites, collected the brass and smoothed out as many tracks as they could. The Rocks were too bulky to tear down.

Captain Solomon was flabbergasted when Jerry asked if they could continue the cruise. "Of course my friend, it will take that long to find out how you arranged this while you were a prisoner with us here on our Tatiana."

Back at the hotel Tommy was elated, "Sherry, your Jerry should be running the CIA. This was the most exciting thing I have witnessed since being in the Diplomatic Corps. You were always a great lady. I can imagine how you and Jerry became a match."

"Tommy, I gotta say, we were all like family back in church in Mount Bell. Your mama and my mama were good friends. Shucks you had to love anyone named Georgia Belle. Your dad was a character. There was only one Edgar Cope. I know you miss your mom and dad. I certainly miss mine."

"I can't wait for you to meet Jerry. I guess he is riding the Tatiana to some pier near here." Sherry was flooded with hugs and kisses from every one. Josh was so relieved. He hated that he could not be with Megan at the finale, but that is the life of a genius. Josh never said that, but others sure did.

Back on site everyone was talking and very proud of the outcome. All the team would get together to talk about the final *EVENT* of the MVA, but hey, they had said that before. Is there ever a *FINAL EVENT*?

The cleanup was complete and the entire team was congratulated. The vans left and Captain Solomon smiled when he hit the start buttons, and the two engines began to purr. He looked over at Jerry and said, "Thank you my friend. I was thinking, I would never hear the beautiful sound of my engines again." The lines were loosed and they were underway. Looking around and catching Ali's eye, he motioned him to come to the bridge.

"Okay tell me Ali, how in the world did you end up here on the Tatiana? I have been thinking, so let me guess, my friends hired you before the cruise, didn't they?"

"Guilty as charged. Now to this joy I feel, I do not know how you did it, but I was sure we were dead. I was so incensed, I wanted you and me to take out as many of these crazy terrorists as we could. You saved my father's life, I owed you that. By the way, I just called him and he told me how your men freed my family. I am grateful for that."

"You owed me nothing but I must tell you, the notes saying I had a friend aboard were music to my ears. I had no idea what my friends were doing because I had discouraged it. I wanted a vacation like normal people. I have learned that is impossible. But to say again, I did not know what they were doing, but I did know they would do something."

"Mr. Wiley."

"Please Ali, call me Jerry."

"Okay Jerry, when I left your house that night weeks ago, the night I mentioned the Coptic sign, I had no idea it would come into play. My wife felt strongly about it and that was the only reason I mentioned it. Now it causes me many thoughts, and I ask myself, is my wife and my father really in touch with a real God? Jerry, I think coming to the brink of life, I might have learned something. Would you ask your wife to pray for me?"

"My friend, when you left our house, my wife said, 'that is a good man' and I agreed."

The Captain and all the crew had talked by way of cell phones to their families to get the stories and for the assurance they were all safe.

One good side effect was that several high ranking terrorists had been arrested.

Jerry had notified the team of the pier number to which the Tatiana was headed. As the Tatiana approached the crowd was waiting. Once the Tatiana was tied up, the first aboard was Sherry. She could not remember Jerry holding her so tightly. As the tears flowed happily, unabated this time, both of them thought, *Thank you God.*

Chapter 38

Jerry was pleasantly surprised at the response from their friends when he asked if they would like to continue this *uneventful vacation*. The answer had been, very positive. Ed had added, "Jerry, if you do this again I want a tank or at least a bazooka. Also my friend for you, I will wear a diaper again," smiling broadly he continued, "It sure brought back memories of a Poodle diaper though."

Jerry had truly missed the companionship of real friends and he got a good laugh from Ed. It was an inside joke about the diapers. Ed had suffered an unhappy time with a lady who insisted he learn to fold dog diapers.

Jerry then talked to the Captain. A five day stay in Corfu was decided. Jerry agreed to fly every family that wanted to come to Corfu for a short vacation to be flown over. Otherwise the crew members could fly back to France for a few days R & R after the escapade.

Jerry was so relieved and proud of everyone involved that many family members were flown over to spend some time in Greece. Mary Ann and Buck left the group for a few days and met most of Mary Ann's family in Athens. Of course Tommy remembered Mary Ann and made sure they got to see the Embassy. Again it was like homecoming to Tommy because he got a kick out of any one who knew where Browntown was.

Most of all for Robyn, it was a fulfilled dream to stand within the Parthenon atop the Acropolis. Then after trying to imagine activities in Ancient Athens to walk to the edge of the Acropolis and view the grand historical city of Athens.

The family enjoyed several traditional Greek meals but Robyn knew she had to visit the market and enjoy a real Greek Gyro with Mom, Buck, Dusty, Sister Debbie and their families. The family could not get over Mr. Jerry Wiley's reactions when she tried to return the stack of one hundred dollar bill she had taken from the Terrorist. "Lady, I have seen the video of that performance on the pier, and it was worth every penny of that. Take it and enjoy it with your family."

No one got tired of hearing how Robyn had actually slapped a well-known terrorist and then hugged him and picked his pocket. A pretty hard act to top.

Jerry finally got the chance to walk in a park, sit beside the Mediterranean and hold the one he loved. Corfu was no longer the small Island with narrow roads as it was in the 1950's.

Amazingly he was able to locate *that one small café,* still in business, where he had once ordered steak and eggs. Back then the owner had sent two kids for the meal, one to get the steaks and the other to get the eggs. The café was at water's edge. Now with Sherry, he again ordered steak and eggs. The café now had its own reefers and the makings were on site. Jerry sat, looking across the table at Sherry. He was enjoying a dream that at times in the past few days he was not sure would happen.

What a week this was. Nice, now they were vacationing again with no cloud over their heads. As Jerry had planned, he was able to show his dream Island of Corfu, but this time just for fun and entertainment. At times they saw the protectors that Tuck and Buddy had assigned. The orders and finances for the protection of course came from Wiley Industries. When the protection was deemed necessary, during the discussions Dallas had told Buddy, "The security is more financially wise than the alternative. Lesson learned."

The rest of the vacation was uneventful as far as danger went, but the thrills and education was top shelf. It was a vacation of a lifetime, one that would be talked about for years.

An ending, but not **The End**. Life continues for Sherry and Jerry.........................

Epilog

World News carried a story of an unusual falling out of terrorists on a small Greek Island.

At Tommy's notification, the CIA along with Greek authorities, took the video cassettes from the cameras for analysis. Due to the many possible ramifications the facts were not released to the international media concerning the work of an elusive group called the MVA; therefore, Tommy could not gloat openly. Within the Embassy, it was a different story. New respect was gained for the little town of Mount Bell.

Back in the USA, in the town of Mount Bell a local church was enjoying a new attendee. Ali was attending with his wife and family. As Ali had told his father and his wife, it had to be a miracle, *I knew we were dead men, but all of a sudden it was over and we were all free. It was amazing.*

And the old man said, "Praise God!"

Books by Jack Darnell

Available as Paperback or e-books

Sticky… Adventure

Rags….. Kids and the Street person, Rags

S'Gar…. The birth of a Vigilante group, the MVA

Finally Love… Adventure, excitement plus Senior love.

Mary Ann….. A kidnapping involving a senior

Gracefully Grasping for Dignity… Senior advice

Why Not Forever… Marriage advice

Toby's Tales… The tales of a turtle as he travels across country from Arizona to Texas. Also featuring poems by **Pauline Lieck.**

Praise for 'The Vacation' (con't)

As I read The Vacation, I appreciate more the love I have for my wife and how much I am enjoying growing older with her. This book is not only enjoyable but a blessing to me. As I read I think about those travels and how I wish I could take my wife on a trip like this. One day I will live in a place that will make Jerry's Vacation look, for lack of a better word, poor. One day I will live forever in a perfect body in a perfect place where the real Jerry Wiley is now, in Heaven.
Thanks, Thanks, Thanks..
Larry Wiley, Bishop, Moultrie, Georgia

www.ingramcontent.com/pod-product-compliance
Lightning Source LLC
Chambersburg PA
CBHW030414180626
46812CB00005B/2008